SHADOWLESS

VOLUME ONE: OUTLIER

L.J. HACHMEISTER
WITH ILLUSTRATIONS BY M.J. ERICKSON

SOURCE 7
PRODUCTIONS

Copyright © 2017 by Source 7 Productions, LLC
www.triorion.com
First Edition*
ISBN-13: 978-0984979882

Colophon

Cover art and design by

The typefaces used are Adobe Caslon Pro for the body text and mix of Cinzel and Cinzel Decorative for the titles.

Source 7 Productions, LLC
Lakewood, CO

SHADOWLESS

VOLUME ONE: OUTLIER

CHAPTER 1

Running away from home seemed like the best option. At least until the shrieking howls of a coguar cut through the trembling surf of trees.

Can't go back, Sen told herself, forcing her way through a tangle of bushes.

Images of the coguar's razored teeth, red mask, and feline paws flashed through her mind. Bedtime stories and old nursery rhymes didn't do the predator justice, not after seeing the deep scars on her mother's arms, and the tormented look in her eyes any time someone gazed too long at her wounds.

Home is worse.

Moonlight streamed down through the swaying trees, giving rise to dancing shadows that played into her fears. Going out into the Dethros forest at night was dangerous for the favored—but for an ungifted Outlier like her, she would be lucky to survive until morning. The other kids her age loved to tell her nightmarish stories of untamed, carnivorous vegetation, feral animals, bloodthirsty Shifters, and rogue swarms that dominated the outlands. But nothing her fourteen-year-old mind could conjure up compared to the cold bite of the winds, and cries of the unseen creatures lurking in the shadows.

Still, risking the dangers of the forest rated more favorably than facing her parents' shame the next day.

Tears blurred Sen's vision as she picked off the burs hooked into the exposed skin on her arms.

Why couldn't I be something—anything—even a Shifter?

A second howl, this time much closer, broke her from her thoughts.

Re-securing the straps of her satchel across her shoulder, she hoisted herself up the large, corrugated trunk of a felled rigalwood tree. Despite the nearly-full moon lighting up the night sky, she didn't see the nest of purple cradel spiders until she felt tickling legs scurry up her right arm and under her shirt.

"Ow, get off—get out!" she cried, slapping at her arm and shirt as the tickling sensation turned into fiery pinpricks. Not minding her feet or her balance, she fell forward, landing hard on her side. Dizzying motes clouded her vision as she gulped for air, unable to fill her lungs.

Can't breathe—

The spasm in her chest subsided. Sen breathed in again, and loud enough to alert the entire forest. As she propped herself up on her elbow with a groan, she noticed the pervading silence.

No insect sibilance, no midnight cawing from the white-feathered gailyns.

Sen curled her legs up into her chest, afraid enough to forget the worsening burn from the spider bites, or the terrible ache in her ribs.

Something large and lumbering crunched down on twigs littering the forest floor. A second footstep, then a huffing snort.

She hugged her legs to her chest even tighter, fresh wounds throbbing. Squeezing her eyes shut, she imagined herself at home, safe within the Lightning Guild stronghold in their dwelling carved into the white rock of Hirak mountain, her mother and father not too far away, ready to rush to her bedside should she even make a concerning sound. The comfort of her own bed, silk sheets soft against her skin, the humming sound of the Scylan mother tree drifting in her bedroom window—

Branches snapped.

A dark figure emerged. Two legs appeared, then four. Sen could make out its curved spine and sharp claws that dug into the leaf-strewn ground. Whatever it was, it stayed between the trees, its jet-black fur blending in with the shadows.

She held her breath, too afraid to move, unable to take her eyes off the colossal thing standing only a few feet away.

The creature took another step forward, this time with a noticeable limp in its step. Moonlight revealed a dark canine face and unusual eyes, one with a yellow iris but a blue sheen. The other, pale and cloudy, the surrounding socket badly scarred.

What's that?!

No schoolroom rumors spoke of such a creature.

Spotting her, he crouched down, pulling back his lips over sharp teeth.

Sen shimmied back as far as she could until her back flattened against the tree trunk.

"Please…" she said, her voice breaking into breathy whispers. "…please…"

The creature limped forward, his low growl vibrating straight down to her bones. Wide-eyed, she watched as the coarse hair on the back of his broad shoulders bristled, making him appear even more massive than before.

But as he limped forward, she saw more of his wounds, dampening her fear with the unnamable feeling she always got when she realized someone else's pain.

"What happened to you?" she whispered, her eyes tracing his badly twisted back paw to the gaping sores on his neck, arms and backside. Some of his injuries looked older, like the scar across his left eye and the shredded ear. But it was his protruding ribs, and the skeletal look of his legs and arms, that snagged her attention.

He's starving.

The excited caterwauling of the nearby coguar made her jump, as it did the creature before her.

What if the coguar isn't hunting me...

Without taking her eyes off the creature, she slowly brought her hand to her satchel, unbuttoned the front flap, and dumped out all of the contents: A few sweet rice buns and a stuck-together mass of cherry dumplings.

The creature's growl intensified, his lips curling back even farther.

"That's everything," she said, scooting away on her hands until she came to a kneeling position.

She saw the glint of the creature's claws in the moonlight just before he swiped his enormous paw in her direction. Yelping, she threw herself backward. In less than a heartbeat she scrambled back over the fallen tree trunk and shot through the thorny underbrush, a feeling of heat and dread nipping at her heels.

Don't look back don't look back DON'T LOOK—

Catching the toe of her boot on a tree root, she came crashing down, smacking her head against hard ground. She tasted something coppery in her mouth before she could register what happened.

Old memories cut their way through to the forefront of her rattled mind.

"Senzo, why are you always running?"

"Father?" she said, touching a wet spot on her forehead. When she brought her hand in front of her face, she saw the red smear on her fingers.

Nausea licked the back of her throat. All the blood left her arms and legs. *Come on, for once in your life, tough something out.*

Roars and screams erupted through the forest. Something large crashed against a tree, splintering bark, rustling leaves.

That injured animal—

She could hear her father's admonishments, telling her to make the smart decision, but she couldn't deny the stronger pull spurring her onto her feet and running back to the site of the fallen rigalwood.

The shadows and trees hid most of the red and black clash, but Sen could make out the injured creature, and the deadly coguar vying to sink its teeth into his hide.

Her father's sensibilities still tried to sway her mind: *How does this benefit you?*

Her answer came in the search for something—anything—to help the injured animal. Sticks and leaves wouldn't do.

But those rocks—

Sen scrambled over to a pile of rocks near the rigalwood, scooping up as many as she could in one arm and then climbing back up the tree trunk to take aim. With a stunning blow, the coguar knocked down the larger creature, and circled around, readying for the kill.

"Leave him alone!" she shouted, throwing rocks at the coguar. The feline predator hissed and shrieked, surprised at her appearance. With flattened ears, it batted at her projectile assault. Despite her weak arm and terrible aim, she landed one good hit on the coguar's sensitive nose. Tucking its tail, it spun around and took off, back into the protection of darkness.

Breathing hard, she waited for what felt like forever until she braved leaping down and checking on the injured animal.

New bite marks scored his already wounded body. Laying on his back, she saw the ragged rise and fall of its chest, and the murmur of his once resonant growl.

Not knowing what else to do, she looked around until she spotted the food she had dumped out on the ground. Most of it had been mashed into the leaves and dirt in the fight, but she picked up the few remaining morsels.

She approached the giant beast, taking a smaller and smaller breath with each step. A loud grunt made her jump back, but even as his head lolled her direction, she dared one last advance.

Both eyes—even the pale, cloudy one—watched her every move as she bent down and placed the last of her food near his mouth.

The creature bayed, and then whipped his tail in her direction. She ducked in time, just as the spiked tip flew over her head.

With tears in her eyes, she took off in the only direction left, away from the roaring beast, the glowing blue lights of the stronghold behind her as she plunged deeper into the heart of the Dethros.

▲▽▲

By the third day, the spider bites had changed from stinging nuisances into inflamed sores with purples streaks aimed toward her heart. If it weren't for the bites, she might have paid more attention to the worsening pain in her ribs, or the pounding in her head.

Sen leaned against a tree trunk, clutching her side, sweat pouring down her face and neck. The heat from the warm afternoon sun didn't right the chill coursing through her body. Shivering, she pulled at tattered ends of her shirt, not understanding why she couldn't find warmth.

Nothing makes sense, she thought, looking around at the towering trees and familiar game trail she could have sworn had taken her on a never-ending loop through the same patch of forest. Even the white mountains behind her, home to her people of the Lightning Guild, should have been a directional marker, but they never appeared in the same place, swirling away and in on themselves in some crazy nightmarish vision.

I'm sick.

She finally allowed herself to think it. Reality struck another rapid succession of blows: *No food. Alone…and injured in the Dethros.*

Dethros. The divide, the place that separated the Realm from the outlands, the favored and the forsaken.

"A place suitable for shadowless cowards," she could hear her father saying.

With every footstep, she felt her strength peeling away. Her head, too heavy to hold up, bounced back and forth as she teetered forward.

The ghostly outline of her mother's face appeared in the grasses near her feet, green-tinted eyes telling more than her words ever could.

"Don't give in, Sen. Don't end up like me."

Mother. Father.

Home.

I didn't want to leave—

"I'm sorry," she whispered to an unseen audience. She stumbled into a bush, her clothes catching on the branches. Losing her balance, she fell forward, thorns scratching her face and arms.

With a monumental struggle, she turned partway onto her back, enough to see up through the tree tops, to the sun shining down on her from the bright blue sky.

Memories surfaced in random waves. She saw her father under the Scylan mother tree, telling her the proud history of the Lightning Guild, of a people that could control the storms, but most importantly, channel lightning. She saw the expectation in his eyes, the need for his only child to bear his immense gift.

A lithe figure, a wisp of a smile breaking through a mask of buried pain. Her mother, dressed in brown silk and flowers, the telltale green vine of her Virid lineage wrapped up her left arm, looking down at her with her own expectation.

"I am not like you either, Mother," she mumbled.

No. Not a shock jockey, not a greenthumb. She couldn't attract and control lightning any more than she could help a plant grow. *Not that I belong in any of the five denoms.*

Older memories pushed their way in front of her waking eye. She saw herself, much younger and already afraid of what she wasn't, clinging to her mother's hand under the safety of a Scylan tree. They both watched in awed silence as her father, chancellor of the Lightning Guild, raised up his arms and summoned the gray clouds from the east. Other Guild members circled around him on the mountain peak, lifting up their arms, their skin glowing blue as the air around them charged for a strike.

"What if I fail the Trials?" she asked her mother as a bolt of lightning struck her father and dispersed amongst the other members.

Her mother never took her eyes off her husband, not even when Sen pulled on her hand and asked again.

"You have something special, Sen; something I haven't seen in a long time…"

"No… I don't," she said, tears sliding down her cheeks.

The winds, from the north, swept through the trees. Someone was summoning a storm to Hirak mountain.

Maybe father…

Does he miss me? Does he know why I left?

Of course he does, she chided herself. *And he's not going to come after me.*

Something hissed, and then growled. She tried to turn her head, but couldn't fight the hold of the branches. Struggling only made things worse, sapping the last of her strength.

Out of the corner of her eyes she saw a flash of red, a mouth crowded full of long teeth.

The coguar—

She screamed, emptying her lungs of all the terror and pain that had come to dominate the last few days of her life.

A second figure rushed through the trees; a streak of black, a hint of yellow. Another predator to compete for her kill? It didn't matter.

I didn't want to shame you, she thought, imagining her mother and father. She closed her eyes as the growling intensified. *Please forgive me.*

Overcome by fever and grief, Sen felt herself slipping away as a looming figure blotted out all evidence of the sun.

CHAPTER 2

"Nya, I forbid this; it's too late for a hunt."

Osan's gruff words reached her ears, but went no further. With little more than a grunt, Nya slung the last of her weapons over her shoulder and gave a curt nod to the other clan members gathered around their chief. Firelight from the central meeting area made Osan's bushy white beard and eyebrows overshadow the rest of his leathery face.

"It's suicide," he said, this time grabbing her arm as she tried to pass him.

Nya stopped in her tracks, but did not look at the old man. Instead, she kept her gaze fixed on the edge of the Dethros forest, the dying orange rays of the setting sun casting foreboding shadows amongst the trees.

"We can't go another day without food," she said, not keeping the anger out of her voice. "And the sick need fresh herbs."

"You can go out with Kaden tomorrow morning."

"Not everyone will survive 'til morning," Nya said, nodding her head toward the cluster of tents on the farthest edge of the camp. The sickest stayed inside, too weak to join the rest of the clan by the fire.

Osan didn't take his eyes off her, mashing the remaining nubs of his teeth together as he weighed her defiance against the awful truth of their situation.

"I give my life for the Chakoa," she whispered, trying to tip the balance her favor by appealing to his sense of clan loyalty.

"Just don't do it foolishly," he said, letting her go.

The other clan members saluted her with fists over their hearts, staying back to guard the camp against the successive attacks that had been happening night after night since they crossed the Mohaj desert and into the Koori lowlands that butted up against the divide. Never in her life had she thought that the various Outlier clans would have to fight each other for food and supplies, but raiding the Realm's border town stocks proved harder with each year, especially with rising tensions between the denominations. Something had upset the precious balance between the Virids, Lightning Guild, Swarm, and the Order of Nezra, and from what she overheard whispered by the guards standing watch near the Realm borders, it sounded like Vulgis, Deathlord of the Order, hadn't shown up to the yearly Gathering of the Elders.

War is coming, her instincts screamed as she passed through camp, but as much as she had warned Osan, he didn't do much more than prematurely celebrate the end of the Realm and all of its favored inhabitants.

A few stars poked out from the deepening purple sky as she ran west, the sun slipping away behind her. The Koori lowlands, dotted with hearty bushes and scraggly trees, jutting rock formations, and pockets of red sand, reminded her of some tale she heard as a child. Something about two siblings who dared leave the protection of the Realm, and wandered into the outlands. After encountering the dastardly fiends that roamed the Godless lands, they fled home, eager to go through the Trials and realize their denom so as to never become one of the forsaken.

"Fools," she muttered to herself, squeezing her hands into fists. Old wounds, awakened by her rage, competed for her attention, but she wouldn't have it.

Gotta get at least a deerkat, she decided, climbing up the steep shelf that marked the edge of the forest. Even the thought of a prospective meal made her stomach gurgle. At this rate, she'd eat anything, even a bowl of squirming wyre worms.

She wasn't more than fifty paces within the trees when she sensed movement behind her.

Unsheathing her knife, she cocked it back before spinning around to take aim.

"Peace, Nya—it's me!"

Recognizing the trim outline of her fellow hunter putting up his hands, she sighed and re-sheathed her knife.

"Could'a warned me."

"Lost you for a second, but I didn't want to shout and scare away our dinner."

As Kaden stepped into a shaft of moonlight, she saw the worried look he tried to hide behind his heavily tattooed face. At only twenty years old, he carried more burdens than some of the old men, and had twice the scars and ink to prove it.

"You shouldn't be here," she said, clasping her hand around his forearm.

He returned the greeting. "Neither should you."

"My wife isn't sick," she said. "You need to be with her."

"Without me, you'd bring home a good meal, but I'm not sure my wife wants to start shaving," he said, one corner of his mouth poking up into a half-smile.

Nya shoved him off with a frown, not caring that he slammed into a tree.

I'm never going to hear the freaking end of that, she thought, picking up her pace to spite him.

"You're too easy, Nya," he said, catching up to her and trying to get her to slow down. "You're not the only one that screws up herbs, alright? I once mixed up an udi mushroom with a revis. Got the entire clan sick. I swear it burned a new hole in my—"

"Quiet," she said, yanking him by the neck of his tunic to a crouching position beside her. She indicated what she saw with a nod of her head.

Kaden followed her line of sight, through trees and broken beams of moonlight to a grassy knoll. Something massive, bigger than a coguar, lay inside a dugout shelter of mud and stone.

"What is that?"

Nya answered by stringing her bow with an arrow and taking aim. But as she tried to zero in on a lethal target, a lazy cloud slipped over the moon.

Gonna have to get closer, she thought, crawling toward the creature. She could hear the sonorous sounds of its breathing, and despite the darkness, spotted the regular expansion and relaxation of its torso.

She waited for Kaden to get in position, watching him ready his throwing axes out of the corner of her eye.

In better times, she might have asked herself what the beast could be, but hunger and desperation narrowed down the scope of her reasoning to primal instincts. Something this big would have enough meat on the bone to feed the entire clan for days.

But as she pulled back on her arrow once more, she felt something from deep inside her whisper through. The same feeling she got right before she stepped up to the denom elders for her own Determining, and when she first met Sho, piqued her mind; a knowing, a foresight she couldn't possibly have.

"Screw it," she said, waiting as the cloud slid past the moon, and once again revealed the monster.

Curled up in a giant black ball, the beast had markings and features she hadn't seen before. A canine face, a broad torso, reptilian accents and a spiked tail. It appeared injured, with multiple wounds, all in various stages of healing.

And then she saw something that made her pause. An arm draped over the side of the tail.

He's probably protecting his meal—

No. As much as she tried to convince herself, something didn't fit.

Kaden gave a low whistle. She looked over to him and shook her head. Not understanding her hesitation, he made to take the first shot.

The arm disappeared. Someone went into a coughing fit. The beast lifted its head, growled, and then gently used its black nose to nudge whomever—or whatever—lay within its clutches.

Nya loosed the arrow just as Kaden cocked back his wrist. The shaft whistled through the air and hit its mark with a *thunk*. Stupefied, her companion looked at her with one eyebrow cocked upward, and a frown that hinted at all the expletives she'd be hearing once they got back to camp.

Wait, she mouthed to him, motioning for him to calm down as he freed his axe from underneath the arrow embedded into the tree.

The little commotion they made alerted the beast. In the blink of an eye it crouched above a much smaller figure, baring its teeth in their direction.

That's…a girl, Nya realized, watching as the figure stirred and rolled over onto her side. *And she's injured, too.*

In all her nineteen years, she couldn't fathom how such a menacing, battered creature would come to protect a girl, but she didn't have time to put much more thought into it as it charged at their position.

Nya shot up a tree, bounding from branch to branch until she gained enough distance to take better aim once it got in her sights. Following suit, Kaden climbed up the nearest tree, readying his axes if the beast chose to attack his position.

But the monster didn't come near. It didn't get farther away than twenty paces from its human, though it barked loud enough to awaken the ancient spirits.

Nya kept one eye on the beast, and the other on the girl stirring in the dugout shelter. With shaky arms the girl pushed herself up to a sitting position, and tried to clear off the matted hair from her face. The look of confusion and tears in her eyes struck Nya in such a way she couldn't help her reaction. Readying another arrow, she took aim at the beast's bony chest.

"No!"

The girl's cry rose above the din, silencing the beast and jarring Nya's focus. Her arrow flew through the air, but hit the ground three feet in front of him.

"No—please—stop!"

"Who are you?" Nya demanded, stringing another arrow and taking aim once more.

Coughing, the girl fell to her side, clutching her chest and throat.

Are those spider bites? Nya lowered her arrow a bit and looked over to Kaden through the break between the branches. The young warrior didn't take his eyes off the mark, ready to deal death as Nya dictated.

"Please…" the girl said between hacks. "I—I'm nobody."

Nya sighed, returning the arrow to her quiver and re-slinging her bow. Coming to the same conclusion, Kaden lowered his axe and looked over to her for direction.

We don't need another mouth to feed, she thought, indicating with two fingers across her neck to leave.

Besides, she had left others behind before. Other unfavored rejects that couldn't pass the Trials, or ran away before their Determining, too weak and unprepared for the harsh life outside of Realm. Mercy and pity could be afforded by the rich and privileged—not by Outliers struggling with day-to-day survival.

"Fine, nobody. Just get your beast off of us and we'll be on our way."

"Don't leave," the girl said, her voice barely audible above her companion's persistent growl.

"Why? What could you possibly offer us?" Nya said, not caring how awful she sounded to the poor kid.

Silence. The kid couldn't come up with anything, not even a threat.

Weakling, Nya thought, climbing back down the tree.

"No, don't!" the girl cried as the beast took a few steps toward Nya and Kaden's position.

The beast stopped in his tracks, then returned to the girl's side, shielding her with his massive body.

As Nya hustled through the brush away from the girl and her beast, Kaden caught up to her and grabbed her by the shoulder.

"What are you doing?"

Shrugging him off, she picked up her step, running toward the thicker underbrush. *There's gotta be a stream up ahead, and if there's water, there'll be game trails, maybe even—*

"Nya, stop!"

Nya reared around and drew her bow and arrow before Kaden could unsling his axe. "Don't even think about it."

"You're just going to leave that girl? She commands that beast!"

"It's probably just a stray Shifter. And she's sick."

"Fine, so what if that beast is a Shifter?" Kaden said, not moving his hands away from his axe. "He'd scare off half of our attackers."

Nya shook her head. "No. She's a burden."

Frustrated, Kaden tossed his axe down into the ground. "Why do you refuse every new kid?"

The question got to her, digging under her skin in a way she wasn't expecting. Old hurts ghosted past her mind, but in the heat of the moment, she shut them out.

Lowering his voice, Kaden delivered an even lower blow: "Sho would take her."

Anger clouded over reason. "She's a waste, just like the rest of our sick."

Kaden's lips compressed into a thin line as his hands tightened into fists. Nya didn't care how big he was, she'd take him down all the same, and he knew it.

"You don't know what's right anymore, do you?" he said, staring her dead in the eye.

"I don't care about being right." Without realizing it, she touched her right forearm covered in tribal ink indicating the five years she'd survived in the outlands. "Not if it doesn't help us survive the day."

"We should split up," he said, his voice going flat. "I'll meet you back at camp."

Before she could even react, Kaden disappeared into the forest, leaving her alone amongst the insect chatter buzzing between the trees.

He's going soft, she thought, picking up her route again toward the stream. *We can't have that in the clan.*

But as much as she tried to convince herself, she knew her ire wasn't all about her hunting partner's inkling of compassion. Having someone who could control a beast would prove a valuable asset. So why did she refuse the kid?

He's right; Sho would have taken her.

The thought of her ex-boyfriend made her stumble.

No, she cautioned herself, pushing the memory of Sho away as she came to a halt. She loved that boy just as much as she couldn't stand him. The way he argued every point she made, questioned every decision—not a day went by that they didn't have some sort of verbal altercation. Yet she couldn't bear to be reminded of him, and the sense of loss left in her heart when he disappeared on a scouting mission several months ago.

Tracing the tattoos spiraling out from middle of her forearm and up to her shoulders, she silently recited the Chakoa creed: *Without a shadow, I seek only the comfort of darkness, and the freedom of its emptiness.*

And her own: *Without attachments, I am invincible.*

After a few calming breaths, she distanced herself from unwanted feelings, and refocused on her objective.

Under the light of the waning moon, she finally came upon her first deerkat sign: A few hoof prints depressed in the soft ground, a scrap of hair caught in the outstretched branches of dead bush. Her stomach growled with anticipation.

I'll take that thing down with my bare hands.

As she carefully wound her way through the thicker foliage, she heard the sound of the stream trickling through forest, and lowered her stance.

Thunder sounded off in the distance, toward white mountains. She didn't have to look back to know what was happening. Blue lightning lit up the sky around Hirak mountain, and men and women with white hair and glowing skin would be dressed in ornate robes, stretching out their arms to the sky.

The rapid succession of thunderclaps made her pause. *Sounds like someone's not happy in the Guild.*

Not that she cared. No Outlier would involve themselves in the convoluted politics of the denoms, not even if the entire Realm fell into war and chaos.

The northern winds felt good, brushing up against her cheeks and the shaved sides of her head, ruffling the few loose strands in her braided hair. For whatever reason, it made her think of Sho, the annoying way he used to sneak up on her and gently blow his breath against her face.

Slurping sounds caught her attention, but she could not identify the source. Nya bent down and froze, listening and looking through her limited vantage behind a bush. Movement up ahead, too big to be a deerkat; she didn't recognize the awkward jerks and twitches.

What is that thing?

The smell of sulfur touched her nose, and she brought her hand up over her face to stifle the imminent revolting of her stomach.

Don't make a sound—

A shrill animal cry pierced the night air, but faded with a whimper. Something larger rustled through the bushes, closing in on its victim.

Nya dared a better look over the top of a bush and across to the other side of the stream. The twisted horns of a blue elk lay in a beam of moonlight, the rest in shadow.

Drawing her bow, she prepared to kill whatever predator felled the poor elk, not caring if it was a bully bear or a dragon, her hunger driving out what little sense of caution she ever possessed.

Until she saw its face.

A Nezra!

She made herself as small as possible as the pale death-dealer glided up to its kill, its bloodshot eyes and gaunt cheeks standing out even amongst the shadows.

What's it doing here?

No denom—not even the fearsome death-dealers—ever ventured outside the safety of the Realm.

The Nezra descended upon the blue elk, raising its black-tipped fingers and wiggling them at the fallen animal. Nya covered her ears as the elk bucked and screeched, uttering sounds she didn't think possible from the living.

Why isn't it finishing the job? she wondered as the elk bucked and kicked, trying to free itself of the visceral attack. *Doesn't make sense.* Even with her limited experience, she had never seen or heard of a death-dealer doing something like this.

Before she could think out the potential consequences of her actions, Nya loosed one of her arrows at the elk. Precise aim and a strong arm left no room for err. The arrow pierced its neck, delivering the merciful death blow that the Nezran would not give.

The Nezra hissed and growled, looking around for the disrupter.

Nya carefully notched another arrow, not taking her eye off the Nezra as it sniffed the air and twitched its fingers, honing in on her life signs.

Footsteps, excited whispers. More figures moving in the shadows.

There's more than one—

As soon as the realization hit her, she took off running, pumping her legs as fast as they would go.

Kaden. Low-hanging branches slapped her face and underbrush scratched her exposed skin, but she forced her way through. *Where are you—?*

She could see him now plucking flower petals and placing them in his leather sack, unaware of the impending assault that would turn his bones to dust.

Slowing only for a second, Nya stuck her thumb and first finger in her mouth and gave off a high-pitched whistle. Seconds later, she heard the hooting response.

They met up at the steep shelf that dropped them back into the lowlands.

"What happened?" Kaden said, putting his hands behind his head and trying to catch his breath.

"Nezra," she said. Wiping the sweat from her brow, she tried to sound more composed than she felt.

The dark-skinned warrior looked at her with one brow lifted. He knew better than to question what she saw, but she saw the doubt etched into the furrows of his knotted forehead. "We should go back for the girl."

"No, it's too late for her."

"Nya—"

"It's not safe here. We'll have to move the camp," she said, starting her descent down the striated shelf.

Kaden didn't follow right away, staring out ahead, past red sands and into the dark horizon of the Wastes, where even the bravest of the Outliers didn't dare travel.

"Move it, Kaden; we don't have time," she said, swinging down to a firmer hold between jagged strips of rock. When she glanced up, she saw his hard expression in the moonlight, the bitterness that had already carved its way into his heart.

Nya didn't allow herself to think of those who wouldn't make it through until morning—and the others that wouldn't survive their abrupt move in the middle of the night. Or that worthless girl and her injured beast.

Holding on to her anger, she cursed her rumbling stomach, and the ocean of stars shining down on to them with cold indifference.

▲▽▲

CHAPTER 3

"My name's Sen—what's yours?"

No matter what she tried, the giant beast paced back and forth in front of her, still agitated from the excitement of the people in the trees. He vacillated between standing on two legs and flitting his ears in every direction, to limping around on all four.

"It's okay, they're gone," she said, trying to prop herself up by the elbow. Everything felt harder to do than it should, every movement requiring a tremendous amount of concentration and dismissal of the aching protests of her body.

Still, she couldn't despair. She made a new friend, even if he stood ten feet tall on all fours, and had fangs the size of her head.

"Ahh," she moaned, pushing up to a sitting position. That got his attention. Her furry companion crawled over on all fours and nudged her with his cold wet nose.

"Okay, okay," she said, laughing as he sniffed her neck and face. With a grunt and a low growl, he sat back on his haunches, still scanning the forest with his one good eye.

"You're kind of a grumpy fella, aren't ya?" she said, reaching out and touching his back leg. She marveled at the smoothness of the black fur covering his upper body, and the slick feel of the scales covering his hind quarters, legs and tail. Sitting beside him, she spotted the webbed folds of skin between his waist and arms, and when he shifted forward, she saw how it went taut.

Like wings!

But the rest of his anatomy didn't make sense for flight, especially not the heavily spiked tip of his tail, or the sheer size of his frame. That, and the extent of his injuries.

We're both in pretty bad shape.

Something in the distance howled, then tapered off in a garble, as if the cry had been strangled right out of it.

Don't wanna to find out what did that.

"We can't stay here," she said, running her hand along his tail, trying to divert his attention.

Clouds gathered near the moon, threatening to thrust them into total darkness. Sen looked around, trying to memorize the narrow paths between the towering trees, but she knew better than to think she could possibly navigate safely in such conditions.

"Please." Gently, she pulled herself up by his fur. "We need to find help."

Her animal companion emitted a deep bass rumbling from his throat, but lowered his body enough for her to haul herself up onto his back.

"I think I'll call you… Akoto," she said, holding on tight to the bony prominences between his shoulder blades. "It means 'friend.'"

Whether he understood or not, Akoto made his way through the trees on all fours, his nose to the ground, sniffing and snorting. Sen held on best she could, but her swollen right arm would have no part in any prolonged exertion. Electric pain coursed up her arm and into her chest, sending wave of nausea up her throat.

Switching to a single hand-hold, she bit down on her lower lip and went through her options.

Can't go back.

And I don't have anything to offer those people.

Even outside the Realm, she couldn't escape her lot.

I'm not good enough, even out here.

Sen swallowed hard, fighting the tears that threatened to fall. But instead of dwelling on the impossible, she pressed her head against Akoto's back, feeling his coarse fur, and the outline of his vertebrae and ribs against her face. "Thanks again for saving me… I wish I had more cherry dumplings for you."

The thought of food made her pause.

When was the last time I ate? Counting backward, she estimated at least four days. *Why am I not hungry?*

From the few times she paid attention to her mother's teachings on plant medicine, she recalled one pertinent lesson: *"If you suspect an infection, and the patient has lost their appetite and has a fever, have them chew on a vega root."*

She leaned over to the side, trying to get a better view of the ground, but Akoto protested the shift in weight, and tried to move her back in the middle by flicking his shoulders.

"Akoto, no—!"

Tumbling off, she landed in a cushioning tuft of feather grass. Akoto wheeled back around, his eyes dilated with concern.

"It's okay, friend. I know you didn't mean it," she said, scratching his inquisitive nose. Using his arm, she hauled herself up with a groan, and resumed her search.

As the moonlight waned under the veil of clouds, she found a patch of the familiar green and blue sprouts near a stream. She gave up trying to use her right arm after a few painful attempts to grasp at the stems, and instead kept it pressed to her chest as she dug into the ground with her left. Too exhausted to rinse off the dirty root, she gave it a shake, and then stuck it in her mouth. The bitter taste made her lips purse, but she gave it a few chews, swallowing the foul-tasting juices.

Bleh! Who would even try this in the first place?

Wearily, she dug up a few more and placed them in her satchel. She offered one to Akoto, but after he took a whiff, he made a disgusted face and snorted.

"You don't know what you're missing," she said, half-grimacing as she swallowed another mouthful.

Akoto's one and a half ears perked up, and he rose on his back legs as he gazed upstream.

"Wha?" Sen said, half of the root dangling out of her mouth.

Darkness blanketed the forest.

"Akoto—" Sen whispered, spitting out the contents of her mouth and reaching out to find her friend. She felt the scales of his back leg, and held on tight.

Growling, the giant beast lowered himself down on all fours. She felt his entire body tense under her hand.

Something's out there, she thought, sensing the pervading silence in the forest.

Heart pounding, she groped around Akoto's side until she found a secure enough handhold to bring herself up onto his back. He didn't wait very long, taking off at the fastest pace his injured body would allow. The choppy gait made it difficult to hold on, especially with only one good hand.

"Run faster," she bade her friend as chill shot down her spine.

Something's behind us.

No—

Her eyes widened as images unfolded before her in the dark.

—inside me.

Looking down, she saw the faint outline of a hand passing through her shirt and reaching inside her stomach. Cold fingers raked against the back of her spine, sending waves of bright light up into her skull. Voices, emanating from all around her, filled her ears until she couldn't separate herself from their caustic whispers.

Underneath her, Akoto faltered. He stuttered, teetering to the side before coming to a standstill.

"No!" she screamed, throwing her arms around Akoto's neck. *Don't hurt him!*

Light blossomed from around her hold, spreading out across Dethros like an expanding halo. Something bellowed, making everything around and inside her shake, but the sensation passed, and she felt a great release.

"What was that?" she said as she tried to catch her breath. "You okay?"

Akoto huffed, shifting his weight until he righted himself. As he continued to agitate and fuss, she checked her stomach, finding it as intact as it was before. *Was that real?*

Maybe it was the vega root, or the poison from the spider bites, she told herself.

The passing clouds released the moon, and she could make out most of her surroundings. In front of them lay a blue elk, its eyes frozen wide with unseen terror. She didn't recognize the black streaks around its mouth and nose, or what could have possibly made it contort into such an odd shape.

Part of her wanted to stay, to somehow comfort the poor lifeless elk, but fear and a sense of someone—or something—lingering in the shadow tore her away.

That's real.

"Run, Akoto," she whispered, kicking him with her heels.

He took off, faster than before, making her hold on for dear life as he jerked along on only three good paws.

As she pressed herself close to Akoto's back, holding tightly with her legs and good arm, she wondered why her parents never told her of such unconscionable dangers in the wilds.

Grief replied: *…because I wasn't supposed to live outside the Realm.*

Hugging herself even closer to Akoto, she felt the vibrations of his stride as his paws slapped the ground, jarring her body and her wounds. She remembered the words of her father after the first time she electrocuted herself on a Scylan trying to understand the power he and the rest of the Guild shared with the lightning trees.

"Can you still feel pain?"

"Y-yes."

"Good. Then you're still alive."

"I'm still alive," she told herself again. After all she'd been through, she'd somehow survived. Maybe that meant something.

As they reached a steep drop-off, she called out to Akoto: "Slow down—wait—what are you doing?—*no!*"

Her animal friend didn't slow as he came to the sharp decline. Instead, he sped up, and as he reached the lip, he spread open his arms, the webbing between his upper limbs and waist going taut. Sen clung to him as hard as she could, but when she felt the air catch under his wings, she peeked one eye open.

For the brief span of their flight, she forgot about her parents, the people in the trees, her injuries, the spider bites—even the dead elk and the horrifying encounter in the forest. A cry of joy rose in her throat, and as she tilted her head back, she let herself be known to the shining stars up above.

As Akoto glided down to patch of open sand between gnarly trees, she wiped away the tears from her cheeks.

"You're great, Akoto."

The beast snorted.

Sen looked back as Akoto continued east on foot, not seeing or sensing anything dangerous. The edge of the Dethros, perched above the steep drop-off, gave no acknowledgement of her departure, sheltering the darkest of its secrets amongst the whispering trees.

Is this the Koori lowlands? she thought, gazing out ahead at the vast expanse of high desert.

She made it—at least out of the divide. Now she faced the real danger. Being an Outlier didn't mean that any one of the many clans would accept her. And she didn't even know if that's what she wanted—not that she had much of a plan in the first place. After all, the girl in the tree had a point. What did she have to offer?

I'm not smart or strong… and I'm not a fighter…

And that was beside the immediate problem. The vega root might help with the infection, but she still needed an antidote for the circulating spider poison. She didn't brave looking at her arm, not when it felt too swollen for the sleeve of her shirt, and burned with even the slightest movement of her fingers.

I got maybe another day in me.

She bumped her arm against Akoto's back, sending a fiery shock up her shoulder, taking her breath away.

…or maybe until morning.

Akoto grunted, breaking her from her pain. As he slowed his steps, she saw a flicker of light out in the distance.

"We've got no other choice," she said, shifting herself higher onto his back to take some of the strain off her good arm. Akoto growled and whined, but she nudged him forward with her heel.

"Let's just hope they're as sweet-tempered as you."

CHAPTER 4

Nya had been keeping an eye on their tail long before Kaden or any of the other warriors were even aware of their presence.

"Nya—"

"I know," she said, cutting Kaden off as he trotted up beside her.

"How long?"

"The last hour. They've been slowly gaining."

Kaden processed this information, scanning their surroundings and reviewing their numbers. Nya didn't need to look. The strongest towed their belongings behind them in wooden carts, while the sickest rode upon the few six-legged horses they had left. Osan, the leader of their clan, walked in front, guiding their trek across the treacherous open desert toward the rock Spires that would afford them a better protection.

But half of us might die before we get there.

"We've got to break soon," Kaden said in a low voice. "I don't think we can reach the Spires in one shot."

Nya kept her eyes trained forward, not acknowledging his exhaustion, or hers. Every footstep in the sand and dirt felt heavier than the next, and did nothing to lessen the impossible distance between them and the Spires. Even with the moon shining brightly she could barely see the reddish-gray rocks, sculpted by ancient rivers long since vanished, jutting above the twisted trees and rolling sands.

"Are you sure of what you saw? The Nezra, out here—it doesn't make any sense."

She understood why he questioned her. Moving now, in the middle of the night, would be too much of a strain on his already sickly wife. Still, she offered him no comforts. "Yes."

As Kaden walked alongside her, she could hear him succumbing to old nervous habits, popping the knuckles on his hands.

"Does Osan know?" she asked.

"About our tail? I came to you first."

Nya thumbed the weapons strap across her chest and glanced over her shoulder, in the direction of whatever monster creeped steadily toward their position. Despite the full moon, she couldn't get a sense of who or what it was, only that it blended in with the shadows, and did well staying out of her direct sight.

"Keep the group going. I'll fade back and check it out."

Before Kaden could protest, one of the elderly women went into a violent coughing fit. Unable to hold herself up on her horse, she slid off, slamming onto a pocket of red sand.

Nya let the others rush to her, keeping watch of the shadows behind them. Warriors subdued the frightened horse while Natsugra, the clan's medicine woman, scuttled over with her sack of herbs.

"How bad is it?" Kaden asked.

"She's dislocated her shoulder," Natsugra said over the weak cries of the old woman. "Nya, come help."

Still keeping an eye out to the west, Nya went over and held down the old woman while Natsugra popped her shoulder back into place.

"We need to stop," the medicine woman said, looking directly at Nya.

"We can't."

Osan came over, resting heavily on his walking stick. "What's the problem?"

"If we don't stop, we're going to lose at least two more tonight," Natsugra said as she comforted the injured woman in her arms.

Nya glanced back to the west. No movements in the shadows. Then again, she could have missed something when she helped Natsugra with the woman's arm.

"Nya?" Osan said, reading her serious expression.

"We stop now, we all die."

The Chakoa chief ground his remaining teeth together, looking between the two of them. Nya, his best warrior, and Natsugra, the shrewd, acerbic healer who wouldn't let him hear the end of it if he disagreed with her.

"We rest long enough for you to treat her and get her back on that horse. Same goes for the others. No later," he said, motioning for the other warriors to help the sick off of the horses and start a fire. "Nya, a word."

The young warrior followed the chief into the dark, away from the few torchlights that illuminated their path. Under the light of the moon, Osan withdrew his last dusty strip of dried meat from one of the pouches on his belt and broke it in two, offering her the bigger half.

"When was the last time you ate?"

"I'm fine."

"I asked you a question, warrior."

She had to really think about it. "Since the last attack."

The old man nodded as he broke the dried meat into smaller bites and swallowed them without chewing. "I need you here with me, Nya."

"I am."

"No, you're not."

Cheeks blooming red, she tried to keep the emotion out of her voice, but his passive accusation cut straight through her. "I've let go of Sho."

"I wasn't talking about Sho, but that adds to my point. We are without attachments here, Nya, but that doesn't mean we don't take care of ourselves, and each other."

Reluctantly, she took the jerky from his outstretched hand. She had survived much longer without food, and in much worse conditions. Any sort of charity felt insulting.

"There's something tailing us. We can't stay here."

"I know," he said, waiting until she took a bite to continue. "Take Kaden and Sahib, circle 'round. Do what you have to do."

Nya touched the inked hashes on her left forearm, indicating the many kills in her short lifetime. "My life for the clan."

A proud smile crossed his face. Osan touched his forehead to hers, whispering a prayer in his native tongue. Years ago the sentiment would have brought butterflies to her stomach, but she had found ways to bury those wasted emotions, focusing all of her energy on the only purpose she found worthy.

As soon as he released her, she tucked the rest of the jerky away in her belt and made her way back to the group, searching for Kaden in the makeshift camp. She found him easing his wife to the ground and carefully propping her against a folded up tent. Leyla's half-opened eyes didn't track any movement, and her head bobbed side to side as he offered her water.

"Kaden, arm up. We're going," she said, already searching for Sahib.

The young man bowed his head. "She's dying."

No attachments, she thought to herself. Why didn't he understand that? Life in the outlands demanded it.

Nya spotted Natsugra helping one of the children. When they met eyes, Nya indicated her question with a nod toward Leyla. Natsugra slowly shook her head and resumed her assessment of the sick boy.

"You can't help her."

"I won't leave her," he said, not looking at Nya.

"Fine," she said, not filtering her disapproval. "Stay here."

But as she turned to find Sahib, a feeble voice called out from the shadows.

"Hello…?"

Every warrior, even some of the sick, raised their weapons. Nya grabbed one of the torches planted into the sand and directed it at the origin of the sound. "Show yourself!"

A large figure, too big to be human, came into view first. Midnight fur, a large mouth full of razor-sharp teeth; different colored eyes that zeroed in on her position. Only after she saw the scrawny girl riding on his back did she recognize the pair.

"You again?"

"I need medicine…spider bites…," the girl mumbled, barely lifting up her head.

"Who is that?" Osan said, coming up beside Nya.

Unsheathing her twin short swords, Nya narrowed her eyes. "A problem I should have taken care of in the Dethros."

The girl half fell off her beast, landing haphazardly in the red sand.

"No, Akoto…" she whispered as her beast snapped his massive jaws at the circling warriors.

"You have nothing we want," Nya said, her voice rising to a shout.

Crawling on her hands and knees, the girl made her way toward Nya with rasping breath. When the girl grabbed her satchel, Nya lifted her swords, ready to make a quick end of the sickly outcast and her beast.

"Wait," Osan said, slapping the back of his hand against her shoulder.

With a heaving breath, the girl tossed the satchel at Nya's feet, the contents spilling out into the sand. Nya kicked around the pitiful fare of a few dirt-encrusted roots and some half-eaten leaves.

"We don't want your garbage—" But as she made to aggress the young girl, the beast roared, setting the entire clan back a few feet.

"For God's sake, Nya," Natsugra said, waddling up beside her. The old woman bent down with a groan, and with knobby fingers, collected the meager offering. "Didn't I teach you anything?"

Osan grabbed one of the roots from Natsugra's hands and brought it closer to his cloudy eyes. "Ah, vega root. Good medicine." With a grunt, he looked at the semi-conscious girl, the beast, and then to Nya. "She's yours."

Gritting her teeth, it took everything she had not to protest his ridiculous order. The last she wanted, especially now with half of their people sick and rival clans looking to finish them off, was to look after some half-dead, newbie Outlier.

"I want two warriors on guard. The rest of you—get back and help the sick," Osan said, turning around.

As the rest of the clan returned to their temporary camp, Nya stood outside the circle of light, the semi-conscious girl at her feet, and her beast one swipe away from taking her head clean off.

Nya eyed the beast, not lowering her swords. "Are you gonna play nice?"

The girl mumbled something and rolled onto her back. When she reached up with one trembling arm, the beast responded, coming up to her side and licking her face.

For reasons she couldn't understand, Nya found herself both rankled and envious of the interaction.

"Listen," she said, plunging her swords into a mud patch and kneeling down besides the girl. "Give me a reason—any reason—and I finish you both off. Got it?"

The girl partially opened her eyes. Nya expected anger or fright, but not the smile that lit up her dirty face. "Thank you."

Surprised and confused, Nya watched the girl for a moment, trying to understand her strange reaction.

She's insane, she rationalized.

"And you're probably just as weird as her, huh?" Nya said, removing the last of the jerky from her belt. The beast sat back on his haunches, watching her hand holding the dried meat with a starving look in his one good eye.

Sighing, Nya broke the small piece in two and tossed him a morsel. "This is a onetime thing, get it? Only 'cause you may prove useful."

The beast caught and swallowed the offering in one quick snap of his jaws. Instead of a tail wag, or any sort of thank you, he lowered his head to his front paws, still keeping watch of his charge.

"Hey—don't fall asleep," Nya said, slapping the girl on the cheek. The poor kid coughed herself back awake and hugged her injured arm close to her chest.

"What's your name?"

"…Sen…" the girl choked out.

"Sen? What's that short for?"

A pained expression crossed the girl's face, and she turned her head away.

That's all I need, Nya thought. *Another shadowless weakling.*

Grabbing Sen by the collar of her shirt, she dragged her back into the torchlight of their temporary camp, the dutiful beast following. She caught sight of Kaden feeding bits of the vega root to his wife, whispering words of encouragement into her ear.

Nya averted her gaze, biting her lip to keep from screaming as others tearfully rejoiced the new medicine. *Stupid girl. That root won't do much. It's just false hope.*

With a clenched jaw she searched through one of Natsugra's herb sacks, trying to find the cradel poison antidote in the clutter of wash bowls, rags, and crude medical equipment.

"Northern bluebell—small sack," Natsugra said as she passed by distributing the vega root to the sick.

I knew that, she grumbled to herself as she snatched up the dried indigo flowers, a mortar and pistol, and returned to Sen.

Natsugra joined Nya's side with one of the torches as she inspected the girl's wounds. Nearly unconscious, the girl didn't make a sound, even as Nya poked and prodded the infected spider bites.

"This one's been through hell," the medicine woman remarked, planting the torch in the sand next to the girl's head.

"The worst of it seems to be the spider bites," Nya said, unimpressed by any of it.

Natsugra patted down the many pockets of her layered robes and dress until she found a spool of cat gut and needle wrapped up in an old silk handkerchief.

"Tend to those lacerations," she said, motioning to trade the suturing kit for the dried flowers. "I'll prepare the antidote."

"No," Nya said.

The old woman looked up sharply, blue eyes cutting straight through Nya's defiance. "Nya—"

Nya firmed up her voice, forcing herself to look at the hairy mess of her own terrible mistake. "Let me do this."

The old woman huffed, but took back the kit and shifted down to take care of the deepest cuts on the girl's legs.

Working in silence, Nya ground up the ingredients for the antidote, overly aware of Natsugra's watchful eye. Every so often the girl's beast would grumble and gruff, but made no move to menace their action.

"Are you done yet?" Natsugra asked as Nya stared at the blue paste in the wooden bowl.

She couldn't remember if she needed to add anything else, but the medicine woman's urgency made her rush to answer. "Yes."

"No!"

Natsugra snatched the bowl out of her hands and shooed her away with a wave of her hand. "You could slay a dragon," she said, taking pinches of other herbs out of the pockets of her dress, "but you're too impatient to see what's right in front of you."

"This is ridiculous," she said, standing up and kicking the sand.

As she stormed off, she heard Natsugra's remark to the girl's beast: "I tried to teach her."

Nya took to the cover of a red juniper tree a good distance from the edge of their camp. Refusing to look up at the ethereal night sky, she turned her gaze to the western edge of the Realm, the glowing blue walls a reminder of all that was denied to her.

"If you're still alive, Sho…" she said through gritted teeth as she removed the hunting knife from her belt. With anger in her heart and an unnamable hunger in her veins, she whispered: "Come back to me."

▲▽▲

CHAPTER 5

Sen heard her mother's voice far off in the distance:

"You have something special… something I haven't seen in a long time…"

Confusing images and sounds followed. A flash of a bearded woman, the sound of hoof beats. Reddish-gray rocks piled high, all the way to the stars. Someone screamed; more cries followed, as well as the shriek of something hideous and inhuman. Hands and feet appeared all around her in a frenzied commotion.

Where am I?

Raising her head felt impossible, like lifting a boulder. The smell of blood and sweat filled her nose, making her gag.

"Akoto…" she mumbled through numb lips.

Somewhere close by she heard his roar, followed by the sound of splintering teeth and crunching bones.

What's happening?

Terrified, she forced her eyes open, only to squeeze them back shut.

Not real not real not real—

Dozens of men and women, robbed of all the color from their skin, attacked the people around her with charred limbs and bloodied mouths. Painted warriors fought off the hordes with spear, arrow, and sword, but even a direct hit to the heart didn't seem to stop their nightmarish attack.

Sen screamed as a blackened hand wrapped around her leg and yanked her out from the protection of the circle of warriors.

"Akoto!" she cried, digging her hands into the sand, trying to find purchase.

Another hand slapped down on her back. Nails raked down her spine. Bucking wildly, she freed herself enough to flip around. A ghostly woman loomed over her, vacant-eyed and panting like a feral dog.

Sen froze.

"Fight back!" someone shouted.

In the corner of her eye, Sen saw a woman with dark braided hair and a sword in each hand taking down the attackers in droves.

"Fight back," she repeated as she fended off two human-like creatures coming at her on all fours.

Strings of cold saliva hit her face from the woman's open mouth. Paralyzed by fear, Sen looked past her rotting teeth and down her gaping throat, unable to breath, her heart pounding its way out of her chest.

No no no—please—help me—

Then she heard it—or at least she thought she did. Somehow, amidst the pandemonium of screams and guttural cries, the raw thudding of sword against flesh, she discerned a whisper, a desperate plea from a place beyond the dying woman's lips.

"*Save me…*"

Shocked by the voice, Sen broke from her fear, her hand drawn to the woman's pale face by a need she felt down in the marrow of her bones.

A streak of silver. Warm wetness splashing against her face.

"Get up!"

Rough hands grabbed her by the armpits and got her to her feet. Sen could barely process her beheaded attacker, or the young warrior woman forcing her toward the others regrouping by the tallest rock spires.

"Stay under cover," she said, shoving Sen near a juniper tree where other clan members, sickened and injured, huddled together under the twisted branches.

Sen brought her knees to her chest, afraid and bewildered by the raging conflict. *Got to get out of here—*

"Don't worry," one of the injured women said, touching Sen's shoulder and then pointing out to the young warrior woman deftly cutting her way through a wave of shrieking attackers. "Nya will save us."

As dark as it was, Sen could follow each slash and stab as moonlight coruscated off the silver blades. In all her life she had never seen such savage grace. Every denom in the Realm relied on their gifts, not the vulgar wielding of an antiquated weapon.

Warriors hooted and hollered, rallying at Nya's ferocity. Dodging bites and clawed attacks, she flipped over the last wailing pale one and beheaded him in one clean stroke.

As the clan cheered for their victory, Sen struggled to her feet in a panic.

"Akoto," she cried, stumbling over felled attackers and broken weapons. "Akoto!"

A weak grumble answered, followed by a whine. Squinting, Sen tried to discern the many fallen bodies in the dark, picking her way through the jumbled mess until she spotted the giant ball of black fur near one of the spires. At least ten of the pale ones lay around him, their faces covered in a mish-mash of black fur and blood.

"Akoto… no…"

Fearing the worst, she approached him, shaking and holding her breath. *Please be okay.*

When she touched his back, she felt the wet patches of hair, but no movement.

"Hey, kid—get back here!" someone shouted.

Forgetting everything and everyone else, she spread her arms and buried her face in his coarse fur. "Stay with me."

You're all I have left.

A light formed, somewhere off in the distance, separate from the pitch black she saw behind closed eyelids. She watched in disbelief as it grew in synchronicity with the beat of her heart until she could tolerate the brightness no longer, and opened her eyes.

What was that?

"Akoto?"

The beast stirred, bumping her away with his shoulders as he rallied to his feet. With tears streaming down her face she hugged his arm, not letting go until he licked her face hard enough to make her fall backwards into the sand.

"I told you to stay under cover."

The stern voice jarred her from her moment of joy. Sen looked over her shoulder, spotting Nya approaching her, eyebrows pinched together in a scowl.

"But Akoto—"

Eyeing the beast, the warrior woman stopped abruptly, keeping a good distance between herself and Sen's friend. "Huh. Didn't think he made it."

"No, he's okay," Sen said, stroking the fur on his arm as he licked his fresh wounds.

Nya reverted right back to her aggravations. "If I tell you to do something, you do it. Unless you want to try surviving out here on your own."

As the remaining clan members spread out with lighted torches, searching the battlefield for anything or anyone to salvage, Sen finally got a good look at the young woman. Imposing scars, war-paint and tattoos covered her exposed skin, and she sported a partially shaved head and braids that wrapped up into a high ponytail. Even though she appeared just above average height, she had a muscular frame, and carried herself with authority.

She's just a teenager, Sen thought. Even so, her initial impression didn't last long. Nya's eyes, rimmed with dark makeup, didn't gaze at her with the youthful exuberance Sen expected from someone her age. There was a hardness there, a cold determination forged in the fires of survival and pain, something which Sen recognized, but could not understand.

Just as Sen looked her over, Nya returned her gaze in a way that made Sen nervous.

She sees right through me—

She knows I'm not worth anything.

After all, she could not handle a blade, and she did not know anything about survival in the outlands.

Sen lowered her gaze. "I'm sorry."

"Look over the dead," Nya said, her tone bereft of pity. "Take whatever's useful."

"W-what happened? Who attacked?"

A pause. Sen braved looking up. Nya knelt down next to one of the pale ones, inspecting the blackened limbs and distorted face. Rolling over another one of the bodies, she pointed out a series of animal tattoos descending down the blanched torso.

"These are Soushin. Another clan of Outliers. We've had some problems with them, but they've never waged a full-out attack on us like this."

"They look sick," Sen said, still clinging with one hand to Akoto as Nya shoved over another body.

Nya didn't answer. At least not immediately. Frowning, she inspected the charred fingers of a pale one much too small to be an adult.

That's a child! Sen realized. *Why would a kid be part of an assault?*

It didn't make sense to her, and by the way Nya scoured the young attacker's body, she gathered it didn't add up to her either.

"There's a lot of sickness going 'round right now." Nya stood up and put her hands on her hips. "...but this isn't right."

"Wait," Sen said, following after Nya as she made her way back to the gathering point near one of the spires. "What's wrong?"

Nya didn't answer, her gaze fixed on the older man with dark skin and a bushy white beard. Leaning heavily on a walking stick, the decorated elder appeared in deep conversation with a woman about his age dressed in layered robes. The woman motioned to the sick, still huddled under the juniper tree, a grave look in her eyes.

Is that...? Sen blinked her eyes several times, thinking her mind to be playing tricks in the moonlight. *Does that old woman have a beard?*

"Chief," Nya said, approaching the two elders with a rush in her step. When they turned their attention to her, she placed her hand over her heart and bowed. "Your council, please."

The old man nodded, placing his hand on her shoulder. He looked once at Sen, and the large beast that followed behind her, before indicating to the bearded woman to give them privacy.

Confused, and closer to tears than she realized, Sen didn't argue when the bearded woman steered her away to allow the old man and Nya their conversation.

"So, you are Sen," the bearded woman said, looking her up and down with one eyebrow lifted. "Not much of a fighter, are you?"

Heat rushed to her cheeks, coloring them bright red. Thankfully, the old woman didn't wait for her to acknowledge her battle weakness.

"And what is this great beast you command?"

"I don't command him," Sen said, backing up into Akoto and staying pressed against his body. "He is my friend, Akoto."

"A Shifter?"

Sen thought about it before answering. Shifters couldn't stay in one form—including their original human cast—for as long as she'd been with Akoto. "No."

"What is he? Where is he from?"

All the questions made her uncomfortable. Still tending to his wounds, Akoto didn't seem to care one way or the other, as she fielded the bearded woman's curiosities.

Sen shrugged.

"Well then how did you come to be 'friends?'"

The question put a smile on her face. "We helped each other out in the Dethros."

With a sigh, the old woman gave up on digging for any more information. "My name is Natsugra. I am the medicine woman for the Chakoa."

The clan name sounded familiar. *"Give me a reason—any reason—and I finish you both off. Got it?"*

(I'm not wanted.)

His dour face appeared in the back of her mind: *"Shadowless savages. I will wipe out the Chakoa myself!"*

Cringing, she averted her eyes to avoid showing any kind of recognition.

"You seem to be doing well enough now," Natsugra said, reverting her attention to the rest of the clan. "Make yourself useful."

Before Sen could respond, the medicine woman returned to her station, tending to the sick and those injured in the battle under the juniper tree. Still unsure of herself or her circumstances, Sen watched from a distance, observing the heated dialogue between Nya and the clan chief between spires. Those who had salvaged from the battlefield returned to help, setting up fires and putting up tents.

"I remember the bearded lady's face from my dreams. I think she saved me," Sen whispered to Akoto. As Nya repeatedly pointed to the west, she recalled another memory. *"Give me a reason—any reason—and I finish you both off. Got it?"*

(I'm not wanted.)

The realization circulated through her mind, dredging up all the reasons for running away in the first place.

(They'll never accept me—)

(They'd be better off if I never even existed.)

A shiver ran through her body, and she pulled at the remnants of her clothing to quell the sudden chill.

Akoto groaned and stretched out, knocking her forward. As she tripped over her own feet, he righted her with his tail, bringing her back in close.

"Thanks, buddy," she whispered, patting his shoulder.

I should help, she thought, seeing Natsugra attending to so many people. *But what can I do? I'm not good at anything.*

But as she clung to Akoto's fur, the soreness of her spider-bitten shoulder registered on a new level. She pulled back one of the torn flaps of her shirt. Instead of an ugly purple, she saw dark pink skin. *They saved me.*

Taking a deep breath, she whispered to Akoto: "Stay here."

The midnight beast grumbled and settled into his spot in the sand.

With tentative steps she approached the Chakoans. Her father's warnings came to mind as she studied their weather-worn, painted faces:

"Outliers are dangerous, Senzo. They represent all that our ancestors feared."

Sen hugged her arms close to her chest as the cries of the sick and injured escalated. Too afraid to look, she saw out of the corner of her eye as several warriors held down one of their own as another approached with a heated blade.

"Their medicine is weak, their bonds forged in brutality."

An overly sweet, pungent smell filled her nose as a black smoke drowned out the moon. She traced the dark trail down to the pyre of burning bodies off in the battlefield. Several warriors ringed the flames, chanting in ancient tongues, their arms outstretched to usher the dead to the skies.

"They are not part of this world."

Every part of her shook, from her head down to her toes. But still, the apprehension she felt for the band of shadowless, forsaken people did not outweigh the fear that drove her out into the wilds in the first place. With each step she took toward the Chakoan camp, she felt one step farther away from the Guild, from her mother and father, from her responsibilities as the sole child of the world's next great leader.

As Natsugra rummaged through one of the brown sacks, she spotted Sen hovering at the edge of the camp. "Come here, Sen."

Sen knelt down next to the medicine woman, looking back and forth between her and the woman lying on a ratty animal hide. Wan and bleary-eyed, the woman moaned between half-spoken whispers, her hands squeezing and releasing something or someone Sen could not see.

"There is a lot of disease out here," Natsugra explained as she produced several different herbs from the pockets of her dress and robes, and put them in a stone mortar. "And unfortunately, we don't have access to the good medicine they keep in the Realm. But we do what we can."

Natsugra ground the herbs and dried flowers into a paste, adding water from a bladder and pinches of black seeds from one of the pouches attached to belt around her waist. The sour smell that wafted up made nose scrunch up, especially when Natsugra added the vega root. "Tilt her head forward."

Sen did as instructed, holding the woman's cool, sweaty head in her hands, trying to be as gentle as possible as she brought her head forward so Natsugra could pour the brown mixture into her mouth.

"That vega root you brought is very special. Only certain folks know how to identify it," the bearded woman said, using her thumb to wipe off the excess mixture from the woman's lips. "We don't get many Outliers from the Virid denom; the Mazes usually keep Outliers from escaping the Gardens…"

Sensing the woman expected a response, Sen answered what she could without delving too much into her origins. "I'm from the Guild."

"So one of your parents is a greenthumb, the other a shock jockey. Interesting."

Sen didn't like the silence that followed, or the gurgling in the sick woman's throat. The medicine woman pulled close another one of her sacks, muttering to herself until she found what she wanted: a handful of capped vials containing various colored liquids, and a tattered old cloth. After selecting a few oils, she soaked the cloth and applied it to the woman's forehead. Within seconds, the woman had enough strength to clear her throat before drifting off into a sedated sleep.

"You'll not find solace out here, child, if that is what you seek," Natsugra said as she put away her things. "The outlands are unforgiving, as are we to those that cast us out."

Sen pulled up her knees to her chin, counting the sick woman's breaths to counter the tension building in her chest. Surrounded by agonized cries, the stench of blood, burnt flesh and disease filling her lungs, she could not withstand Natsugra's mordant stare. For the briefest of moments, she wished herself in her mother's arms, safe under the Scylan tree.

"Do you know why we are called 'shadowless?'" Natsugra said, taking Sen's hand and raising it up in the firelight. The resulting shadow stretched out over the sick woman's face, and into the darkness behind her. "Because we are invisible in the eyes of God. And yet what do you see?"

Sen tried to pull back her hand, but Natsugra held firm. The old woman's blue eyes, pellucid as mountain lakes in the fall, cut through her like sharpened glass.

"I—I don't know."

The medicine woman's lips came together as if she tasted something bitter. Without looking at Sen, she struggled back to her feet, her knees making a popping sound as she straightened up.

"You don't have to stay with her," she said, motioning to the sick woman.

"Is she going to make it?" Sen asked, touching her pale arm. Feeling the cold, waxy skin, she immediately retracted her hand.

"No," Natsugra replied, turning away.

Despite the millions of questions running through her head, Sen kept her mouth shut as Natsugra turned her attention to the other sick or wounded Chakoans.

What do I do? she thought, too terrified to run back to Akoto and leave the camp, but equally fearful of staying. *I don't belong here. I don't belong anywhere.*

The woman coughed, her head falling to the side nearest Sen. Through the slits of her lids, Sen saw into the woman's glossy chestnut eyes, and sensed something beyond the sickly confines of her body.

Curious, Sen placed her hand again on the woman's arm, hoping to look deeper. Nothing. Only the woman's ragged breath, and the yeasty smell of whatever disease ravaged her insides.

Stupid. I can't do anything to help her.

Still, she remembered the odd occurrences as of late: throwing her arms around Akoto in the Dethros, and the halo of light blossoming out from her hold. Seeing the pulsating light within him when he was dying. Hearing the pale attacker's whispered words in the din of battle—and reaching back to connect with someone or something she couldn't name. Impossible things—

—Things her father would dismiss and punish her for even entertaining.

Who am I kidding? I'm shadowless.

With tears in her eyes, Sen scooted closer to the dying woman, setting her straight, and positioning her body in a way she thought would be most comfortable.

"I'm sorry," she whispered, touching the woman's stringy blonde hair. She set her other hand in the sick woman's frigid grip. "I wish I could do more."

As the cries and moans of the Chakoans died down, Sen saw more than the firelight reflecting off of the dying woman's unseeing eyes. She saw herself, the same small and wiry girl she'd always been, with a shadow that cast out farther than she could see.

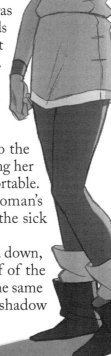

▲▽▲

CHAPTER 6

Sahib caught up to Nya at the mouth of the river where the terrain began to change. Patches of dirt and red sand gave rise to hardy grasses, shrubs, and sun-bowed trees. Rock spires grouped together, fabricating long channels threaded by rushing winds and water. Just a little bit farther, and the walls would come together, creating the formidable maze of the Ko'pai canyon lands.

"Nya," he called out. When she wouldn't stop, he ran up beside her and grabbed at her arm. "You shouldn't do this alone."

"Go back. Osan can't spare you," she said, pushing back the low hanging branches of the brittlepines, not caring if the young man got out of the way or not.

"No more than he can you."

Furious, she reared around and grabbed Sahib by the throat and pinned him against the tree. "This isn't a time to lick our wounds," she said through gritted teeth. "If we don't act now, we'll be wiped out."

The young warrior pawed at her hands, veins popping out on his forehead as he gasped for air.

Realizing herself, Nya let go. Sahib fell to his knees in a bed of grass, heaving and coughing until he righted his breath.

Nya looked up, through the tangle of the treetops, to the waking sky. Blue light shuttered out all but the brightest stars. *Can't stop. Only an hour left before he heads back to the Realm.*

Finding Sulo wouldn't be hard, but in her condition, and without a bribe, she didn't think he'd take her seriously.

A hand grasped her leg. Nya looked down. Though he didn't look directly at her, Sahib offered up a half roll of bread.

"I'm not trying to stop you," he rasped, his cheeks suffused with blood.

Nya refused to feel anything, for the boy, for their situation, or how delicious that week-old bread looked in his dirty hands. But she needed to eat.

Take it. You can't appear weak in front of Sulo.

Nya accepted the bread and offered Sahib a hand up.

"What did Osan tell you?" she asked.

Brushing off his animal skins and re-securing his weapons, Sahib nodded to the west. "That you wanted to make contact with the Shifter. You're worried about what happened to the Soushin could happen to us. Osan only agreed to you going as long as you took someone with you…not that you listened."

"You're here now, aren't you?" she said as she downed the bread. Sahib rolled his eyes. "Stay close to me. And when we meet with Sulo, you're not to say a word."

"What is he?" Sahib asked as he ran behind Nya alongside the river.

Sometimes she forgot how young Sahib was. Cast out of his home at fourteen like the rest of them, the Swarm reject had only been with the Chakoas for two years, but in that short time, he had made a name for himself as a warrior in the outlands. Faster than any Outlier, he could run down a deerkat, and wasn't too bad with a bow and arrow. But even though he had been tested and proven in the wilds, he had yet to engage in the clandestine world of subversion and espionage.

Nya slowed to a stop, touching the damaged bark of one of one of the brittlepines. Dragging her fingers over the scuff marks, she remembered her first—and almost last—encounter with the infamous Shifter.

"A bully bear…" Sahib said, touching the denuded bark of another tree. "Wow. How does he move in and out of the Realm? Isn't he branded?"

Ignoring his questions, she looked for other clues of Sulo's presence. A few discarded seeds from a yellowberry bush. Tufts of soft brown hair and golden quills lodged into the thorny branches of the river bushes. But most importantly, the distinctive claw marks and five-toed paw imprints in the sandy mud of the riverbank.

He's blowing his summer coat, she thought. *And fattening up for winter.*

"I mean, wouldn't a powerful Shifter like that be assigned to one of the denom leaders? Or a world council member?"

Annoyed, Nya turned to Sahib. "He's charged to protect one of the Virid sages who happens to have a lot of interest in 'forbidden' outland vegetation and will turn a blind eye."

That seemed to satisfy the kid, at least enough to shut-up for the moment.

Nya scanned their surroundings. The multi-hued canyon walls, carved by nature over millions of years, held secrets and dangers that in optimal conditions she'd take no less than ten warriors. Even the other Outlier clans steered clear, fueled by their own myths and legends of the lost souls and demon spirits that lurked in the twisted stone maze of the Ko'pai.

I hate this place, she thought as the first rays of morning light touched the vast expanse of sandstone and surreal, time-sculpted rock formations. In another time, perhaps in another life, she might have appreciated the compressed layers of deep reds and burnt oranges of the noble stone walls, or tenacity of each tree and bush that staked their claim to meager plots or crevices near the winding river. But acknowledging beauty—in any form—went against her core beliefs. After all, nothing lasted forever.

"Even the mountains will fall," she could hear Sho say.

Movement up ahead. Nya sensed it before Sahib, and pulled him back behind a pile of boulders to wait to see who or what emerged.

Grunting, huffing. A sizeable animal lumbered through the brittlepines, knocking down hearty branches with its bulky frame. But as Sahib drew an arrow, she spotted the golden-brown bear, and stepped out from behind the rocks.

"Nya—"

"His eyes. Look," she said, pointing at the bear's face as it reared back on its hind legs and sniffed the air.

Sahib lowered his bow and arrow as his jaw fell agape. She doubted he understood what she was trying to point out as the bully bear snarled and dropped back down on all fours, but it didn't matter.

That's old Sulo alright, she thought, seeing his distinct eyes that once reminded her of the first buds of spring, the kind of vibrant green that shook away the long hardship of winter. But knowing him now, seeing how the decades of slavery eroded what little was left of his humanity, she saw something different.

"Peace, Sulo," she said, keeping one hand on her weapons belt, and the other in front of her, palm facing the aggravated bully bear. Keeping her voice even and shoulders relaxed, she continued to talk to him as the quills on his shoulders and back raised. "It's Nya, from clan Chakoa. I come with concerning news. I need your help."

The bear scratched at the mud and sand, retracting his lips over rows of serrated teeth.

Why isn't he changing back?

Out of the side of her eye she spotted Sahib shifting his weight and tensing his muscles.

Something's not right.

"It's Nya, Sulo. I need your help," she said, losing the calm in her voice. The bully bear slapped his paws on the ground, unleashing a roar that shook the walls of the canyon. "Come on, dammit—I don't have time for this!"

Nya rolled up the sleeves of her shirt and spread out her arms, exposing the scars and tattoos that marked more than her rite of passage into the Chakoan clan, or her many battles. "Wake up, Sulo! You're not the only one who's pissed off."

The bear shuddered, then groaned. A horrible grating sound reverberated off the canyon walls as bones shrunk and muscles deflated, brown fur and golden quills retracting and softening into tan skin. When the transformation finished, Sulo sat naked on the other side of the river, covered in a shimmering film, heaving for breath.

"What was that all about?" Nya said, pulling her sleeves back down.

Sulo shook his head and wiped the film from his eyes. Most days she liked him, but today she couldn't find the patience to wait for him to sort himself out from his animal.

"Wasn't expecting to see you until next month," he said after hawking up something thick from his throat and spitting it on the ground next to him. "Can't sneak up on a bear like that."

"Thought you had better control."

Sulo quirked up an eyebrow at her. Not many people—especially an ungifted Outlier—had the gall to antagonize a Shifter, let alone one that could transform into a bully bear.

"I'll lose myself to the bear soon enough," he said, leaving any hint of pity out of his voice as he casually draped an arm over one of his bent knees. "But you—you won't make it past winter with the animal eating up your insides."

As they exchanged a heated silence, Sahib came up to her side, nervously looking at her for direction. He didn't understand the code of conduct, the measures that each of them had to take to ensure the other hadn't gone soft—hadn't turned on their true loyalties.

"You're still a thorn in my side"

"And you're still too easy," Sulo said, standing to meet her as she crossed the river. After they had clasped forearms, he looked to Sahib. "Who's this?"

"Another thorn," she said, crossing her arms as Sahib offered his arm in greeting to the Shifter.

Instead, Sulo grabbed the young warrior by the shoulders and assumed an overly serious tone. "You should learn to keep better company, kid. Nya isn't known for her good graces and charm."

Nya made a mental note to punish Sahib later for grinning. "I need your help."

The Shifter ran one hand through his gray-and-black speckled hair as he scratched at the scruff of his grizzly face. "I figured as much. Nobody has seen or heard from Lord Vulgis in months. There's all sorts of conspiracy talk between the denom elders."

"I know; I've heard the border guard rumors. Something's happening within the Order of Nezra. I don't like any of it."

"But that's not why you came here," he said, his eyes finding the fresh stains on her tunic and trousers. She caught him sniffing the air again, his inner predator heeding the call of blood.

"There's new sickness," she said, recalling the battle near the spires. Whatever happened to the Soushin seemed beyond what regular sickness could do. She had never seen skin sapped of color like that before—at least not among the living—nor such impossible contortions and mobility from limbs bent in the wrong direction. It seemed like dark magic, an illness spun out of ire and curse. A feat only one denom could manage.

As she described the battle to Sulo, she watched his reaction, gauging what little she could from his stolid gaze. An older Shifter, Sulo had endured over three decades of slavery, outlasting most of his kin, and bearing the burden of his experiences alone. He didn't react to her tale of bloodshed, or even to her descriptions of the Soushins' appearance—but he did stop her when she mentioned her encounter with the dying blue elk in the Dethros.

"Are you sure of what you saw?"

The question infuriated her, and she didn't hide it. "You know better than to doubt me."

Sulo stood up, sunlight reflecting off his naked body. Refusing to avert her eyes, she stared him down, even as he stretched out his arms and legs.

"Why are the Nezra going outside the wall?" he wondered out loud.

"And torturing animals and infecting the Soushin."

Sulo gave her the side-eye, but didn't disagree with her assumption about the other clan of Outliers.

"I'll ask around," he said, scanning the horizon. "See if I can't get some intel from one of the Shifters serving the death-dealers."

"Good," she said.

"Whoa," he said as she turned to go. "You interrupted my hunt and you've got nothing to offer in return?"

Nya clenched her jaw. No, she had nothing. At least nothing that would satisfy a Shifter or possibly give him something to barter with to get back in the Realm unharmed.

Unless...

She thought of that new girl, and the great beast she commanded. Akoto—or whatever stupid name she had assigned. She'd never seen an animal like him, if he could even be classified as one.

He's rare, unseen.

Valuable...

Her gut pulled her in one direction as her needs yanked her the opposite way.

The girl is useless in battle, she thought, remembering how Sen froze under attack. *But that beast could be trained.*

Thinking of Sho, of what he would do in her situation, she made her decision of whom to sell out.

"New runaway wants to join our group. Goes by Sen. You could return her for a reward."

"Nya..." Sahib whispered, a look of confusion and concern pinching up his eyebrows.

This is survival, she thought, not looking at the young warrior.

Sulo's eyes widened. "Sen—as in Senzo Hikari? I heard she'd gone missing."

The name sounded familiar, but she couldn't summon any details. "Isn't that a boy's name?"

"I know of her," Sahib chimed in. "She's Kajar Hikari's daughter."

"What? She's the daughter of the Lightning Guild chancellor? I thought he had a son."

"No—he wanted a son... He did everything he could to make her what she's not," Sulo said.

"Wait—how do you know so much about her?" Nya asked.

The spark of emotion in his eyes surprised her. "I knew her mother," he said, his voice tightening.

Nya felt her hands twitch for the twin blades strapped to her back, and the eight throwing knives secured to her belt and thighs. *He's not going for it.* "Where does that leave us then?"

The Shifter didn't answer right away, his eyes focusing on something beyond her, well past the horizon. "Keep her."

"Someone that valuable?"

Sulo looked her dead in the eye, all the gruffness returning to his voice. "Found out where they take them."

"Who?" Sahib said, leaning into their conversation.

Nya slapped her hand over Sahib's mouth. "I thought I told you not to talk."

"Outliers, kid," Sulo answered. "The ones that don't escape the Realm. They take them to a place called 'the Sanctum' at the base of Hirak mountain, just inside the western Garden Mazes."

Having never heard of such a place, Nya cast her doubt into her response. "All Outliers are killed. You're saying there's something worse?"

Sulo nodded. "There are worse things than death, Nya."

That she could agree on.

"How did you find out?" she asked. Some part of her, which she refused to give recognition, sent her stomach into a nervous flutter.

Anger flashed across Sulo's eyes. She heard a low, baritone rumble, saw the black hair on his chest thicken. Something about that question inflamed him enough to trigger a shift, but he flexed his fists, and fought against the change.

"You owe me," he said, barely getting the words out through gritted teeth.

Nya firmed up her voice. "I'll make it up to you. I'm good for my word."

Tipping his head back, Sulo allowed himself to fall back into his own fury. Golden quills erupted alongside great lengths of brown fur. Nya grabbed Sahib and took off as the sounds of stretching skin and cracking and reshaping bones echoed across the canyon.

The bully bear's roars followed them for the first several miles, but once they reached the edge of the high desert, she only heard her own rapid heartbeat, and the distant clashes of a violent lightning storm raging around Hirak mountain.

"Why would you sell out the new girl?" Sahib asked, wiping the sweat from his brow as she stopped to assess the route. "We haven't even given her a chance to—"

"She's not one of us," she said. Not minding the coldness of her tone, she added: "Don't you ever question me again."

Sahib took a step back, his head tilting to the side as he tried to comprehend her hostility. When she wouldn't acknowledge him any further, he broke out into a sprint, running as fast as he could back toward their camp. Within seconds his long, lanky figure turned into a speck against the red sand and stone.

He's going to pay for that, she thought, kicking back into a run. Not that she could even hope to catch up to him until camp.

After only a few minutes she slowed to a stop, her heart beating madly in her chest. Exhaustion and hunger faded away as Sulo's words rewound and played again, over and over, in her mind: *The ones that don't escape the Realm. They take them to a place called 'the Sanctum'…"*

She looked straight east, out to the sun, her eyes burning as she stared into the fiery orange disk.

They don't kill Outliers.

Terrible and wonderful possibilities filled her mind.

Sho.

With all of her strength, she closed her eyes and fought the surge of emotion, but to no avail. She felt his muscular arm around waist, his calloused hand cupping her cheek as if he stood right in front of her.

"There are worse things than death, Nya."

Sulo's warning pushed away all other senses, leaving her with a pitting fear she hadn't felt since her parents' arrest, before she had learned to control her emotions.

"I'm coming, Sho," she said, digging her fingernails into her palms hard enough to draw blood. Once her heart rate steadied, and she found her breath again, she looked back to Hirak mountain, back to the great blue wall separating the Realm, and whispered. "And we'll end this ugly world together."

▲▽▲

CHAPTER 7

Sen woke up with a start, bewildered by sight of the stone spires scraping against the starry night sky, and the unfamiliar—and mostly unpleasant—smells competing with the smoky aroma of evening campfires. As she tried to roll onto her shoulder, she saw the gigantic black tail draped across her hips, and remembered her circumstances.

How long have I been asleep?

From the scratchiness of her throat, and the stiffness of her body, it could have been more than a day.

"Akoto," she said, looking up to the beast partially curled up around her. Her friend stirred, but only cracked open his eyes for a second before falling back asleep with a huff.

The last happenings came back in a rush: emerging from the cradel poison daze in the middle of a horrifying battle with people that looked more dead than alive. Freezing under attack, only to be saved by Nya, the warrior teenager who could take down an army with her two silver swords. The medicine woman's harsh words: *"You'll not find solace out here, child."* Tending to the dying woman, wishing with all her heart that she could do more than just stay by her side as she slipped away.

"Where is—?" Sen looked to her right, but instead of the sick woman, she found a depression in the ratty animal hide next to her.

Maybe she got up?

"Sen," the medicine woman said, rounding past the campfire. Holding the end of her dress up, she walked toward Sen with a purpose. "Come with me."

Oh no… she thought, heart sinking at grave expression on Natsugra's face.

Frightened, but not knowing why, Sen pressed back into Akoto, wanting him to wake back up. But he wouldn't stir, not even when she shook one of his paws, or lifted up his eyelid.

"Don't bother; I gave him a tranquilizer. You won't be able to wake him until tomorrow morning."

"Why?" Sen said, holding on tight to Akoto flaccid arm.

The medicine woman looked her up and down, weariness inflected in her serious tone. "It's time for your Determining."

Sen shrunk into herself, shoulders caving in as her spine rounded out, legs pressing against her chest. She wanted to scream, but no breath would come up from her lungs.

No—impossible—

They're Outliers! There aren't supposed to be the same rules here.

"Come, child," Natsugra said, turning back around and heading off toward the circle of Chakoans gathering near the central fire.

"Akoto," she whispered, trying one last time to wake her friend with a vigorous shake. No luck. Instead, his tongue flopped out of the side of his mouth, and he snored so loudly that it dispersed the wake of vultures picking over the unattended remains of the battlefield.

Sen couldn't find the volition to budge.

Why would they do this to me?

—I'll fail.

(I'll die.)

"Hey, pssst."

Sen snapped her head to the left. A boy not too much older than her, but bearing similar ink and scars to the rest of the clan, paused as he walked toward the central fire. Keeping his eyes trained ahead, he whispered: "They already know who you are."

Sen didn't know how to interpret what he said. At the moment, it seemed like a warning, but as his words sunk in, a visceral heat started up in her belly, and moved out to her limbs and face.

No, they don't, she thought, cheeks flushing with anger. Not her old schoolmates, not her teachers—and especially not her parents. Nobody did. But that didn't stop anyone from telling her who she was or wasn't.

"You are not what I had hoped," she remembered her father saying as he turned away from her and stared out of his office window, hands clasped behind his back. *"What have I done to deserve you?"*

Sen got to her feet, leaving Akoto behind as she walked right up to the remaining clan members in a semi-circle around the central campfire. The man with the bushy white beard stared expectantly at her from behind the fire, holding something bundled in a ceremonial cloth under one of his arms. Natsugra stood to his left, and Nya, with an especially brooding expression, to his right. The rest of the clan fanned out on either side, fresh war paint darkening their faces, including the boy who had whispered to her just moments ago. Something about his round cheeks and bright blue eyes looked familiar, but she didn't have time to put any more thought to it.

With a wave of his hand, the clan leader commanded the remaining Chakoans to sit. Upset and confused, Sen remained standing, pulling at the ragged strings at the end of her shirt, waiting for the chief to say something.

Stop messing with me, Stop messing with me, Stop messing with me,

Seconds passed like hours as the waning moon poked through the clouds and rock spires, casting amorphous shadows across the high desert.

Stop messing with me, she thought, angry and terrified of what the Chakoan leader could possibly want her to do for their version of the Determining. If she had gone through with her own back in the Realm, she would have been brought before the council of elders from each of the denoms. After looking her over, the council would have decided which test she should take for her Trials: Swarm, Virid, Guild, Order.

If I even got that far.

Even now, trembling before the Chakoan clan, she didn't see how they could suspect anything from her, even a lesser ability to Shift.

Don't you see? I'm nothing! she wanted to scream, tears forming in her eyes.

"I am Osan, chief of the Chakoa," the old man finally said, resting his hands in his lap. "Why do you come to us?"

Sen summoned all of her strength to answer, but little more than a mouse squeak came out. "Because… I'm shadowless."

All except Osan answered her in unison: *"Without a shadow, I seek only the comfort of darkness, and the freedom of its emptiness."*

Osan grabbed the bundle he had set down beside him and tossed it over the fire. A crude sword, spear, and broken battle axe landed near her feet, in addition to four sealed jars that tumbled out of the ceremonial cloth. "Choose one."

Every muscle in her body stiffened. She had weathered her fair share of bullies and physical harassment at school, but no altercation had ever devolved into a full-blown fight. And since she didn't have any brother or sisters, or cousins that paid her any notice, she'd never tested herself beyond her father's trials in the Scylan grove. But practicing breathing techniques and channeling stances didn't compare to a bloody fight where she faced graver injuries than electric shock.

"I don't fight," she said, surprised that the words made it past her tight throat.

Nya stood up, saluted Osan, and then assumed a position opposite of Sen, on the far side of the fire. In an ordinary moment, Nya could level anyone with her gaze, but now, with her twin blades drawn and blue eyes shadowed by a streak of black war paint, Sen felt smaller and weaker than ever before.

"W-why are you doing this?" Sen asked, shuffling back.

The other warriors stood and spread out, making a circle around Sen, Nya, and the roaring fire. A low hum started amongst them, building in intensity, strumming her fears.

"Fight or die," Nya said, spinning her blades around in an impressive display. The other warriors hooted and hollered, chanting phrases in foreign tongues that only seemed to liven the fire and darken Nya's face.

Sen looked back, past the unbreakable circle of warriors, to where her sleeping friend lay. *Wake up, Akoto!*

A blade swished past her face, nicking her chin. The pain shocked her back a few more steps as Nya continued to hack and slash at Sen.

"Stop, please!"

Adrenalized with primal fear, Sen dodged Nya's attack while frantically searching for something—anything—to help her stop the fight. She scrambled across the ground, rolling every which way. Sand got in her hair, her face, her mouth, choking her breath and confusing her senses. But as the teenage warrior's blades sliced closer and closer to their mark, she felt a distinct chill, and her worst fear realize.

Fight or die.

Cold sweat broke out across her brow as she backed up on her hands and feet, moving dangerously close to the fire. Just behind her lay the weapons and the mysterious jars, to her right, the central campfire.

"Stop!" Sen screamed, flailing out as Nya spun on of the blades behind her back and geared up for a final blow.

Something broke inside of her as the blade came screaming down toward her head. A rush of energy came out from a place beyond her perceptions, undamming her fears, and awakening all of her senses at once. The jars behind her shattered, the fire blazing up to the stars. She heard every heartbeat, every halted breath as light exploded all around and inside her, and radiant beams shot forth from behind her closed eyes.

Heaving for breath, she waited and waited for the pain, the death strike, that never came. Instead, she felt pressure against her body, something coarse rubbing up against her skin. When she opened her eyes, she found herself underneath a great wall of fur, trapped by a spiked tail and a furious growl.

Akoto?

Nya and the warriors shouted at each other.

"I thought you tranquilized him!"

"How did he do that—?"

"The fire—he came from the fire!"

Osan's voice rose above all the rest. "Stand down!"

From her limited vantage point, Sen peeked out between Akoto's arms and saw Nya scrambling back to her feet, sand all over her face, hair and clothes, as if she had been blasted backward. The rest of the warriors followed suit as Nya moved away from the agitated beast, slowing lowering her weapons.

What just happened?

Sen didn't believe her gut feeling, or the tingling sensation coursing through her body. *Did Akoto and I... Did he just travel through light?*

No, not possible.

But as she shimmied out from underneath his body, she thought she saw a fading iridescent swirl around her palms.

No, impossible, she told herself again.

Still shaking, she got to her feet and placed her hands on Akoto's chest as he barked and growled at the Chakoans.

"No, please. No more," she said. When he calmed, she turned to Osan. "I don't want to fight."

Osan looked at her with a conflicted expression of fear and wonder. "What is that great beast?"

Sen didn't know how to answer, keeping herself close to her friend. "Please—we don't want to cause trouble. I just—we just—needed…" She wanted to finish the sentence but couldn't, the words sticking to the lump forming in her throat.

"She's dangerous," Nya said, pointing one of her blades at the pair, "and that thing is even more dangerous."

Osan closed his eyes, pressing his hands together and bringing them to his chest. Swaying side to side, he mumbled to himself, then opened his eyes and lifted his hands to the stars. All but the crackling fire fell silent as they waited for his decision.

Keeping his hands together, the Chakoan chief walked back to the ceremonial cloth. Sen didn't understand his action as he meticulously inspected the shattered jars and the spilled contents. Coiled plants, scurrying ants, a moldy, severed crow's head, and the seeds of a Scylan tree. Aside from their broken containers, all of the items appeared unaffected by the strange event.

"She is shadowless," he announced with satisfaction.

I don't understand, she thought, confused at how he could draw such a conclusion.

All the warriors, save Nya, fell to their knees, shaking their fists at the stars as they chanted and cried.

"But what about that thing?" Nya countered. "We don't know what it is, or what it's capable of."

"He's not dangerous!" Sen said, her voice rising.

Osan pointed an arthritic finger at Sen. "How can you be certain of that if you don't know what he is?"

The question bothered her in a way she didn't expect. *Am I too trusting?*

Looking in Akoto's one good eye, the yellow iris with the blue sheen, she lost sight of his canine teeth, or his blackened wings and foreboding stature. Instead, she felt the strength of his arms, the sensation of flying through the air on his back, the way his entire body eclipsed hers as he protected her at her most vulnerable.

She brought her hands to his muzzle, and placed her forehead against his. "You don't need to know what someone is to know if they're good."

Akoto growled, then licked her face.

"She can't stay; it's dangerous to keep someone as high-profile as her, even if she is an Outlier," Nya said.

Her stomach dropped to her knees. *They do know!*

How would they accept her now?

"What do you say to this, child?" Osan asked.

Turning to Osan, Sen kept one hand on her furry friend. "I-It's true. My father is Kajar Hikari, chancellor of the Lightning Guild and rightful ascendant to the world throne, and my mother is Lyn Mor, daughter of Virid sage Hiran Mor. I'm worthless to them an Outlier... Not any better for you. I'm not fast, or good with weapons, and I run away from fights."

"So maybe we should keep your friend, and send you back to the Realm?" Osan said.

Sen heard a waver in his voice, detecting not a threat, but a challenge. Old angers stirred in her chest as she thought of all the times her father tried to trick her, to stress her into making a snap decision in the midst of a crisis. "I'm not good at anything," she said, hands turning to fists. "But that doesn't mean I won't stop you from taking him away."

Osan smiled. Out of the side of her eye, she saw Natsugra nod her head.

"So there is fight in you after all," Osan said.

Nya's scoffed. "Fight? Her monster just rescued her pathetic—"

"Enough!" Osan said, silencing the entire clan with a wave of his hands. He turned to Sen, firelight casting dancing shadows in the hard ridges of his forehead. "What do you wish, child?"

Exhausted and despondent, she couldn't hold back the need that slipped past her lips: "To belong."

She anticipated laughter, chiding, but not the still silence that followed.

"I will make my decision by the morrow," Osan announced, touching his hands together underneath his chin.

"No!" Nya shouted, "we don't have time for this. Our missing warriors—"

"Vision, Nya," Osan said, spreading his arms. "We are two dozen left. What do you expect to do?"

"Not leave our people behind," she shouted, jabbing her hand in the direction of the great wall.

"You don't know that Sho and the others are alive, nor have you confirmed what the Shifter said is true."

"Chief, I—"

"I have made my decision," he said, glaring at her.

Sen watched the dynamic shift as Nya begrudgingly stepped down.

As the clan dispersed, Osan and Nya heading in opposite directions, the boy she recognized came up to her.

"I've never seen anything like that," the boy said, grinning ear to ear. Though he stood several feet away, he looked up to Akoto with awe. "You're something special, big guy."

Sen relaxed a little. "His name is Akoto."

"Nice. I'm Sahib," the boy said, offering his forearm. Sen didn't know their customs, and jumped a little when he clasped his hand midway around her arm. "We sorta know each other from Gatherings."

Not those... she thought, shuddering at the thought. She hated the annual competition between the denoms. Her father always made a big deal out of watching the tournaments, and forced Sen to attend the boring after parties for the politicians and statesmen. Not that he allowed her to talk, or do more than sit still and behave while he made his rounds to forge alliances and secure his ascension to the world throne.

Cheeks turning rosy, she withdrew her arm. "Sorry—I hated the Gatherings. I just tried to make it through without embarrassing my parents too much."

Sahib shrugged his shoulders. "I know the feeling. And I hated dressing up, all the drama and pressure."

"Me too," Sen said, twisting her fingers around the shredded ends of her shirt. "I was always happier away from all of that."

"You'll forget your parents here." The young warrior looked up at the stars. "In the clan, you'll have freedom and family. Real family—not the kind that will throw you out just because you can't bend a plant, make mold, take a zap or whisper to bugs."

A shy smile touched her lips. As Sahib continued to talk, she looked over his face and lean body, amazed at the contrast of tribal ink and scars against the glimmer in his eyes and sweetness in his voice.

"I'm not sure I really belong here," she said, staring at the series of inked lines on the back of his arm. "Nya's right about me. If it weren't for Akoto—"

Sahib made an exasperated sound with pursed lips. "Nya. Don't worry about her."

"What do you mean?" she said as Akoto nudged her forward to make room for himself to stretch out on the sand. As he yawned, his giant tongue curled beside her head, wetting her cheek.

"Nya's tough, don't get me wrong," Sahib said, looking to the left and right as if he didn't want to be overheard. "But she's hard on everyone. It's just her way."

"She tried to kill me!"

Sahib didn't offer her the comfort she wanted. "Trust me—we wouldn't be talking right now if she really wanted you dead."

Unable to wrap her mind around his words, or any of the recent events, Sen fumbled with her hands, mad at herself for the hot tears sliding down her cheeks.

"Sen, a word."

Sahib acknowledged the medicine woman with a salute and returned to the tents, leaving Sen alone with Natsugra.

As much as she tried to hide her tears, the bearded woman caught her using her sleeves to dab at the corner of her eyes and pushed her hands down.

"So, you're Kajar's child," Natsugra said, still holding on to her wrists. "Not the desired son, and even worse yet, shadowless. If ever there was an Outlier, it would be you."

Wiggling her wrists free, Sen looked for a way to escape the conversation, but could find no reprieve within the foreign clan, or the dark landscape. Even Akoto, falling back asleep once again, didn't provide her any protection as Natsugra pried open her secrets.

"Do you know why we tested you today?"

"No," she said, surprised at the anger in her voice. "Like you said—I'm an Outlier."

"And we had to make sure of that," Natsugra said, rolling up her right sleeve to reveal clumps of zig-zagging scar tissue across her forearm.

Those are scorpion bee bites! Sen thought, automatically hugging her arms against her chest. One of the older bullies at her school could control the nasty fist-sized bugs, and sent a few after her once for a laugh. The sting felt worse than getting electrocuted, and it took some of her mother's strongest medicine to neutralize the poison and control the swelling. But even with the best treatment she still got scars—but nothing as bad as Natsugra's. *She could have been killed...*

"Years ago we let in a young boy who said he ran away before his Determining, claiming like you, to be an Outlier. After he learned our secrets, he killed three of our warriors with his bugs, returned back to the Realm, and sent drones after us to clear us out of our homes in the lavafields."

"He was like a spy from the Swarm?"

"Yes," Natsugra said, covering her arm back up. "So now you understand why we have our own 'Determining.'"

It all made sense to her now. The jars, Nya's vicious attack. "If I had talent, I would have used the contents of the jars to protect myself."

"Or Shift, if you had even the lesser ability."

So it's true...I'm not anything.

Fresh tears started up, but she bit down on her lower lip and refused to let them fall.

"You have something special Sen; something I haven't seen in a long time."

Her mother's words competed with the ugly truth circulating in her head until she realized that her hands had turned into shaking fists.

"We've all experienced this anger," Natsugra said, her eyes searching Sen's reddening face. "It will pass once you realize what you are capable of."

What I'm capable of…

Sen thought about Nya, the way the teenage warrior cut down swaths of attackers with expert precision, and could so easily dismiss her without a hint of regret. *I'm not like that.*

Nor was she like Sahib. She couldn't fathom allowing her skin to be inked with tattoos, or scarred to denote battles and rites of passage. Or so easily forgetting her parents. *I'm not like any of them.*

"Come," Natsugra said, taking her hand and leading her back toward the tents. Digging in her heels, she refused to part with Akoto for more than a few feet. "Child, please; he's more than capable of taking care of both of you—even in his sleep."

Sen couldn't help herself; a burgeoning smile turned into a suppressed giggle.

"Go now," Natsugra said, pulling back the flap of the tent and gesturing for her to get inside.

Sen didn't understand, nor did she recognize the shadowed figure curled up on a bearskin.

"Chenzin requested your company."

Chenzin? Sen thought, ducking her head into the tent. As the woman rolled over, she couldn't believe her eyes. *The sick woman! But—*

"She lived," Natsugra said. "So perhaps you have some use after all."

Sen didn't mind the tears that came now as Chenzin reached up with a trembling arm.

"So… beautiful…" the woman rasped.

Scooting next to the Chenzin, Sen clasped her hand in both of hers, a terrified joy filling her heart with all of the possibilities she would not let herself consider.

▲▽▲

CHAPTER 8

As expected, Kaden interrupted her impromptu knife and sword practice atop one of the rock spires.

"Go away," Nya said, jabbing her knife and slashing her sword against invisible attackers.

Kaden grunted as he hauled himself up to the flat top, heaving for breath. On some level she registered his feat. Climbing a seventy-foot spire in the middle of the night, with only the moonlight and the stars to guide his ascent, if only to chase her down for a hearty nag, impressed her even in her worst moods.

As he sat at the edge, not saying or doing anything, she sensed a shift in his demeanor, even without looking directly at his face.

Finally, after felling another invisible attacker, she sheathed her weapons and turned to him.

"What then?"

After clearing his throat and averting his gaze, Kaden responded. "Leyla didn't make it."

Nya suppressed her initial reaction, relying on her learned response. *"Without a shadow, I seek only the comfort of darkness, and the freedom of its emptiness."*

Freedom from attachment, distancing oneself from comfort and compassion. The Chakoa way, the Outlier way.

Her only way.

Squatting down in front of him, she pointed to the hunting knife hanging off of his weapons belt. "Did you perform the severance?"

Kaden nodded, steeling himself to her gaze. Even in the pale light of the moon she saw the burst capillaries reddening the whites of his eyes, the veins that popped out on his forehead.

He's been crying.

She thought less of him until she noticed the frayed ends of the jet-black hair where he had cut off the braids, and the beaded necklace his wife had given him missing from around his neck. Through a complete purge and cleansing, he let his wife go, as their most sacred customs dictated.

Or at least he should have.

He's still holding on to something, she sensed as she watched his eyes mist over.

Regardless, she turned to the stars and emptied her lungs with a scream that filled the night, letting the Godless land hear the ferocity in her that would not die, even if every last one of them fell.

"Don't," Kaden said as she withdrew her own knife. "Save your strength."

"What?" Nya exclaimed.

"We'll need everything we have to find Sho and the others."

Nya couldn't believe any of his words—that he would tell her to defy custom, or dare speak of going against Osan's command. Then again, as much pain as she had endured in her nineteen years, she had never allowed herself to foolishly love like Kaden had, and know such loss.

Her own credo surfaced: *Without attachments, I am invincible.*

"Who would you bring? Only you, me and Sahib are healthy enough to travel."

"The girl and her beast,"

"Sen?" Nya scoffed. "Her beast, maybe, but she'd just get in the way."

Kaden shook his head. "You see the weakness in others. That makes you a great warrior. But you dismiss potential."

"Potential?"

"Sahib could barely string a bow when he got initiated. I couldn't throw an axe more than fifteen feet. Even you—you can't tell me you were born with blades in your hands."

"What if I did?" she said, a smile hinting at the corner of her lips.

"Be serious, Nya. And give her a chance. Everyone deserves a chance, especially our kind."

Nya bristled at the thought. *Sen is not 'our kind.'*

Then she stopped herself. As much as she wanted to get rid of the wimpy girl, Kaden's words cut beneath her skin. *"Everyone deserves a chance."*

Squeezing her eyes shut and gripping the hilt of her knife, she tried to keep unwelcome memories from surfacing. 'Deserving a chance' got her rejected more than once—by her parents, her adopted parents—by the entire recognized world. Emotion tore through her carefully constructed logic. Anger bade her to lash out, to reject any notion of accepting Sen, while something else—a feeling she refused to acknowledge—made her hesitate.

Nya looked out to the west, to the glowing blue walls of the Realm, layering her rage over all the good memories that tried to play out in her mind. The feel of her mother's surprise kiss on her cheek, her father's firm grip as he held her tight until she submitted to the hug. A bed to sleep in, a roof always over her head, warm food in her belly. Memories of a different time, an entirely different life; of a promise broken on her fourteenth birthday when her parents tried to shelter her, keep her from undergoing the Determining, only to be arrested and taken away.

They knew, everyone knew, what she wasn't. As all her schoolmates predicted, the orphan child of Outlier parents left at the gates of the great wall turned out to be just as forsaken as her biological parents.

I didn't deserve anything, she thought, spitting out the bitter contents of her mouth. *And neither does Sen.*

"She is not 'our kind,' Kaden," she said, dousing her words in fury. "At the very least, she has to prove herself, just like the rest of us have."

"That beast could be the difference between a rescue and a suicide mission," Kaden countered.

Nya sighed and unsheathed her swords again, resuming her fight against imagined foes. "You're assuming Osan will accept her."

"Osan didn't turn away Rigen. He won't turn away Sen."

Rigen. Her blood boiled at the mere mention of his name. Although she only met him briefly, right before he betrayed the Chakoa and ran back to the Realm, she remembered the look in his eyes. The cold calculation, the anger. Things she could relate to, but not the greed that crafted his disingenuous smile. Something about him never sat right with her, but then again, as attractive and well-spoken as he was, she couldn't help but hate herself for falling for the same trap the rest of them had.

Carving up the wind with her blades, Nya balanced on one leg, then somersaulted forward, bringing down both her swords in a sweeping arc that made even Kaden, who had watched her practice for years, shift back.

"Rest up," she said after she finished her kata. "We'll leave first thing in the morning."

Kaden acknowledged her with a nod, then climbed back down over the lip of the rock, disappearing into the night.

Without missing a step, Nya launched right into the next kata, fighting through the memories of the past, of Leyla's death, of the pressure building beneath her breastbone. She embraced the chill of the night air, the surrounding darkness, the persistent hunger gnawing at her belly as she swung her blades, and committed herself to the only truth, the only purpose, she knew.

▲▽▲

When Nya returned to camp in the morning, Osan's acceptance of Sen into the clan didn't surprise her, but the sudden storm did. From the ground-shattering booms of thunder, and the frequency of the lightning strikes, she had a good idea why she didn't see it coming.

Looks like the Lightning Guild got into a fight, she thought, standing out in the rain with one hand shielding her eyes. The icy sheets cut through her animal skins, right down to her bones, but she didn't waver. Not when her gut pulled at her to understand something she couldn't yet see.

"Nya, get inside already!" Osan shouted from inside the protection of his tent.

The rescue mission would have to wait.

Grumbling, Nya took one last look at the black, congested clouds in the sky and trudged back over to her tent. When she pulled the flap back and saw the hazel eyes peeking out from underneath her deerskin blankets, she threw up her hands. "What are you doing here?"

"Natsugra said—"

Nya didn't care to hear the rest of her pitiful explanation. Even if the medicine woman needed to stay with Chenzin to continue her treatment, or if there wasn't enough in any other tent, why did she have to pick hers?

"Where's your beast?"

Sen pointed outside. Ducking her head back out of the tent, Nya spotted the black mass in a flash of lightning. The gigantic monster curled in on himself into a tight ball underneath one of the rock segments of a fallen spire.

"Why aren't you out there with him?"

Shooting out from underneath the blankets, Sen scurried over to the tent flap. "I thought he was okay—his fur—he seemed okay—oh no—should we bring him inside?"

With a sigh, Nya pushed the girl back to the blankets. "He's fine. Forget it already."

As the girl looked nervously back and forth between the flap and Nya, she unbelted her weapons and started shedding her wet clothes. "You've got a lot to learn if you really want to be one of us."

Nya hated Sen's expression. Innocent confusion; a face unscored by bitterness and years of disappointment. And those big hazel eyes, wide and still searching for answers, not expecting the worst.

"First thing: your beast out there—"

"Akoto," Sen interjected.

With a huff, Nya continued. "*Akoto.* Don't get attached. No day out here is guaranteed."

Sen's brow scrunched together, but she didn't argue, just curled her knees up to her chest and watched Nya's every move.

Several flashes of lightning preceded a peal of thunder. Nya checked the oil in the clay lamp atop the small wooden bench housing her collection of personal items. Judging by the low levels, they'd need to scavenge or go on a raid for more supplies in the next day anyway.

Nya stifled a smile as she pulled off her drenched top. *This is how I'll convince Osan to authorize a raid.*

(Sho...I'm coming.)

"How did you get those?"

The question jarred her from her thoughts. Nya grabbed her shirt and covered up the criss-crossing scars on her stomach.

"That's not your business."

Sen's shoulders hiked up to her ears. "Sorry…They just don't look like the rest."

No, they didn't. All the other scars on her body came from battles or rites of passage, forming either a singular mark or a distinct pattern. Not the chaotic, successive strokes that simultaneously sheltered and projected her darkest secrets.

Nya continued to disrobe, this time shielding the old wounds she did not want to explain. As she pulled on a thin pair of pants and shirt, the only clothes other than her armor left in her possession, she caught Sen still eyeing her up and down.

"You got a problem?"

Looking down at her fumbling hands, Sen muttered the word, no, but then paused. "You've got more muscle than most boys."

Nya tore down her smile before it could even form. "You're still seeing the world from the other side of the wall. Out here we don't have great feasts with cream cakes and cherry dumplings to make us fat. And our women fight just like the men, not get married off to forge false allegiances and pop our heirs in some ancient tradition that already died once."

Sen licked her lips, as if the mere mention of cream cakes and cherry dumplings awakened her hunger pains.

Finished with their conversation, Nya pulled out one of the blankets from underneath Sen, making her yelp as she toppled over. Without giving her so much as an apology or a glance, the teenage warrior made a place for herself near the wooden bench, counting the lightning strikes and thunder crashes.

Must be a big fight, she thought, sitting cross-legged in front of the clay lamp.

As she tried to concentrate on more important things, she saw Sen out of the corner of her eye pushing her brown hair behind her ears, only to have it fall back in her face. The girl studied her for a while, then rearranged a spot on the remaining blanket to lay down.

Nya went through her mental list of supplies they'd need for the rescue mission until she heard the girl humming to herself.

"Stop that."

"Stop what?"

"That ridiculous humming."

"Sorry," Sen said.

The silence only lasted another minute before the girl found something else to pester her with. "You weren't really going to kill me for my

Determining, were you?"

Sahib, Nya guessed, rolling her eyes. "Keep bugging me and find out."

But after a moment, curiosity got the best of her. "How did you do that fire trick with Akoto anyway?"

"What fire trick?"

That pissed her off. "Don't play stupid, kid. The explosion of light that threw me back. It looked like it came from the fire. Then he appeared right on top of you."

Sen bit down on her lower lip, looking like she feared what her answer would elicit. "Dunno."

"Useless," she muttered, turning back to the candlelight and closing her eyes to meditate.

"No."

The sharpness of Sen's tone got her attention. "No?"

"No. I'm not useless."

Nya grabbed one of the knives strapped to her weapons belt on the tent floor and threw it into Sen's lap. The girl reared back as if expecting a subsequent blow.

"Can you hunt? Can I count on you in battle?" Lunging at Sen, she grabbed the knife she threw into the girl's lap and held it to her throat. "Can you kill?"

The tears in the girl's eyes didn't surprise her, but her response did. "Maybe I won't have to."

"What?"

"You don't always have to fight."

Sitting back on her feet, Nya dismissed the girl with a hearty laugh and lobbed the knife back near her belt. "Tell Osan that for your initiation."

"Initiation?"

"Yeah. That's when you choose your weapon, and we take you on your first hunt."

Sen's eyes darted back and forth as she started scratching at the healing spider bites on her right chest and shoulder.

"Stop that. *Stop that,*" Nya said, pulling Sen's hand away and inspecting the wound. "You're just making it worse."

With a sigh, she reached into one of the sacks belted into the waistband of her armored pants, and offered Sen a pinch of crushed red leaves.

"Chew on these, then rub the paste on the wound. It'll stop the itching."

Sen hesitated, her hand poised above Nya's.

"Take it," she insisted. *If she even mentions Natsugra's beard, I'm going to—*

"Thanks."

The girl's smile brightened her dirty face. Even after all her conditioning, Nya caught herself reacting, feeling something more than the bite of her foul mood.

Returning once again to her blanket, Nya assumed her cross-legged position and tried to gain meditative focus. She managed to ignore Sen's loud chomping until a dozen lightning strikes flashed in rapid succession, followed by concussive roll of thunder.

"Nya…?"

"What?!"

"Someone's attacking the wall."

Nya reared around. "Why do you think that?"

"That's a *mor'tye,*" Sen said, removing the mushy red glob from her mouth and smearing it on her shoulder. "A twelve-point attack pattern used by the Guild post."

"You know attack patterns?"

Sen nodded. "My Father was a captain in the guard before he got into politics…"

This is good, Nya thought, not caring that Sen's gaze drifted off or that her brow furrowed from some painful recollection. *She knows more about the Guild than any of us do.*

In fact, Nya couldn't recall the last time they ran into a Guild Outlier, even from another clan. Of all the denoms, the shock jockeys kept the tightest reign on their citizens. A child escaping before their Determining just didn't happen.

"Wait a minute—how did you escape from the Guild?" Nya asked, casting her suspicion into the question. "Especially if your father is Kajar Hikari. They would have kept you on lockdown right before your Determining."

Sen twirled her brown hair around her finger, not looking directly at the warrior. "I ran away in the middle of the night."

"Yeah, sure. Just climbed out of your bedroom window."

"N-no. Jumped."

Nya scoffed. "Jumped?"

"Onto the canopy tree my mother's been growing in the palace garden. It's huge. Almost to my window. Really giant bouncy leaves."

Scrutinizing the girl's face or her posture didn't give Nya any reason to doubt her. Still, part of her refused to believe the gangly looking kid before her had the gumption to take such a leap.

"Then?"

Sen picked at the toes of her boots, keeping her head down. "I climbed up some overgrown vines to get over the wall… and then…"The young girl opened her hand and made a poof sound. "Disappeared."

Nya waited until another series of lightning flashes and thunder crashes passed, watching Sen's growing concern. *She knows more than she even realizes. Might get some use out of her after all…*

As wind and rain pelted the tent, Nya considered all of what Sen had said, and decided to push for anything else she could get out of her. Especially if it could help her find Sho. "So who's attacking the wall? What kind of enemies does your father have?"

Sen looked to the tent flap, as if she wanted to run outside, right into the storm.

Back to her father, Nya realized.

"Don't know."

"Come on, he's got enemies. He's ascending the throne, taking over world power from the Virids…"

The girl didn't take the bait. Instead, worry spread across her face, widening her eyes and making her lips tremble. "Do you think he's okay?"

"Why do you care?"

Sen looked shocked at the question.

"You want to go back? What—you think they'd take in an Outlier like you, especially after you ran away like a 'shadowless coward?'"

"But if he's in trouble, maybe I can—"

"You'd be killed," Nya said, not cushioning the blow. "Or worse."

Dismay crushed the girl's shoulders down, making her appear even smaller than before. "I know."

"You know what?"

"My mom never really talked about it, but she had a brother, Haebi. She told me once that he and I were a lot alike. Everyone but my mom said he killed himself before his Determining. Either way, my family made sure he disappeared," Sen lifted her head, looking at Nya with large hazel eyes. "If I return, I'll end up like Haebi. Forgotten, erased. Dead one way or another."

Before Nya could push her agenda, Sen added: "But that doesn't mean I can just give up on them."

Nya sensed her opportunity. "Once this storm passes, I'm leading a rescue mission. Some of our people are trapped in a place called the Sanctum."

"What's that?"

"A secret place they keep Outliers. Maybe your uncle is there."

Sen perked up. "Really?"

"Yeah. It'll be dangerous. We don't usually venture that far into the Realm. You and Akoto want in?"

"But what about my parents?" Sen asked, absently scratching at her wounds.

"We'll be passing through Guild territory. We can check up on them."

A skeptical look crossed her face, but ultimately Sen's need triumphed over any doubt. "Ok."

"Good," Nya said, going back to her meditative position.

After a long silence, one that almost had Nya convinced that the kid could be quiet for more than a minute, Sen whispered: "Nya… we're friends then, right?"

Nya sighed, trying to figure out some way to avoid answering such a stupid question. "Get some rest, kid."

Thunder boomed overhead. Nya lost track of all the lightning flashes, and the occupants of her tent as she concentrated her energy on her objective.

Nothing will stop me from reaching you, Sho.

She opened her eyes, looking into the candle flame, seeing the entire world afire.

Nothing.

▲▽▲

CHAPTER 9

As the storm started to dissipate, Sen squeezed out from underneath Akoto's wing and ran through the drizzle to Chenzin's tent. Inside, Natsugra sat cross-legged next to the sick woman, eyes closed and waving her hands up and down her body. Sen recognized a few words to her chant, but not many.

Sounds like beetle-tongue, she thought, cramming herself inside the tent. *Maybe Natsugra's from the Swarm!*

"What are you doing here?" Natsugra said, popping one eye open and frowning. "I told you to stay with Nya."

"Nya's not very fun."

The medicine woman pretended to pat down her beard to hide her smirk. "Do you know any of the Virid medicine?"

Sen wrapped her arms around her ankles and shrugged. "My mom was a healer, but…"

The old woman looked her up and down. "But she didn't teach you?"

"No, she tried." Sen caved under Natsugra's patient silence. "I just never paid much attention."

"Ah, I see. So you're a daydreamer," she said, grabbing some wooden bowls and mixing herbs together as she talked. "We've had a few like you in the clan. These lands will toughen you up…"

Natsugra paused as she held Chenzin's head up to offer her some water from a clay pitcher. "Or take you."

Pulling her legs in close, Sen dared to dig a little deeper. "They used to teach us in school that there are only savages, monsters, and disease outside the Realm. I thought they told us that to keep us from sneaking over the wall."

Natsugra huffed. "They're right. What did you expect?"

The question made her scrunch up her brow. "I didn't think I'd find people like you."

"Savages?"

"No. Survivors."

With a faint smile on her face, Natsugra placed her palm on Chenzin's forehead, whispered another prayer, and then turned back to Sen. "Our clan has been through much, child, but these last few years have thinned our ranks and have taken down the best of us."

"Sickness?"

"Disease, clan warfare, denom hunters—and yes, those monsters you mentioned. That's why we have our credo— *Without a shadow, I seek only the comfort of darkness, and the freedom of its emptiness.* Invisible, we are without attachment, we seek no God, and therefore, are free."

The clan logic didn't make sense to her. "But then why help each other? Why have a clan at all?"

Natsugra elbowed Sen out of the way to get what she wanted out of the sack next to her hip. "We are without attachment, but that does not mean we are without loyalty to each other. After all, what purpose is there to life if not for your clan, your family?"

Family.

Her mother and father's faces flashed through her mind.

Choking back the lump in her throat, she waited until she thought her voice wouldn't falter before speaking again. "Is that why Nya wants to lead a rescue mission inside the Realm?"

Natsugra reared her head around. "What?"

Regret and fear spiked her heart. *Oh no—maybe it was a secret!*

"Answer me, child—what did Nya say?"

The old woman gripped her wrist, but the look in her eye portended concern more than punishment. With a wobbly voice, Sen tried to absorb some of the damage she'd already caused. "She wants to save some of your group that got taken. Family is important to her."

"Too important," Natsugra mumbled, letting go of her wrist and shaking her head. "It's critical to know when to let someone go, Sen. You can't save everyone—and sometimes the greater good outweighs an individual life no matter how special they are to you."

Feeling the weight to Natsugra's words, Sen waited for the medicine woman to continue.

"This is about Sho," the old woman whispered. "Her greatest love—and her greatest mistake."

Confused, Sen didn't know how to respond. *How can loving someone be a mistake?*

She thought of her father, and his grave disappointment in all that Sen wasn't.

"I understand," she whispered.

Natsugra checked on Chenzin, feeling for the pulse in her neck and the temperature of her ashen skin. "Her spirit grows distant. I'm not sure if she'll wake up again."

"But I thought she was getting better?"

"Aye, me too. Perhaps she just rallied for you."

Not sure how to take Natsugra's statement, Sen watched as the medicine woman applied a poultice to her forehead.

"You need to start taking *charaza*," Natsugra said, reaching into a sack out of Sen's immediate view. She returned back with a handful of black seeds that she offered to Sen. "These will help boost your immunity, give you some protection against what's out here."

"You mean sickness?" Sen said, accepting the black seeds and inspecting them up close. She hadn't seen anything like them before, not even in her mother's guidebooks.

"Yes. There's always something new infecting our people. Why do you think the favored hide behind that wall?"

Sen put a seed in her mouth and took a bite. At first she didn't taste anything, but then she felt as if she had swallowed dirt.

"Ew—"

"Don't spit it out," Natsugra said, covering Sen's mouth with her hand until she complied.

"Blech," Sen said, wiping off her tongue with her sleeve.

"It's better than dying, yes?"

Sen sighed, put the rest in her satchel, and rested her head on her knees. "It's not going to give me a beard, is it?"

A look of shock, then anger, crossed Natsugra's face, but as Sen shrunk back, Natsugra chuckled. "Nya's our best warrior, but she can't tell a petal from a thorn."

"I know," Sen said, pulling at the neck of her shirt to show Natsugra the concoction Nya had given her to smear across her spider bites. Curious little green shoots sprouted up from the red paste, some of them already budding yellow flowers.

"For God's sake," Natsugra mumbled, pulling Sen closer to her to have a better look. Still muttering under her breath, the medicine woman pulled over a bowl full of water and a washcloth, and indicated for Sen to take off her shirt.

"Scrub that off—and then put this on it," Natsugra said, handing her a pinch of crushed blue leaves.

After cleaning off and applying the correct medicine, Sen put her shirt back on and returned the dirty water bowl to Natsugra.

"Thanks," she said, "for helping me—again."

Natsugra's expression vacillated between a smile and a frown, and settled on revulsion when Sen scooted closer and reached up to her beard.

"What are you doing?"

"Braiding," Sen said, separating the gray and white hairs with her fingers.

The old woman stayed stiff for a moment, but as Sen continued to work, she eased up. "You're a strange one, you know that?"

After finishing, Sen reached into her satchel and pulled out one of the strings that had held down the cherry dumplings inside the rice paper, and used that to tie off her work. "Better."

"Better?"

"Yeah."

Natsugra shook her head, but didn't undo Sen's creation. "Go now. The storm has almost passed, and I must keep my focus on Chenzin."

"Yeah," Sen said, sitting back on her heels and staring at the ground.

Running her fingers along her new braids, Natsugra studied Sen's face, and deduced her worry. "Nya asked you to go with her, didn't she? Is that why you came to my tent?"

Sen nodded.

"I see. You're worried why she wants you?"

Picking at the toe of her boots, Sen sighed. "Not me. She wants Akoto. It's not like I'm a fighter."

"Maybe not like Nya, no."

Sen couldn't find the words to go on. Instead, she dropped her gaze so that the medicine woman wouldn't see what she couldn't express.

"You don't want to go back at all," Natsugra said.

"I want to make sure my parents are okay, but…"

"Being afraid doesn't mean you're a coward, Sen."

"You don't know my father," she whispered. Shame made her hesitate. *No—Natsugra has to know. They should all know.*

She removed her boots and socks, and held up one foot at a time for the medicine woman to see.

"You tried to channel lightning?" Natsugra said, inspecting the exit wounds on her feet and then reaching for her hands.

"My father insisted that I practice."

Tracing the branching scars on her Sen's palms, she didn't accept what she saw. "Even before your Determining? How could he know you were favored for the Guild?"

He didn't, she thought, too embarrassed to answer out loud.

"What he did is forbidden. You could have been killed!"

Sen took back her hands and sandwiched them in her armpits. "That doesn't matter. The Guild, and upholding his denom's place as the greatest world power, is all that he cares about."

"How does electrocuting his only child make the Guild strong?"

"He wanted to prepare me. For battle, I guess. To be stronger. To be like him."

"I see," Natsugra said, her voice quieting.

As the rain continued to patter against the tent cloth, Sen listened for thunder and watched for a flash of lightning, but none came. *The battle's over.*

That meant that Nya would want to leave soon—if she hadn't already talked to Osan, and gathered Sahib and Kaden.

Natsugra folded her hands across her lap. "Why did you come to me, Sen?"

Lips trembling, she forced herself to look up as she pleaded for her best friend. "Will you watch over Akoto if I get taken back? He doesn't have anywhere else to go."

Natsugra reached around Sen and pulled back the front flap to the tent. Breaks in the clouds allowed for beams of yellow sunlight to fall from the sky and illuminate the wet sand and dirt.

"He seems just fine on his own," the medicine woman observed. Growling and digging at the base of a weeping cacti, the gigantic black beast uncovered a nest of squirming white grubs. Within seconds he devoured the entire nest, and the unprotected roots of the cacti. "Even if he doesn't have the best tastes."

"Please," Sen said, tugging on the end of Natsugra's dress.

"Fine," she huffed, squaring herself back to Chenzin and shooing Sen with a wave of her hand. "Be off now. Stop pestering me."

Sen paused before ducking out of the tent, feeling something left unfinished. As she crawled back to Natsugra's side, she gazed upon Chenzin, drawing closer and closer to the sick woman's body until she found herself holding her icy hand.

"What are you doing?" Natsugra asked.

If she had an answer, she would have responded, but Sen didn't know herself what force drew her in.

Sensing a distinct gap between herself and Chenzin, one much greater than the space between them appeared, she called out, only to surprise herself by projecting the thought instead of speaking the words. *Hello?*

No answer.

Stupid—what did I expect? she thought, ready to pull away.

But then she saw something, a twinkle of light superimposed against Chenzin's chest. Without thinking, she reached out, grasping for what couldn't exist, feeling ridiculous as her fingers raked through air, and then came to rest on the sick woman's chest.

"Sen—what is this?" Natsugra said, pulling her hand off and holding her away.

"S-sorry, I don't know," she said, cheeks burning red. "I thought I…"

What's wrong with me?

A thousand excuses ran through her head. *Maybe there's still cradel poison in me—I'm hallucinating. No, it's from Nya's mixed-up medicine.*

I'm crazy. Stupid. I don't know—

"Chenzin?" Natsugra said, bending over the sick woman.

Chest rising and falling more rapidly, Chenzin's limbs tensed, her hands and feet curling in on themselves.

"Give me that," Natsugra said, pointing to the wooden bowl full of a purplish ground paste. "Hurry!"

Sen knocked over all of the bowls and pitchers in between, but managed to grab what Natsugra wanted and handed it to her just as Chenzin arched back, all of the muscles in her neck bulging and taut. Taking a scoop of the paste with her fingers, the medicine woman applied it to Chenzin's lips, chanting in a foreign tongue.

"Give me your hand," Natsugra said.

Sen complied, allowing the medicine woman to raise her left arm, following suit with her right as Natsugra's chants escalated.

Frightened, Sen shut her eyes and held her breath. *Did I hurt her? What did I do?*

The same light, much brighter than before, appeared behind her closed lids, illuminating the outline of Chenzin's body. Next to her, a second light emerged, one that gave form to Natsugra.

Sen squeezed her eyes shut even harder. *Not real—*

Golden light branched out from her chest, connecting with the shining stars to her left and in front of her. A wave of energy stole the breath from her lungs, and she gulped for air, opening her eyes and lurching forward.

"I'm sorry," she said between breaths. "I didn't mean to—"

"Be quiet," Natsugra said, leaning down and putting her ear to Chenzin's lips. The sick woman, no longer animated or tense, laid in front of them unmoving.

Heart beating in her ears, Sen waited for what felt like eternity. *Please be okay. Please be okay!*

Chenzin gasped, and sat up at the waist, eyes wider than saucers.

"Peace, Chenzin," Natsugra said, trying to get her to lie back down. "You're safe."

"Stars, no sky ..." the sick woman said, her voice rising and falling. Turning her head, she saw Sen, tears brimming over her eyelids. "You... sunlight..."

Natsugra mirrored Sen's confusion as she tried to quiet Chenzin. "Please—"

"So beautiful," Chenzin said, reaching out to Sen with quivering fingers.

Feeling the pulse in Chenzin's wrist, Natsugra's insistence turned to panic. "Your heartrate is too high, Chenzin. Please, you must lay back!"

But no matter what Natsugra tried, Chenzin stayed sitting up, her eyes locked on Sen, arms extended. Torn between what she felt and what she feared, Sen froze in place, not knowing what to do.

"Na...nas..." Chenzin sputtered, her arms dropping to her side. Falling back, Chenzin's eyes rolled around in their sockets.

"What's she saying?" Natsugra said, bracing the woman's shoulders.

"...ci...nas...ci."

Sen tilted her head to the side. "Nasci?"

"No—that's not possible—"

A sigh, long and relaxed, escaped from Chenzin's lips. Her eyelids closed, and her movements stilled.

Natsugra laid her hand on Chenzin's face and whispered a prayer in her native tongue.

"Is she...?"

The old medicine woman pulled an animal skin blanket up over Chenzin's face. "She's gone."

Sen's legs took charge before her mind could catch up. Bursting out of the tent, Sen sprinted into the rain, the droplets hitting her exposed skin like cold needles.

What did I do? Guilt clawed at her heart, making her legs pump even faster. *I killed her!*

Directionless, she didn't care where she went, as long as she got as far away as she could from the red sands and dirt, the imposing judgements of the towering rock spires, and the whispered words of the dying woman.

Stars, no sky—

Sunlight.

Nasci...

"Sen!" She saw Nya and Osan in her peripheries as she passed by the last tent where they stood outside arguing. "Where are you going?"

Ignoring Nya's shouts, she ran even faster, her lungs burning, her eyes blurring with wind, rain and tears. A dark shadow appeared just behind her, but she didn't need to look back, hearing his limping gait and occasional snort.

Akoto—

Canine jaws clamped around her ankle. Falling forward, she face-planted into the ground, sucking in sand into her nose and mouth. Coughing, she yanked her leg back and freed herself, only to have him bat her back and hold her down at the chest with his giant paw.

His baritone growl rumbled across the desert, shocking the cry from her lips. Teeth bared, he raised his hackles, pressing down on his paw to her chest.

Can't breathe—

Pounding her fists against his paw, she squeaked out her last breath. "Get off!"

Dark spots danced across her vision.

Why?! You're my friend!

Lowering his head to hers, she saw into his eyes, one scarred and pale, the other clear yellow as the sun. The distance between them vanished, the pain of his weight against her chest, the grating feel of sand against her skin. As the world stilled, she heard her mother's voice whisper across the expanse.

Nasci…

▲▽▲

CHAPTER 10

Twin blades drawn, Nya soared through the air, ready to deal a death blow to Sen's attacker. Forgetting everything else—Sen's professed friendship with the midnight beast, the strange bond between the two—and ignoring all other possibilities, she zeroed in on the meat of neck where sliceable arteries would make for a quick kill.

But as she came down, time slowed, so much that she perceived more than just her target, but the animated world around her; the wind soughing through the spires, rain still sprinkling from the skies and hitting her cheeks, the insect sibilance humming across the desert sands. Her own heartbeat transformed into a visible pulse behind her eyes, and the sweat flying off her forehead and the back of her neck connected her to the environment around her.

Akoto snapped his head in her direction just as her blades hissed down within inches of his neck. As soon as she saw into his golden eye, an explosion of light, energy and sound blasted her away. She hit the ground hard, knocking the air from her lungs, and tumbled across the sands, losing her weapons in the fray.

She looked up, vision see-sawing, not understanding what she saw. A fire-yellow halo swirled in and around Sen and Akoto, binding them together as the beast growled and bared his teeth at the young outcast.

"Nya!"

The chief's strong arms got her to her feet, but she couldn't seem to make them work just yet. Leaning on Osan's shoulder, she watched in silenced awe as Sen hugged Akoto's paw and rested her forehead against his muzzle. The light around them surged, then faded away.

Other clan members caught up, standing beside them, weapons drawn.

"What happened?" Kaden said, axes in hand.

"I don't... Akoto... light... exploded," Nya tried, but she couldn't get the racing thoughts in her head to come out making any sense.

"Sen!" Sahib took a few steps closer to Akoto and Sen than the others braved. "Sen—are you okay?"

Disoriented, Sen looked their direction, but didn't seem to recognize her surroundings until Akoto released her, and she rolled out from beneath his paw.

"Sen! Explain yourself," Osan demanded, handing Nya over to Kaden. Keeping his walking stick out in front of him, he approached the strange girl and her beast. Sahib trailed close behind the chief, notching an arrow in his bow. Infuriated, Nya shoved off Kaden and stumbled to her weapons lying in the sand, picking them up and assuming a teetering attack stance.

"Nasci!"

The old medicine woman's cry stopped them all in place.

"What did you say?" Osan put out his hands to stop his advancing warriors.

Nya looked back and forth between Osan, Sen, and Natsugra.

What the…did Natsugra braid her beard?

"Don't harm either of them," the medicine woman said, hobbling along as fast as her arthritic knees would carry her. "I saw something—we all saw something."

Osan huffed. "And you claim 'nasci?' There hasn't been a nascent being in over 1,000 years."

Kaden and Sahib acted just as dismissive. "It's that monster!"

"Maybe he's from the Wastes—could be a mutant of some sort."

Other clan members gathered around, whispering and pointing at the young outcast still hiding beneath the midnight beast. Sensing the rising tension, Nya reaffirmed her grips on her blades, and dug her heels into the sand, ready for even the slightest provocation to battle.

"Don't hurt him," Sen said. Her feeble voice hardened as she knotted her fingers into Akoto's fur. "He didn't do anything wrong."

"Then why did he attack you?" Nya said.

"He didn't. Well, no. He was…" Close to tears, Sen struggled for every word. "He stopped me from running away. I got scared. Sorry."

"All of you—go back to your tents, now," Osan ordered. "Nya, Natsugra—stay here."

As the rest of the clan returned to the tents, Nya kept her eyes on Sen and the beast.

Something's changed. She sensed it in her gut, though she couldn't quite put her finger on what as she stared down the girl. Nothing in Sen's eyes, or the awkward way she carried her skinny frame; just something around or about her—a spark in the air, a new lightness to her step.

"Stand your beast down," Osan said as Akoto stood protectively over Sen.

Whispering to Akoto and pulling on his fur, she got the dark giant to lay down behind her, though he took to it with his regular grumble.

Finally feeling steady, Nya re-sheathed her swords, but kept her hands by the throwing knives strapped to her waist and thighs as she joined Osan's side across from Sen.

"Sit," Osan commanded. He waited until Sen, Nya, and Natsugra took their places until he assumed his cross-legged posture.

"Do you know what a nasci is, Sen?" the chief said, watching her every move.

Stupid question, Nya thought. *No kid ever knows about that dumb legend until they escape the wall.*

To her surprise, Sen nodded. "My mom told me about it once, but she made me swear not to speak of it, especially in front of my father."

Osan looked as shocked as Nya felt. "What do you know?"

"She said that a 'nasci' is an emergent being; the first person to form a harmonic bond with a spirit. Someone who awakens a power."

"She's right. There hasn't been a nasci since the awakening of the last denom, the Swarm, over 1,000 years ago. And as far as the people inside the wall are concerned, there are only the five denoms: Virids, Lightning Guild, Order of Nezra, Swarm, and the Shifters. To even speak of a sixth denom inside the Realm would mean lifetime imprisonment. I'm curious: how would your mother come to know this? Only we shadowless can whisper of such legends."

Sen wound the frayed ends of her shirt around her fingers. "Dunno. Maybe because she needed find something to believe in. About my uncle, about me."

The sadness embedded in Sen's words made Nya cringe, then incensed enough so that she smacked the ground with her hand. "Rubbish. It's the beast, for bloody sake. That thing isn't from these lands. Kaden's right—what if he's from the Wastes? What if he's some sort of mutant with new disease?"

"Nya—" Osan said, raising his hands to calm her.

"No—there's no way that kid is a nasci. To even entertain that idea is an insult to every Outlier that's ever lived and died out here!"

Sen's shoulders got lower, her brow knitting together, but Nya didn't care if she hurt the kid's feelings. A nascent being wasn't anything to joke about. It opened up possibilities she didn't want to consider, especially after learning to survive on the one thing she could always count on in the harsh outlands.

"Set aside your anger, Nya, and consider what we all saw," Osan said. "That light surrounded both of them."

"And you did something to Chenzin," Natsugra added, looking at Sen. "She came back, if only for a moment."

Nya flung a handful of sand outside their circle. "This is a waste of time. Don't you remember Ostora, Kenzin, or Eray?"

"Who are they?" Sen interjected.

"Dumb kids—like you—from other clans. Everyone thought they were nasci—that they could elevate all of us from shadowless to… to…"

She couldn't think of what.

"Screw it!"

Storming back toward camp, Nya determined not to let any more distractions stop her mission. *Not the weather, not Osan—and certainly not some stupid kid.*

"Nya?" Kaden said as soon as she rounded the tents and came to the central fire. Both he and Sahib sat cross-legged, sharpening their weapons with their backpacks stuffed and ready to go besides them.

"We're going. Now."

But both warriors looked past her, eyes narrowing, no longer interested in tending their weapons or listening to her command.

Instinct kicked in. In one fluid motion, she spun around and drew her swords, ready to take down whatever summoned their attention.

"Sulo, no—"

The words barely left her mouth as she sprinted toward the bully bear stumbling across the sands. Bloody and beaten, she wouldn't have recognized him if not for the sharp green of his eyes, and what remained of the golden quills descending his back.

"Nya! Stop!"

More than one clan member screamed her name, but she lost herself in Sulo's pain as he crashed into a spire, and slid down onto his side.

Forgetting his state, she tried to approach him, but as soon as she neared his face, he lashed out with gnashing teeth and desperate swipes of his paws.

"What happened to him?" Sahib said, catching up to her, but keeping his distance.

No animal did this, she thought, sheathing her swords and looking over the grievous wounds. Great lacerations split down his back, branching down into his hind legs like a charred tree. Angry red blisters covered the raised ridges of swollen tissue where his golden-brown fur had been burnt away.

The storm—

She heard Sen's words in the back of her mind. *"That's a mor'tye…A twelve-point attack pattern used by the Guild post."*

"Shock jockeys did this," Nya replied, stooping down to level with the bully bear.

But why?

It didn't matter. Not now, when his breath came in great heaves, and his movements became less and less coordinated.

"Sulo," Nya said, trying to get his attention with the sharpness of her voice. "You need to turn back. I can't help you like this."

Kaden and Osan joined her side, each of them knowing well enough to stand behind her and not antagonize the bully bear.

"The rest of you—back off," she commanded, waving away the clan members emerging from their tents or approaching the scene with weapons in hand. She spotted Sen and her beast not too far off, looking on with wide, curious eyes.

"Who's this?" Natsugra said, pushing aside all but Nya to see the wounded Shifter.

"Sulo. He's my best contact in the Realm."

He can lead us to Sho—

The bully bear growled and snapped at Natsugra as she tried to take a step closer.

"I can't do anything for him while he's shifted," the medicine woman said, looking to Nya. "You've got to get him back or he'll die."

"Sulo, wake up!" she said, stretching out her arms to display her tattoos and scars. The bully bear dropped his head, blood dripping from his ears, saliva frothing from his mouth. "Come on—don't do this, you stupid mutt. We want to help you!"

Yelling didn't help, but she didn't know what else to do.

"Please," she said, dropping to her knees as he rasped and grunted, his eyes no longer maintaining any kind focus. "Shift back. Don't do this to me."

One word, strangled by pain, escaped his muzzle in a wheezy breath. "Nezra…"

Nya's stomach dropped to her knees. *Did the Nezra attack a Guild post? Maybe Sulo got caught in the middle.*

"Can I help?"

"Get back," Nya said, waving Sen away as the young girl took a few tentative steps toward the bully bear.

A wrinkled hand covered in brown spots gripped her shoulder. "Let her."

"What?" Nya huffed, shocked that the medicine woman would even entertain such an idiotic idea. "Like she could do anything."

Natsugra and Osan exchanged glances.

"What other choice do we have, Nya?" Osan said, pointing his walking stick at the dying bear.

Gritting her teeth, but refusing to look directly at the girl, Nya asked: "What are you going to do?"

No response. Instead, Sen shrunk back, clinging to Akoto with a frightened look upon her face.

Come on, Sulo, she thought, holding up her arms again to show him something familiar, hoping to trigger him back to his human form. Remember me. "Don't give in to the animal," she whispered.

A shadow fell over her and the others, and the injured bully bear. Nya looked back and jumped at the sight of the midnight beast rising up of his hind legs, sniffing the air and flitting his ears toward Sulo.

"Keep him back!" Nya shouted, her hands moving to the hilts of her blades.

"Akoto, stop." Sen waved her hands in front of him, trying to get him to back off.

The beast didn't listen. Whipping around his spiked tail, he nearly took Osan and Natsugra's heads off, and forced Sen to dive between his legs.

That's it.

Drawing a knife from her belt, Nya took aim for his throat.

What the—

Akoto's howl, a mournful cry like none other she ever heard, stripped away her intent and sent her stumbling into the bully bear. As she dropped her knife, a memory, not her own, splashed across the surface of her mind: Insects droning, the pain of a thousand stingers piercing her skin. Glimpses of bloody teeth, a denuded hand wrapped in a translucent exoskeleton reaching out for her. A chorus of voices silenced all at once, leaving her hollow and empty, in a place of darkness.

I've never felt such loss—

But before grief could lock into her heart, a light caught her attention.

Is Sen…glowing?

She didn't believe her eyes. A soft yellow light radiated off the young girl's skin as she clung to her beast, her arms wrapped around one of his legs.

No, she thought, resisting the new feeling taking hold as Akoto's haunting song rose in pitch and intensity. For a moment she felt Sen's arms hugging her tightly, in an embrace that cut through her armor.

"Stop!" she screamed, squeezing her eyes shut and falling to her knees.

"Look!" someone shouted.

Nya dared to open her eyes as the bully bear roared. Seconds later, golden quills reabsorbed and fur disappeared beneath tan skin as the man behind the animal emerged.

"A miracle…"

"I've never seen anything like it."

As Osan and Natsugra exclaimed praises and awe, Nya shook off the tingling feeling still coursing through her body and lunged at Sen.

"What the hell was that?" she said, shaking the frightened girl by the shoulders.

"I don't know!"

Osan pried Nya off as Akoto came down to defend his charge. Retreating under Akoto, Sen looked just as feeble and helpless as before as Nya and Akoto stared each other down.

"Nya?"

The weak voice broke Nya's anger, and she shook off Osan's grips to run over to Sulo.

"Sulo—Gods—what the hell happened?" she said, holding up his head as Natsugra waddled over and began tending to his wounds.

"Nezra," he repeated, terror dilating his pupils.

"Did they attack you?"

"No," he said, straining for breath. "They attacked...the wall...Guild tried to fight...death-dealers got through..."

"He's in no condition for questioning right now, Nya," Natsugra said, putting her ear to his chest and pointing a finger at her to get away. "Help get him to my tent, now."

Rounding up able clan mates, Nya assisted the transfer of Sulo to Natsugra's tent. As much as she wanted to question him, to find out more about the attacks, a greater need pulled at her attention.

We've got to go. Now.

Osan came up behind her as she paced outside Natsugra's tent.

"Nya, a word."

The stern look that squeezed down his bushy eyebrows and pursed his lips killed any defiant response.

Following him to the edge of camp, Nya couldn't help but look again and again to the wall. Apart from the stacks of smoke rising from the forest from the lightning strikes, she couldn't see anything concerning. Still, Sulo's injuries and his limited account made her imagination conjure the terrible battle yet unseen.

"How many of us are left, Nya?" he asked, indicating with a nod of his head toward the Chakoan camp.

Already on edge, Nya didn't want to rattle off the short list, or listen to Osan's drawn-out lecture on the importance of detachment.

"Don't make me do this. Please," she said, grinding her teeth together.

The chief pulled at his beard, forehead wrinkles falling over his eyes as he contemplated his words. "I have survived longer out here than you've been alive, Aniya," he said, using her full name. "I do not mourn the dead, and I do not expect the rise of the sun. But what we just witnessed..."

Is the chief crying?

No, not possible. In all her years, she'd never seen Osan show much of any emotion, least of all one that would give him the appearance of vulnerability.

"If you leave now, you risk the miracle we just witnessed."

"Miracle?" Nya snorted.

"Did you not feel that great beast's memories? Or see the spirits rising from Sen?"

Nya curbed the stream of curse words and vituperations at the idea of "spirts rising" from Sen with a quick bite of her tongue. Tasting blood, she took a breath and then answered through a clenched jaw.

"Fine. That beast is special, not Sen. So what?"

"Did Sulo not transform?"

"What does that have to do with me rescuing Sho and the others?" she said, frustration quickening her words. "If the Nezra are attacking, then this is the perfect opportunity to infiltrate the Realm."

"You cannot deny that the girl has a bond with that beast."

Rolling her eyes, Nya crossed her arms but did not argue his point.

"Then we must protect Sen if she is nasci."

Nya's hands turned into fists. "You always taught me that the clan comes first. What are we without our blood pact? Will we become just like the favored, weakened by superstition and myth?"

The fury in his eyes should have stopped her, but it didn't. Instead, she pressed farther, cutting deep into their oldest shared wound.

"I am shadowless. We are shadowless," she said, spitting on the ground. "And I curse all who are ashamed of what we are."

His palm struck her face with such quickness that the pain and surprise registered after she found herself cradling her cheek and kneeling down on one knee.

"You're blind, Aniya, to all but what cannot be."

Spitting near her feet, Osan walked past her, leaving her alone at the edge of the camp.

She didn't realize she was holding her breath until dark specks dotted her vision. With a great inhale, she filled her lungs until she thought they would burst, pushing back the pain, the tears, and the awful feeling tearing into her gut.

I don't need him. I don't need anyone, she reminded herself. Looking up, she set her sights on the wall, her promise to Sho renewed.

I'm coming. And nothing will stop me now.

CHAPTER 11

The second the tips of Sen's fingers touched down on Nya's shoulder, the woman warrior reared around, took one look at her through glistening eyes, and then took off toward the mountains.

"Nya, wait!" Sen shouted after her, but to no avail. Within a few seconds, only a dusty cloud and the uncomfortable feeling in her stomach remained.

"Let her go."

Still looking west in hopes of spotting Nya one last time, Sen didn't turn to face Osan until he called to her again.

"Come, Sen."

"But Nya—"

"Come."

Sen wrung her hands together as she returned to the camp, Akoto grumbling as he followed behind her. Something agitated him too, though she couldn't be certain what.

"Join me," Osan said, opening the flap to his tent to allow her in.

"Stay here," she whispered to her oversized friend. Akoto grunted, but found a shady spot under a red juniper tree to escape the building lowland heat.

Sen marveled at the oddities inside Osan's tent. Old books with dust-covered jackets and yellowed pages served as tables and shelves for strange artifacts she couldn't quite place. At first the jagged metal objects looked like scraps, but upon closer inspection, she realized it looked nothing like the metal she'd seen in the Guild.

"What's that?" she said, pointing to a tiny and chipped red, white, and blue flag painted on a broken name plate.

"Patience," Osan said, directing her to sit down on a cut of animal skin.

After she found her seating, he continued. "Tell me about what just happened with the Shifter, Sulo."

Sen balked. What could she tell him—that she feared for Akoto's life when Nya drew her weapon, so she hugged him with all her might?

It's more than that, a voice deep inside her called. The memory of the warmth that rushed through her when his fur brushed against her face, or the sadness in her heart when she heard his doleful howl.

And then that feeling...

A memory, not her own, playing out in the back of her mind. She couldn't recall exactly what she saw, but remember distinct sights and smells: the dewy air inside her lungs, glowing slugs sliding across porous rock. Then pain, immense and terrifying, drowning out all else. A blood-stained smile and a hand that looked more insect than human; thousands of stars blinking out at once.

"I don't know."

"You know something," Osan said, scrutinizing her face.

Biting her bottom lip, she stopped herself from saying what first came to mind: We saved him.

"Akoto saved Sulo," she said. Fidgeting in her seat, she blurted out whatever else surfaced as Osan continued to study her in silence. "I thought I could do something, but…"

Old doubts jangled her nerves. *Who am I kidding? I'm no one.*

She continued, her voice shaky. "But Akoto's howl—it brought him back."

Osan stroked his beard. "I see. How do you know this?"

No answer came to mind. Instead, she shrugged her shoulders and made herself as small as possible, hoping he'd lose interest in the subject.

"Akoto is special. In all my years wandering the outlands, I've never encountered a beast like him. Where do you think he comes from?"

Sen shook her head. *Why does that matter?*

Muttering to himself, Osan unstacked books and rummaged through a cache of old scrolls until he found what he wanted.

"This is a map of our world," he said, unrolling a large parchment across the little ground space between them, and over several books.

"Wow," Sen said. Eyes wide with wonder, she looked over the intricately sketched map of the Realm, and the surrounding outlands. She'd never seen Hirak mountain drawn with such reverence, or the Gardens represented with the plant associated with each Pod. Even the foggy swamplands of the Nezra and the conical Swarm hives, drawn with only black ink and perhaps charcoal, popped off the paper just like the pictures in her father's books. "This is beautiful. Where'd you get it?"

"I drew it."

"Really?" she said, failing to consider the rigidity in his voice, or the way he avoided her gaze. Instead, she rose on her knees, and ran her hands along the edges of the paper, excited by his talent. "I like to draw, but I'm not very good. Do you draw other things, too? Animals, people?"

"Sen," he said, his voice cutting down her enthusiasm. "Focus."

Pointing a calloused finger to the map, he drew her eyes to the spires. "We are here. This is where Nya found you," he said, drawing a line back to the Dethros. "This is also where you say you met Akoto, yes?"

Sen nodded.

After scratching his chin for a good minute, Osan, pointed back to the map. "Judging by how good his teeth look, I doubt that Akoto is very old, so he probably hasn't strayed too far from wherever he's from. I've traveled everywhere on this map, inside and outside the Realm—the ice forests of the north, the forgotten islands to the east, the southern lavafields—even far west, where the world ends. But I've never been here."

He stabbed his finger just southeast of their position, where the drawing abruptly ended in a furious scribble.

"Where's that?" she asked.

"The Wastes."

Dread pulled down on her stomach. She'd never heard of the Wastes, but by the way he said it, she felt she'd just learned something her father would have surely forbidden.

"This is where no man can travel."

"Why?" she said, her voice just above a whisper.

"Only death, and dragons, lurk there."

"Dragons?"

She thought of her father, and the day she came running into his office to show him the drawing she had done of a big red dragon.

Senzo, you shame me by believing in such foolishness. There are no such things as dragons.

"But—"

"No!" he said, slamming his fist down on his desk. Swiping the drawing from her hands, he set it aflame with a spark from his fingertips.

As she cried, he continued to lecture her. "Never say—never think—of dragons ever again!"

Older kids spoke of the many mythical creatures that roamed the outlands, but of all of them, dragons fascinated her the most. She imagined their dark scales, sharp talons, and powerful wings that spanned the length of a hundred men. The fact that they actually existed made her both excited and scared.

"You've seen one?"

"More than seen," he said. Unbuttoning the top of his shirt, he pulled down at the neck to give her a hint of the impressive claw marks that mutilated his chest. "Barely escaped one on a scavenging mission. I have Nya to thank for my life."

A gasp escaped her lips. *Akoto wouldn't do something like that!* "Akoto's not a dragon."

Osan studied her face with one eye half shut and his lips pressed together in a tight line. Finally, he reached for another scroll and spread it out for her atop the map.

Sen held her breath. The dark creature rendered in harsh brushstrokes and jagged, angry lines before her didn't look anything like Akoto at all, but someone's nightmare, born in the stinking pits of fear and pain. With jagged teeth and cold fire burning in its eyes, Osan's dragon wouldn't know about protecting runaway girls, or keeping them safe against attack. Its larger, webbed wings couldn't wrap around her to keep her warm during the cold night freezes, and with only scales and no fur coverings its massive body, how could she keep hold during rides across the outlands?

"Akoto's not a dragon."

"You can't deny some of the resemblance," Osan said, pointing to the similar tail and hindquarters, and the angle of the nose and jaw.

No, she thought, refusing to make any kind of connection with her friend and the monster on the parchment.

"And this—this power Akoto has—to reach a lost spirit. So similar to what I felt," he said, dragging his finger along the black curl of smoke rising from the dragon's mouth and then circling back under its cold eyes. A tremble found its way into his voice. "A dragon can see into your mind, break open your soul. Imagine if you could possess that gift as nasci."

The need to run became an itch that carried all the way down to her bones. She didn't like Osan's theory, especially the part about her wielding such dark power.

"He's not a dragon," she said, adding quietly: "And I'm not nasci."

"This is important, Sen. There are many secrets out there in the Wastes," he said, handing her the red, white, and blue flag painted on the nameplate she had noticed earlier. "Things that the favored fear; secrets that may save us shadowless, and lead us to a new beginning."

Sen looked at the multicolored flag, wondering if it belonged to a denom she didn't know about. As her fingers rubbed along the brass, she felt inscribed letters, and brought the piece close to her face. She recognized a few of the letters, but not all. *L, I, F...B...*

"I found that, and all these metal scraps, near the border, just before the dragon attacked me. If you take on Akoto's powers, you can command the dragons and lead us farther into the Wastes than we've been able to get before."

Setting down the nameplate, she shook her head. "No."

"No?"

"Neither one of us is what you want," she said pushing away the drawing of the dragon, "especially not me."

Osan frowned. "You disappoint me, Sen."

Jarred by the serious tone of his voice, Sen went rigid, fearing an electrocution that the Outlier chief couldn't dispense. "Then you don't need me, do you?"

"Enough. You're not understanding any of this."

Lectures and lessons coursed through her mind as the increasing weight of her father's expectations crushed down on her chest.

"No!" she said, kicking the map and running out the tent flap.

Akoto caught up to her as she ran as fast as she could away from the chief's tent. Galloping beside her, he snorted and growled, nudging her until she finally took notice. Without slowing, she grabbed onto his fur and swung herself up onto his shoulders. Any other time she would have been impressed with herself, but not now.

When she looked back, she saw Sahib and a few other warriors running after them, but their figures grew distant within seconds.

Sen pressed her entire body into Akoto, even as his uneven pace bumped and flung her in several directions. "You're not a dragon."

As they broke free of the Spires and entered the shrubs and prickly bushes just before the cliffs, Sen pulled back on his hair to make him slow. Something didn't feel right. An unnatural stillness pervaded the air, as if everything around her held its breath. She smelled smoke, but another stench intermingled, turning her stomach. A trail of overturned corpses of ratlings and other small rodents caught her eye, as well as the withered leaves and desiccated limbs of the cacti littering the ground, all leading west into the Dethros.

The Nezra!

But as her instincts screamed to run in the opposite direction, she stopped herself.

Nya.

Sen froze, no knowing what to do.

Nya can take care of herself, she reasoned.

No, a deeper voice called. *You have to help her.*

Maybe she didn't go this way—

She ran this direction, and this trail is still fresh. She would have followed it, found out what happened to Sulo at the Guild post.

What could I possibly do to help her? she countered angrily.

Nya cannot handle the Nezra alone.

But I can't do anything!

Only the sigh of the winds responded, carrying a fresh wave of death to her nose.

No, I'm not going back there, she thought, reflexively touching her right shoulder and reviving the immense pain of the spider bites. Yanking Akoto's fur, she turned him the other way. *I can't.*

But as he turned south, a cry broke through stillness, shaking vultures and ravenrines from a distant group of trees. As the scavengers cawed and circled in the cloudy skies, black wings fluttering, she heard the cry again, this time protracted and frustrated.

She held her breath as a distant sense of pain struck her, making her reach down to free herself from whatever snared her right leg. When her fingers couldn't find the phantom trap, she hiked up her pant leg, expecting to find spikes driven into the bone.

Nothing. Only intact, dirty brown skin.

But as the pain dissipated, all her worries and concerns became singular. *Nya.*

Heart pounding in her chest, she forgot about the real pain in her shoulder and arm, and spurred Akoto with her heel, directing him west down the trail of death and decay, back into the heart of the Dethros.

CHAPTER 12

Pain shot through Nya's ankle where the electro trap bit through her boot and sent white fire up into her leg and hip. Muscles cramping, she fell to the ground, but did her best to raise her head and face her attacker. When she saw his mangled face, and the ghostly look in his eyes, she doubted her own senses.

He's dead—

Instincts corrected her initial judgment. *No, alive. But barely.*

Instead of the usual blue glow that emanated from a shock jockey's skin, purple veins snaked up from the officer's neck and knotted around his eyes. His white and gold Guild uniform, bloody and singed, appeared as if he had suffered an attack from his own soldiers.

A cry escaped her lips as he sent another bolt of electricity from his outstretched fingertips through the air and into the trap. Violent spasms tore through her leg and up into her abdomen, and she doubled over on the ground.

Animalistic fear bade her to claw at the metal trap clamped around her ankle, try to dig it out, even sacrifice her foot, but she kept her head down, and pretended to go unconscious, even as she heard and smelled her own skin sizzling inside her boot. She couldn't fight an officer, especially not one powerful enough not to need a storm, and draw enough electrical charge from his surroundings.

Dragging a broken leg on the ground, the officer staggered toward her, saliva and blood gurgling in his throat. Nya let her eyes relax, expanding her focus. Trees surrounded her on all sides, as well as the few scattered bodies of fallen Guild soldiers. Other electro traps, clamped around the limbs of corpses, and a few other Guild weapons laid within reach. She also had her twin blades, and knives strapped her belt and thighs, but even if she got her hands on them, she'd have only a fraction of a second to act before the officer incapacitated her with another jolt.

One chance.

Her fingers twitched as she slowly let the air from her lungs.

Aim to kill.

As soon as the dirt from his boot kicked up in her face, she bucked backward and grabbed for her twin blades, intending to cut him in half. But as her hands wrapped around the hilts, he sent another zig-zagging jolt of electricity into the trap around her ankle, freezing her in place with excruciating pain.

She expected a snarky remark, a quip about her being too slow. At least she would have thrown a few insults if the positions were reversed. Instead, the officer hacked and slurped, uttering something so garbled she didn't think it could be a language as he raised his other hand.

He's going to kill me.

She recognized the stance as the shock jockey stacked his hands to deliver the death blow, and burn her heart right out of her chest.

Still arched back, she yelled through gritted teeth. "Go to hell!"

But the final strike didn't come. Instead, the officer stood shaking in front of her, his hands intertwined as his face contorted into the oddest expression.

Why's he hesitating?

A howl ripped through the forest, snagging both of their attention. Despite her protesting muscles, Nya managed to turn her neck as a giant black mass came bounding through the forest.

Akoto?

And Sen.

Nya couldn't believe her eyes. The wimpy girl, riding atop her monster, charged at the shock jockey.

"Watch out!" she cried as the officer wheeled around and aimed his hands at the pair.

Akoto dodged the bolt of blue lightning, but Sen didn't duck in time, and caught a lesser discharge right to the chest. Knocked off Akoto, the young girl went flying backwards, landing in a flailing mess in a greyleaf bush.

The few seconds of distraction allowed Nya to regain some control of her limbs, enough to draw her swords. As another bolt blazed from the officer's fingers at Akoto, she swung with all her might, coming down on the back of the shock jockey's legs. A wild branch of blue electricity exploded upward as he tipped back and fell. When he tried to roll over, she finished the job with a hard stab to the chest.

Nya stayed pressed on top of her swords until she felt no movement underneath, and the last of his breath bubbled out of his lungs in a gush of blood. After determining the kill, she turned her attention to the beast and his charge. Akoto took some damage, but aside from some scorched hair and a superficial burn, he seemed unfazed, and more concerned with his pitiful companion yelping in the bushes.

"Ridiculous," Nya muttered as she pried at the jaws of the metal trap biting into her ankle. The leather of her old, patchy boots absorbed most of the damage, but she felt the spikes rubbing up against her bone. Nausea licked at the back of her throat, but she swallowed hard and looked for a weakness in the design.

Those bastards changed the lock mechanism, she realized as she tried to pull down the springs and pin back the jaws. No luck.

"You okay?"

The combination of pain and Sen's annoying, feeble voice made her even angrier. "I'm fine. Get the hell out of here."

Sen looked back and forth between Nya's face and the trap on her ankle, sucking back her lips when she saw the blood pooling around her injury. "Need help?"

"No. I said go!"

The young girl took a step back, but didn't mount her beast and take off as Nya desired.

Grimacing, Nya thrashed her leg back and forth across the ground. Cold sweat beaded on her brow.

Gonna pass out.

"*Shy't,*" she cursed in her native tongue.

The world see-sawed in and out of view. She tasted something metallic in her mouth, felt the hard ground against her cheek. Taking big breaths filled her lungs, but she couldn't satisfy her hunger for air.

"Press your thumbs into the notches and turn your hands opposite directions."

Sen's words sounded distant, muffled, as if she spoken in water. But through the haze of pain and injury, Nya found the notches at the base of the jaws and did as the young girl instructed.

The trap released. After kicking it off, Nya removed her boot and assessed the injury.

What's this? she thought, rubbing off a black ooze from around the bites.

"They started adding putra extract on the teeth," Sen said, still keeping her distance. "Helps conduct electricity, and it makes the prisoner sick."

"I'm not sick," she said, shutting her eyes to keep the world from spinning away.

"It passes in a minute—"

"I'm fine!" she said, throwing a handful of dirt in Sen's general direction.

Akoto growled, and moved to the girl's side.

Breathe it out, she told herself, fighting against the ominous churnings of her stomach. Controlling her breaths, she inhaled through her nose and blew out her mouth, imagining the poison running through her system seeping out her pores. After several breaths, she regained enough of herself to chastise Sen.

"Why are you here? Shouldn't you be all protected and safe by Osan's side?"

Sen averted her eyes and hugged her arms to her chest.

"Don't tell me you ran away again," she laughed.

A low grumble shook the ground, but Nya didn't care if she pissed off the beast by hurting Sen's feelings. *That girl's a coward.*

But as she tore off strips of her shirt to wrap around her injured ankle, a nagging feeling wore away at her crass assumptions. Sen would have heard her cries, seen flashes of the attack, even at a distance.

Cowards don't run toward battle.

Pausing, she offered what little edge her ego would allow her to give. "At least you're a decent distraction."

"Isn't that painful?" Sen said as Nya thrust her injured ankle back in the boot.

"Doesn't matter," she muttered, using a nearby tree to steady herself as she tested out the pressure she could apply. Something crunched as she set down her full weight, sending another wave of nausea up her throat.

It's fine, she told herself, raising and setting down her foot again. This time no crunch, just throbbing pain, and an unstable feeling in the ankle. After taking a few steps, she determined it could hold her up, but complex movements wouldn't be guaranteed.

"Where are you going?"

"To rescue Sho and the others," Nya said in a huff as she searched the fallen Guild soldiers for anything useful.

"But you're hurt and alone—"

Nya ignored Sen, focusing her attention on more important matters. *Why did the Guild attack each other?*

Nudging one of the electro traps on the arm of a dead Guild soldier, she noted the same purple veins streaking up the man's neck and bunching around his eyes. *They look sick.*

She remembered how she felt earlier, when she first saw the officer, and thought he looked dead.

What kind of disease would do this? she wondered, stooping down to get a better look at another soldier. The man's skin, anemic and riddled with discolored blood vessels, triggered a flashback to the battle with the Soushin.

But the Soushin attacked us, not each other. Still, she couldn't ignore the eerie similarity, or the cold dread sinking into her stomach.

"Don't go," Sen whispered, still clinging to her beast. "Remember what Sulo said?"

"I don't care if it's Lord Vulgis himself—I'm going."

"You can't fight the Nezra!"

Nya glared at the young girl as she slung two electro traps to her belt. "Why? Because I'm shadowless?"

With a grunt, she freed another one of the electro traps and flung it at Sen. The girl didn't move fast enough, and the edge of the setting pin caught her side. "Ow!"

"Being smarter, faster—that's all that matters," Nya said, pointing at the trap. "Guild soldiers use those to concentrate their attacks, but if it's not ground into your flesh, you can use it to channel away their strikes—even counterattack."

Sen bent over at took the device in her hands, looking at it as if she'd never seen the weapon before. "Really?"

Sho's arrogant smile flashed through her mind as he ran out against a fully charged strikeforce with only two electro traps in hand. No one else had ever considered using the Guild's prime weapon against them, or been brazen enough to try it in the heat of a losing battle.

Sho, you wicked fool...

Her heart warmed at the thought of him, but on its heels came a fresh injection of urgency. "Really. Now get out of my way," she said, blowing past Sen and Akoto, and heading back toward the wall.

Blocking out the pain of her injured leg, Nya found a path through the trees, spotting footprints of both man and beast alike.

Sulo came through here, she thought, recognizing the five-toed bully bear prints. From what she could tell, he made it as far as the tower lookout erected just before the wall. *He made it to the Guild post—then what?*

A circle of dead grass and trees with dried out, brown leaves surrounded the tower. Different footprints—ones that dragged in the dirt—headed toward the opened gate. All the Guild soldiers were dead, and Sulo didn't get through. *But somebody else did.*

Nya considered her options. If the Guild soldiers got ambushed, they might not have had time to signal for help. And with the battle happening earlier that morning, the attackers would have had plenty of time to penetrate deep into Guild territory, opening up a wide path for her to follow.

This is perfect, she thought, eyeing the wall. Without the soldiers to charge the giant slabs of conductive rock, the blue glow faded, and her confidence swelled. *I hope those death-dealers kill them all.*

An inter-denom war excited her, especially when she thought of the Guild elder who announced the charges against her parents in the public square. Even after five years, she could still remember his austere voice, and the gaudy white gold ceremonial mask that hid his face, as he stood up on the pulpit and declared the world council verdict. *"Aron and Setalla Calatheas—for abetting an Outlier, you will be held in contempt of the Realm, and sentenced to ten years in the Gorge."*

She hoped the Nezra found that bastard first.

As she slipped past the crisscrossing, fifty-foot iron gates splitting the stone, she kept her swords drawn, ears and eyes tuned in to the slightest movements. Finding a winding dirt and stone path, she followed the dragging footprints, noticing the continued mélange of dead animals and foliage along the edges.

From what little she remembered about the Order of Nezra, the reclusive and oftentimes silent masters of death and decay rarely ventured outside their territory in the swamps, and though their elders and leader, Lord Vulgis, used to attend world council gatherings, the death-dealers never squabbled or posed threats to the other denoms.

And they never demonstrated the end of their powers, she thought, eyeing the putrefied head of a ratling. At least not in such a vulgar way as to leave a trail of decomposing corpses.

Still, wild stories and grotesque legends circulated amongst the other denoms, generating discomfort at their presence, and fear of their power. A death-dealer hadn't been elected as world leader in over a hundred years as a result, but Lord Vulgis hadn't protested the injustice.

Until now, she thought, kicking away a fuzzy rabbix with eyes melted out of its skull.

A low growl, the sound of a limping gait.

"Shhhh, Akoto."

Nya stopped in place and huffed. "Why are you following me?"

Silence. Then a hesitant answer. "I'm worried…about my family."

"You need to get back to camp," she said, turning around to face the young girl riding atop her beast. "It's not safe out here."

Sen slid down off her beast, but stayed pinned to his side. "It doesn't matter."

"What?" Nya exclaimed. "After all that nasci business?"

"But I'm—"

"Osan's *shy't* about 'miracles' and ancient legends—a waste of time, delusions for the desperate." Her hand went to her slapped cheek, but when she realized what she did, she tried to play it off. "Don't you see how you've divided the last of us?"

Sen squeezed her eyes shut and shouted over Nya's tirade. "I'm not nasci!"

The girl's voice carried through the thicket of trees, echoing off of the side of the mountain, and rising to the cloudy afternoon sky above. All of the bird song, and even insect trilling, seemed to pause in the wake of her outburst.

"At least we agree about that," Nya said, keeping an eye on Sen's beast. She didn't like the way Akoto's black fur rose on his back, or how he dug his claws into the ground. He's reacting to her, she thought, watching his lips curl back on sharp teeth.

As another baritone rumble emitted from Akoto's chest, she reconsidered her original idea. "You can come with me, but you have to do everything I say."

Sen nodded, her eyes drifting off to the west, where steep mountain passes and the countless hidden dangerous protected the pathway to the Lightning Guild fortress.

"The Nezra aren't headed to Hirak," Nya said, resuming her course down the trail. "This is the back way to the Gardens."

"But you said we could check on my parents—"

"Rescue mission first."

If she had any response, the girl kept it to herself as they traversed their way through the foothills. Succulent plants gave way to ivy and trees with leafy branches that draped to the ground. Bamboo punctuated the forest floor, making it almost impossible to deviate from the established trail. Passing higher, they came across fast-moving rivers that dropped and twisted down rocky channels and spilled over falls into lost lakes. Nya caught glimpses of the mist shrouded, secret blue waters, but squelched any hint of curiosity and wonder with the objective of their mission.

I'm coming, Sho.

Five miles in, hunger pains and the ache of her injured ankle whittled down her concentration, enough so that she couldn't hide her limp.

"I can hear that," she said, picking up Sen's whispers and Akoto's grumble.

"Akoto says it's okay to ride on his back for a while."

Nya resisted the urge to look over her shoulder, not wanting to see the sweet, innocent expression on the kid's face. "No."

"Why not? He's really strong. And you're hurt—"

"I said *no*." Nya turned around, intending to yell at the girl, but forgot that her ankle couldn't handle the sudden position change. She fell to her side, cracking her hip and elbow against one of the dead tree branches littering the edge of the trail.

Cradling her elbow, she scowled at Sen, but it didn't keep the girl from kneeling down a few feet in front of her. "Your elbow—it's bleeding."

"Really?" Nya said, but the girl didn't catch on to her sarcastic tone.

"Here," Sen said, pulling around her satchel to the front and digging through it. When she couldn't find what she wanted, she ripped off a piece of her tattered shirt. "Take this."

"What am I supposed to do with that?"

A look of confusion crossed her face. "To stop the bleeding."

"I'm not using your dirty shirt."

Sen tilted her head to the side, looking at her with a mix of trepidation and inquisitiveness. "Why won't you let me help you?"

The question hit her in a place she didn't think herself vulnerable anymore, least of all when asked by a shadowless fourteen-year-old girl. Her deepest scars, not earned or received in battle, became a pulsating beacon in her mind's eye, even though they lay hidden underneath her layers of armor.

"I don't need help, especially from you."

Sen said nothing, but her gaze dropped the gaping laceration on the young warrior's elbow.

I should cover it up, she thought, frustration subsiding. The scent of fresh blood might attract the Nezra, and since she estimated they trailed behind by only a mile or less, they couldn't risk any exposure.

With a grunt, she swiped the dirty strip of cloth from the kid's hand and bound the wound. "You're a pest."

Sen stared at her, no hint of retort or resentment in her big hazel eyes. Anger surfaced first, her conditioned reaction to such a vexing personality, but then something new and unexpected nibbled at the corners of her mind. Warmth, a memory of comforts long forgotten; sentiments Nya dismissed with a huff before they could be realized. *Stupid kid. This world will eat her up.*

"Here," Nya said, standing up as she drew one of the two ten-inch knives from her belt and handed it to Sen. "You're no good to me if you can't fight."

"What am I supposed to do with this?" Sen held the knife up with two hands, her eyes converging at the sharpened point.

"I want you to practice two moves as we hike. A fake stab, then slice, and a parry and slash. Like this."

Nya drew the other knife and demonstrated the first attack with advancing shuffle steps, and then second defensive/counterattack using a side-step and deep forward stance. Her ankle screamed with pain, but she couldn't falter, not now as Sen watched on with fright and awe.

"You try," Nya said to the girl still sitting on her knees and holding the knife out away from her body.

"N-no, I can't."

"Do it," Nya said, grabbing her by the upper arm and hoisting her to her feet. "Or go back to camp."

Sen gave a half-hearted stab at the invisible enemy in front of her, and an even less enthusiastic and weak-wristed slice. Instead of trying the second move, Sen whimpered an excuse and fumbled with the knife.

"At least he's got some fight in him," Nya said, nodding to the growling beast looming over Sen.

"Sorry, I'm just not good at this stuff."

"No excuses," Nya said, resuming their hike. Glancing over her shoulder, she added: "Keep practicing."

Frustrated grunts and boots scuffing across the dirt followed, but not the sweet swishing sound of coordinated knife attacks cutting through the air.

The question popped out of her mouth. "So, what are you good at?"

Silence.

Nya resisted the temptation to look back. Unsure of why she asked such an idiotic thing, she tried to justify it with the nagging pain of her ankle, empty stomach, or the need to know more about the survival worth of her travel companion. Not that I really care.

"Nothing."

The girl's fragile response didn't surprise her, but nonetheless, summoned uncomfortable feelings from deep within, as if someone shined the spotlight on her, not Sen.

Clearing her throat, Nya afforded the girl no pity. "Then keep practicing."

After crossing a weathered stone bridge, they reached a clearing that overlooked the valley dividing the White mountains and the endless verdant hills. The sun, sinking behind Hirak mountain, cast shadows over the sleepy forests.

"That's the end of Guild territory," Nya said, pointing to the river cutting through the valley at the base of Hirak mountain. "The Gardens are right over there. See the post? That's the entry to the Mazes."

Sen squinted, looking out a mile to the northeast where a group of trees twisted together to form a fortified platform. "Yeah, but why aren't they moving?"

As soon as she pointed out the Virid soldiers frozen in place, Nya dropped to the ground, pulling Sen down with her.

"Quiet," she said, putting her finger over her lips before Sen could question her action.

Though the soldiers on the platform remained unmoving, their strangulated cries carried across the valley. Vines attached to their post sprung up to the sky as if the Virid soldiers made to defend themselves against an invisible enemy.

"What's happening—"

Nya slapped her hand over Sen's mouth. More vines shot up to the sky, and fell back to the ground around the post. Two petal cannons formed from the surrounding pink and yellow floral bed, fell apart, and reformed, as if none of the soldiers bore the concentration to be able to finish the command, let alone aim it at whatever attacked them.

"Stay here," Nya said, pointing to Sen, and then Akoto.

"But Nya—"

"Do as I say!"

Keeping low, Nya descended the trail, looking for any movement in the trees as she made her way toward the tower. Gurgling and slurping sounds, like the ones she heard just before the Soushin attacked, made her reach for her swords.

The shadows up ahead congealed. Nya kept her swords in front of her, taking slower and slower steps, trying to understand what she saw and heard. Something clicking and grating silenced all of the twilight forest song. Not insect sounds; more like bones rubbing and snapping together.

What the hell is that?!

Nya retreated behind a tangle of blue grass, watching the horror unfold at the base of the Virid post fifty feet ahead. Hunched over figures, too dark to see, wiggled long fingers at the soldiers high up in the tower. Vines snaked up the tower, went taut, and then pulled a soldier to the ground with sickening force, shattering his bones and splitting his skull.

A flash of green, the putrid smell of wet leaves. Nya spied a Virid soldier, his green and grey uniform ripped to shreds, his face bloodied and almost unrecognizable, limping toward the other side of the post. Standing at an awkward angle, he raised his broken hands and molded and bent the vegetation around him to his will. Petal cannons reformed, this time taking aim at the tower.

What's he—

Before she could complete the thought, he fired the cannons, sending a spread of pistils at his own men. Nya crouched down and covered her head as a plume of pollen, dust, and wood splinters exploded out from the collapsing tower.

As the wreckage settled, the hissing and clicking sounds returned. Staying crouched, Nya tried to watch from her limited vantage point as the dark figures perused the fallen Virid post, lingering over the dead and dying soldiers trapped underneath vines and wooden beams.

No...

Nya recoiled as a Virid officer, cut in half by a vine, reanimated under the wriggling fingers of the dark figures. Mouth agape, he looked up with bleached eyes at his masters.

"Hissan de templare... Hissan de templare..." the dark figures hissed.

Dropping her swords, Nya pressed her palms against her ears, not wanting to hear any more of the vicious Nezran tongue. Whatever they chanted made her feel weak and powerless, like a mouse trapped inside the jaws of a predator.

The officer shook and contorted, both halves of his body writhing in pain, but he would not respond to the death-dealers' demands.

Their chants escalated, penetrating through Nya's meager barrier, turning her bones to ice. *"Hissan de templare. HISSAN DE TEMPLARE."*

I can't take it, Nya thought, unable to take a breath. A phantom vice trapped her mind, crushing down on all sides. Dread pulled apart reason, allowing panic to calve the last of her rational mind.

Tell them—TELL THEM!

Submitting, the dead officer raised his broken arm, pointing it northwest.

Tears streamed from his eyes as he shrieked for mercy, his fractured jaw dangling from the hinges.

But the torments didn't stop, not even after the officer gave them whatever they demanded. Instead, the death-dealers drew together, pooling their collective talents, decay spreading out from their squirming fingers in fetid waves of brown and black. Flowers wilted and withered in seconds, the grasses, trees, and plants turning into heaps of tarry mold. The dying Virid soldiers and the officers morphed in ways that Nya couldn't fathom in her worst nightmares, screaming out as their skin went from green hues to jaundiced yellow, then to a deathly cracked brown.

Nya fell to the ground shaking, forgetting all but the terrible pain pulling her apart from the inside out. *God, please stop, please stop, STOP.*

A mournful howl broke through forest, silencing the death-dealer chant, washing away their terrible words from her mind. Nya inhaled sharply, taking in a starving breath, filling her lungs until she thought they'd burst. As she fought to right her breathing, she saw all around her with extraordinary lucidity, as if she had a thousand eyes open all at once. She saw each insect scurrying up the trees, the branching veins on the leaves, individual blades of grass; the tiny flecks of dirt that covered her boots. Head reeling, she caught sight of bloodshot eyes, rawboned faces. Despite her fear, she couldn't look away, drawn into the Nezra's hollow stare, the way their mouths hung open with words unspoken, their fingers outstretched in panic, not malice.

Shocked, she closed her eyes, not wanting to see the world with such clarity. As the sensation passed, she heard Akoto's uneven gait, his four paws slapping against rock as he bound down toward her, like a boulder crashing through the forest.

When she opened her eyes, the dark figures in front of had dispersed, disappearing into the sanctuary of the Garden shadows.

"Shy't," she muttered, rolling up to a sitting position as the beast and his rider charged through to her position.

"Nya—are you okay?"

"I'm fine," she grumbled, brushing herself of and using the adjacent tree to help her stand. "Didn't I tell you to wait?"

"Yeah, but Akoto wouldn't stay."

"Do you not have control over your beast?"

"He's not a beast!" Sen said, raising her voice to meet Nya's.

Nya flexed and relaxed her fists, wanting to yell, but realizing more than just her anger. The midnight creature standing before her, his brawny chest, angular jaw, and wolf-like mask, did more than just intimate a great physical power. *His howl…it did something to me.*

Just like it had done to Sulo.

Before, when he howled for the dying Shifter, she saw something of Akoto's past; a glimpse into a memory of pain and suffering that connected her to an experience beyond herself. This time she saw the world around her in the absence of darkness, from angles she never cared to see, in depths and details she once deemed unnecessary. And she saw into the faces of death, seeing less the frightful monster, and more the fragile human behind such evil acts.

No. Not possible. None of this is real.

Unsure of herself, Nya decided to refocus on the most important matter. "Get down. We need to assess the site."

As she picked up her swords and re-sheathed them, Sen slid off Akoto and joined her in surveying the battleground.

Covering her nose, Nya stepped into the distinct ring that separated the living forest from the area affected by the death-dealers. Her boots squished with every step, pushing up greyish liquid from the wet soil. Mold and decay peppered the air with smells that churned her stomach, but she detected no lingering Nezra.

Why would the Nezra run from a howl? she thought, surveying the dead soldiers littering the piles of moldy vegetation and splintered beams. *They had the upper hand.*

The answer seemed within reach, but as she tried to feel out the reason, some part of her pushed her own experiences out of consideration, leaving her frustrated and more confused.

None of this makes sense, she decided, kicking over the withered stalk of a pink quapo flower.

"Hey—Nya—I think he's still alive!" Sen said, pointing to the halved officer lying in the wreckage. "Oh… I don't feel so good…"

Sighing, Nya watched as the young girl turned ashen at the sight of the moaning Virid. "Stay back then."

Nya stooped down next to the officer, studying his blind gaze and colorless lips. *How is he still alive?*

"Hey—can you hear me?" She slapped him on the chest, trying to elicit some intelligible response. "Why did the Nezra attack you? What are they after?"

She got only fragmented, garbled words.

"Nya, stop," Sen said, kneeling down and clutching her stomach. "He's in pain."

Nya grabbed the officer by the collar and held one of her knives to his neck. "Listen—I'll end your suffering. Just tell me why they did this."

"Run…" the officer rasped, reaching for her face with trembling hands. Grazing her jaw with cold fingers, he screamed. "RUN!"

In one swift motion, Nya cut his throat. The light in the officer's eyes dimmed, and his head lolled off to the side.

As she tried to process what had just happened, Sen's quiet whimpering got under her skin.

"Stop that," she said, grasping the girl by the elbow and lifting her to her feet. Sen wouldn't look at her, keeping her head down as Nya continued her reprimands. "Get yourself together. This isn't going to get any easier."

Wiping her nose off on her shirtsleeve, she whispered: "I felt him…"

"What?"

By the pained expression on Sen's face, she inferred that the girl meant more than just having a sense of empathy for the officer's suffering.

Yeah, right—

But then it struck her as she watched Akoto sniffing the dead soldiers, the low rumble in his chest turning into a whine.

No, she told herself, dismissing any possibility that the beast could have feelings for the fallen—or that, even more impossibly, that Sen could tap into those sensitivities.

"Then you should feel nothing now. He's dead," she said, slapping the kid's shoulder. Looking up, she saw the first stars of the night dotting the darkening sky. "Come on. We've got to find a light source before we go through the Mazes."

"T-the Mazes?" Sen hugged her arms to her chest. "But we'll get lost in there without a guide."

The girl's observation did more than just nettle. Yes, the Virids constantly shifted the walls, making it impossible to navigate inside their borders without a greenthumb. Nya thrust one of her blades in Sen's face. "Then we'll just hack our way through."

Worry and fright pinched the girl's face, but she didn't try to talk her out of her terrible plan. The Mazes, alive and reactive, would not stand to be cut or hacked, and would surely put up a fight.

Sen followed behind her, sniffling and clinging to Akoto as Nya stepped outside the decaying battlegrounds and into the Garden forests.

"Wait…rodudendrum or occulrum?" she muttered to herself as she hacked away at the shrubs to get to the floral beds surrounding the grey oak trees. Not that she could discern the coral, blue or purple flowers from one another in the twilight.

"What are you doing?" Sen asked.

"Eating one of these flowers will improve our night vision."

Sen looked at her with a wary expression. "Can't we just make a fire and carry torches—or pick off a lantern bulb?"

"And alert all the Virids—and possibly those Nezra—that we're coming?"

Anxious to get back to the mission, Nya plucked a dozen random flowers and crammed them all into her mouth. If Sen hadn't been watching her, she might have considered spitting them out. The acrid taste alone made her gag, but she couldn't let on in front of the kid.

"Ummm…did it work?" Sen asked after Nya gulped the bitter pulp.

Nya blinked a few times, and looked around the dark forest. The light from the waning moon gave her some sense of her environment, but not much. Still, she couldn't stand Sen's dubious expression. "Yes. Let's go."

After plowing through the underbrush trying to guess her way to the maze entrance, she heard a shudder and moan, as if something immense and inhuman, suffered a grievous injury. She angled toward the sound, stumbling upon the outer hedge wall of the maze.

Just gotta find a way in…

She followed the wall for several feet, but couldn't find the opening. Instead, she managed to get her hair tangled in the low branches of the trees, and snag her shirt in a bush.

"What about there?" Sen said, pointing to an opening in the wall.

Nya didn't like the looks of it. It didn't appear like an intentional entry point, not with the dried leaves and shriveled-up vines littering the ground.

The Nezra came through here, she surmised, running her hand along the dead, brittle interior. Squinting, she made out the subsequent holes penetrating the hedges, giving them a straight shot toward a soft light up ahead.

Sanctum.

It had to be, at least from Sulo's description.

You have to be there, Sho.

Cracking, groaning; the sound of a thousand branches stretching out, trying to reform.

"Run," Nya said, grabbing Sen's hand and pulling her inside. Akoto roared, too big to fit through the hole without taking out more of the surrounding wall.

Gritting her teeth against the pain of her injured ankle, Nya sprinted through the holes, towing Sen behind her, her eyes locked on the light, as the walls around her shrieked and collapsed.

▲▽▲

CHAPTER 13

Sen landed hard on her hands and knees in the grass, leaves, dirt and twigs spraying out around her. In front of her, Nya grunted and cursed, her face turning red as she pushed herself up and stood on her injured ankle.

"Akoto!" she screamed, turning back to see him biting and clawing at the vines wrapped around his chest and dragging him back into the Maze.

Tripping over the plant debris, she stumbled her way to him, batting away the tendrils spilling over the maze walls that sought out the trespassers.

"Sen, get back!"

Nya's shouts didn't deter her, nor did the ominous creaks and snapping sounds coming from behind the outer wall. Only when the spiny heads of the bird-eater stalk lifted above the hedge did she give pause. She'd only ever seen their rosette faces in picture books, not rising above her head, dripping digestive fluids from their pink oral cavities.

Screaming, she dodged one of the diving heads, its trigger hairs brushing the back of her legs. She smelled sweet nectar as its other heads waved back and forth, spraying the air with their intoxicating scent.

"Akoto," she cried, slamming her fists against one of the bigger vines wrapped around his stomach. Roaring, he tried to bite, claw, and wrestle his way out, but the harder he struggled, the more it squeezed down around his torso.

Vines slithered up her leg and wrapped around her hip as she pleaded with her friend to try harder. "Don't give up!" she screamed as a vine circled around his muzzle and pulled his head back.

Focused on her friend, she didn't give enough attention to the vines snagging both her arms, or the bird-eaters spreading out around them, opening up their bladed leaves for the anticipated meal. "Akoto!"

Two knives whizzed past her head, plunging into the thicker vine crushing Akoto's rib cage. Everything around her—the hedges, the bird-eaters, the very leaves—shrieked and shuddered.

"Use your knife!" Nya shouted as she sliced her way toward them with her twin blades.

When the command registered, Sen hesitated, afraid to grab the borrowed blade from her waistband.

I can't—

"Do it!"

Sen cried out as another vine slapped down around her neck while another two lashed around her wrists and pulled her in opposite directions.

Three of the bird-eater heads dipped down to her eye-level so that she could see into their maw, down their ribbed gullet.

Choked by the vines, she could do little more than squeeze her eyes shut as they lunged toward her face.

A terrible cry rose above the din. The vines around her neck slackened enough for her to take a gasping breath and open her eyes.

Silver flashed in the moonlight.

Nya!

But as she watched Nya hack down the vines, she realized it wasn't the warrior's concerted effort that stopped the attack.

The cry intensified, piercing the Gardens with a chorus of suffering. All of the vines retracted, then sprouted back out of the Maze, rushing toward the origin of the sound somewhere up ahead. The bird-eaters followed, their bladed leaves whistling in the winds as they slithered away.

Akoto!

After picking herself up off the ground, Sen ran to the midnight beast shaking off near the hole in the outer Maze wall.

"You okay, buddy?" she said, brushing off the twigs and leaf bits from his fur.

He answered with a grumble, then a snort as he cleared out his lungs.

"Phew," she said, giving him a hug. He growled, but she didn't let up until Nya grabbed her by the elbow and yanked her toward the awful sound.

"Let's go."

"Wait—what's happening?"

"What do you think?"

You don't always have to yell, she thought, keeping pace with the woman warrior.

Lights up ahead hinted at multiple structures hidden within the trees and vines. The closer they got, the more Sen dug in her heels. She didn't like the pitting feeling in her stomach, or the way all of the plants and trees up ahead shivered and shook.

Nya gave her a good tug, making her lurch forward. "Come on—we're close."

Without the bioluminescent bulbs dangling from the trees, she wouldn't have been able to see the fallen branches, curled up leaves and shriveled flowers, or the Virid soldiers lying face-down in the mud. Nya let go of her arm to inspect the dead bodies, her clinical eyes moving from soldier to soldier, and then to the agitated trees.

Not again.

Terrified, she reached back to hold on to Akoto. "Don't leave me."

Nya returned to her, holding her stomach, a thin line of sweat accumulating across her brow.

"Are you okay?" Sen asked.

"I'm fine," she said, wiping her forehead with the back of her sleeve.

She's lying. Even if she had the guts to call her out, it wouldn't matter. The way Nya pushed herself, she wouldn't stop until she was dead. And maybe not even then.

"Up ahead...Nezra...Virids, fighting..." Nya said, gritting her teeth as her color went from pink to green. "...gotta circle around."

Uh oh—it's those flowers, Sen thought, remembering Nya taking a huge handful from the base of the grey oak tree. *I bet she ate the emesilius and occulrum together.*

One of her mother's lessons came to mind.

"The potent emesilius flower, beautiful in its coral color and heart shaped leaves, causes severe nausea and vomiting, unless paired with..."

Sen drew a blank. *Oh no—what did she tell me?*

"...and then it acts as a vitality boost."

However, she did remember the fluffy look of the clouds that day as she lay on her back twirling her hair, gazing at their bulbous formations and dreaming of exotic foreign landscapes—or anything beyond the stone and steel protection of the Guild fortress.

"Sen, are you paying attention?"

"Nya!" Sen yelped as the woman warrior dropped to her knees and lost the meager contents of her stomach in a sun bush. When she tried to hold her hair back, Nya shoved her aside, but didn't have the breath to tell her off.

A fresh wave of desperate cries and shouts came from up ahead, as did animal noises Sen couldn't identify. The ground beneath them trembled, as if thousands of roots and hidden plants charged to assist in the battle.

We can't stay here, Sen thought, eyeing the swaying trees.

"Nya—we gotta go," she said, shaking Nya's shoulders. "We're too close to the battle. The trees are reacting to us."

The woman warrior responded in another round of stomach cramps and upheavals into the plants, her entire body shaking.

Can't stay here—

Can't leave Nya—

Think!

"The potent emesilius flower... causes severe nausea and vomiting, unless paired with..."

"No no no," she muttered, pressing her palm into her forehead. *Why didn't I ever pay attention? I'm worthless—*

Something bumped her from behind. Turning, Sen found Akoto's giant head in her face.

"Akoto, stop," she protested, holding on to his cheeks as he pressed his face even closer, "we need to—"

But as she stared into his blue and yellow eye, she saw a peal of light in the distance, unfolding and blossoming in an impossible space. The cries and shouts of battle, the shaking ground, Nya's violent retching all telescoped away as she watched the light essence form into familiar faces and scenes.

"Akoto…"

Arms falling slack to her sides, she allowed herself to fall into the trance of his gaze, into the light that should not exist.

Sen found herself lying in the courtyard garden, staring up into the cloud-studded afternoon sky. Distant rumblings portended the usual evening storm her father summoned to the Scylan grove, to strengthen the spirit of the Lightning Guild, connecting them from the Realm to the heavens.

"Sen, are you paying attention?"

Glancing to her right, she saw her mother sitting prim and proper, a leafbound book open in her lap. Her mother's gaze, which never lingered long, dashed back to the marked pages.

"This is very important, Sen," she said, tilting her head so that her auburn hair would cover the scars on her neck.

Mother—

As much as she tried, she couldn't deviate from the memory, and though she wanted to cry out for her mother's help, she merely muttered the same desultory response she did months ago. "Yes, mother."

"Even if you have another gift, it's important to learn about Virid culture and medicine. All the denoms are connected, Sen, as are all things in this world."

An old thought crushed down on her mother's words: Except me. I'm not connected. I'm not a part of anything.

Sen cringed, but as her greatest fear pressed its thorns into her heart, she perked to the familiar statement that followed.

"Let's continue. Chapter three, lesson one: native flowers and roots of the western Gardens. The potent emesilius flower, beautiful in its coral color and heart shaped leaves, causes severe nausea and vomiting, unless paired with…"

Sen fought her old self, straining against the stream of imagined places running through her head, ridiculous fantasies of adventure and laudation for heroic deeds she could never accomplish in real life: fighting monsters, finding fabulous treasures, saving the lives of entire villages, cities, even the world—as her mother uttered the answer she needed to save her friend.

Gotta…help…Nya, *she thought, the vision blurring as she zeroed in on the forgotten words.*

"…moonstar root, and then it acts as a vitality boost…"

With the answer she needed, Sen pulled away. But as the images disintegrated into wisps of firelight, she heard the rest of her mother's sentence, no longer drowned out by another daydream adventure:

"...You aren't listening, are you? So much like your uncle..."

And then she added in a sorrowful whisper: "One day they'll take you away, too..."

"No!" Sen shouted, stumbling back, arms flailing. Akoto caught her with his tail, keeping her steady as she reoriented back to the present.

Shouts and screams came from all around her, the trees arcing back and forth. Still kneeling into the sun bush, Nya continued to retch, unable to fight off the effects of the emesilius flower.

The moonstar root, Sen remembered, pushing away Akoto's tail and plucking one of the bioluminescent bulbs from the tree branches. But where do I find it?

Her mother's voice echoed out from the dark corners of her mind: *When searching for the moonstar, rememeber—the sun and moon are never far apart.*

The sun bush... Sen touched the yellow blossoms of the poor bush Nya polluted. *It's gotta be close.*

Holding the glowing teardrop-shaped plant in one hand, she searched the ground for the tiny blue flowers that indicated the medicinal root below.

Come on! she thought, digging into the soft, mossy ground with her fingers.

Footsteps approached, loud and tromping. She didn't dare think of the size of whatever awful thing headed toward them.

Hurry hurry hurry—

Akoto roared, raising up on his hind legs and lashing out his tail as a giant bear knocked down one of the dead trees just feet from them.

"Whoa, Akoto." A tattooed man emerged from behind the bear, sheathing his weapons and holding up his arms. "Peace."

Terrified, Sen scurried backward on her hands, unable to take her eyes off the golden-quilled bully bear growling and baring his teeth.

"Peace!" he shouted again as Akoto took a swipe at the approaching warrior.

"Sen!"

The familiar voice broke through her fright. Recognizing the dark-haired young warrior, Sen scooted up and grabbed on to Akoto's thigh to quiet him. "Sahib? What are you doing here?"

"Oh, for the love—" Nya said before her stomach continued the upwards onslaught.

"Osan thought Nya would be foolish enough to attempt a rescue without us," the other warrior said, approaching Sen with one eye still on Akoto. "Just didn't think you'd follow."

"I'm glad you're okay," Sahib said, offering his hand to help her up. Sen accepted, surprised at the strength of his scrawny arms.

"That's Kaden. And you remember Sulo," the warrior boy said, pointing to injured bear shrinking and reshaping into the form of a man.

Sulo. The injured bully bear that couldn't shift back until Akoto's howl triggered his return. *How'd he recover so fast?*

Lacerations and burn marks still covered his body, but they appeared more healed than she would have expected. *Did Natsugra's medicine do that?*

... Or Akoto's howl?

While Sen watched the last of the bully bear's transformation, Kaden and Sahib attempted to help Nya.

"Get away!" she shouted between heaves.

When the warriors looked at her for answers, she sighed and admitted Nya's deed: "She ate an emesilius flower."

Sahib covered mouth his hand to stifle a grin, but Kaden's face remained as cold as stone.

"We need to find the antidote," the warrior said, grabbing one of the low-hanging bioluminescent bulbs.

"It's the moonstar. It's blue and grows near the sun bush," she said, pointing to the suffering bush in front of Nya.

"I got it," Sulo said, wrapping a canana leaf around his waist before dropping down to his knees and sniffing around. Still covered in a transparent film, he paused at the base of a tree. "Here."

Running over, Sen dropped down to her knees and dug out the moonstar, exposing its white, five-point roots.

"What now?" Kaden said as Sen cleaned off the root on her shirt.

She won't be able to eat it, Sen though, clutching the root to her chest as Nya heaved and spit. "I-I don't know."

"You don't know?" Kaden's voice dropped, his eyes narrowing. Sen hated the way he regarded her, the way his primmed lips denoted his disappointment, or the way his eyes looked her over, as if remeasuring of her worth.

"Give it here," Sulo said, taking the root from her and bunching it up in one of his fists. Sen watched as his hand vibrated, the color going from pink to golden brown, as he channeled the strength of his inner bear. When a few clear droplets came from his fist, he ran over to Nya and, as gently as a bully bear Shifter could, held her head with one hand, and raised his fist with the moonstar over her right eye.

"Hold still," he said, wrestling with her to get the drops in.

"Enough!" Nya grabbed him by the wrist and elbow, and put him in a lock. "What the hell are you doing?"

"He's just trying to help," Kaden said, trying to get her to let Sulo go.

But Nya wouldn't have it. "You giant, mutt-lovin'—"

"Feel better?" Sulo said, twisting around to show her the crushed moon-star in his hand.

Nya paused, swallowed without gagging, and then let the shifter go. "Lucky guess."

"No, guessing is what you do." Sulo rubbed the arm Nya had locked and nodded to Sen. "You'd better thank the kid for figuring out the antidote."

Nya's eyes flicked her direction, but instead of a thank you, she snapped her fingers at Kaden and Sahib. "Show me what you brought for supplies. One minute, then we move."

As the three warriors laid out the supplies and weapons, Sulo walked over to Sen. His lips twitched before a single sound came out, as if he had something to say, but didn't know how.

"You don't recognize me, do you?"

Sen didn't understand what he meant. "You're the hurt Shifter."

The bear man grunted, his vibrant green eyes not leaving her face. She sensed he meant something more, but she couldn't place his grizzly face or hardened features, and meeting him before today wouldn't have made sense. Not with how much her father hated bully bears, and as a result, forbade even the gentle relatives like the okala and senta bear Shifters from even setting foot inside the Guild.

"You did well identifying the moonstar."

Stuffing her hands in her pants pockets, she shook her head. "But I didn't know what to do next."

"The eyes can absorb some liquid medicines. It's not great, but it'll work in an emergency," he said, jabbing a thumb at Nya. "And with that one, you'd better know your herbs, especially the antithesis's."

By his stern tone, Sen couldn't tell if he meant it as a joke, so she kept her head down and shrugged her shoulders.

"So, about your beast," Sulo said, turning his attention to Akoto. "What is he?"

"He's my friend." Sen moved to Akoto's side, putting herself between the two.

"I can see that. I don't remember much after the Nezra attacked the Guild post, but I do remember hearing his howl."

What's he doing? Sen thought, watching as Sulo sniffed the air.

"You know what species he is?"

"No."

Sulo pointed at Akoto's golden-blue eye. "By the looks of it, he may be a Torjin."

"Huh?"

The name caught Nya's attention, and she stopped her conversation with the two other warriors. "Torjins are just myths, Sulo."

Akoto growled, lowering his head to meet at eye level with the Shifter.

"What's a Torjin?" Sen asked, stroking Akoto's fur to try and calm him.

Sulo didn't answer right away, watching Akoto with increasing interest. "Agents of heaven. Or hell."

"We're moving out," Nya announced, handing off extra electro traps to Kaden and Sahib. "Sulo, take us to Sanctum."

The Shifter crossed his arms across his chest, not budging. "I came for the girl, not to guide you in."

Sen didn't understand. *Why would he come for me?*

"Sen?!" Nya said as the shouts and cries up ahead surged. "I thought you didn't want her."

"I don't. But you can't take her in there," Sulo said, his hands turning into fists. "She's untrained; she'll get killed."

"Fine, stay here. I'll find Sanctum without your help!"

"No—wait, Nya!"

Sen tried to run after the Chakoans, but Sulo shot his arm out and caught her. "It's too dangerous. I'll guide you back to the outlands."

"No," Sen said, pushing his arm down. "I promised I'd help."

"There's nothing for you there."

"That's not true," she said, watching as Nya and the others disappeared into the forest. "My uncle might be in Sanctum."

A fleeting look of recognition crossed Sulo's face.

Wait...what does he know?

"Even if he is, you don't know what you're up against. That battle—can you hear it?" A high-pitched, inhuman shriek cut through the forest, agitating the trees. "The Nezra don't just kill you," he said, voice faltering. Eyes growing distant, he finished his thought with a clenched jaw. "They tear your insides apart."

Maybe I should go back, she thought, taking a handful of Akoto's fur in her hand. *What could I do anyway? I'll just get in the way.*

Akoto's low growl rumbled through her body as he turned to her. Tilting his giant head to the side, he looked at her through his pale and cloudy eye. Seeing her gawky body and messy hair reflected in the gauzy pupil made heat rush through her chest and into her limbs.

I'm tired of being me.

She thought of Nya, of all that she didn't want to be anymore, and ran.

▲▽▲

CHAPTER 14

Nya expected a gruesome battle, but nothing in her experience or imagination matched what they found.

"Nya…" Kaden's voice cut out before he could finish whatever admonition crossed his mind as they reached the braided trees that once served as a protective wall for the hidden Virid city. Now, decimated and crumbling, the woven branches and trunks fell apart before even reaching the ground, turning into giant plumes of dust and decomposing plant matter.

Taking cover behind one of the few segments of branches still standing, Nya surveyed the area of destruction. Virid soldiers screamed for their life as bird-eaters gobbled them down, or vines wrapped around them and dragged them away through the courtyard.

But where are the Nezra? Her gut kicked in as she spotted the pathway of dead foliage and gleaming white bones cutting straight through the multi-story bamboo huts. Cries bellowing out from that direction indicated the new battle unfolding. The bird-eaters reacted to their summons, dropping what parts they hadn't digested, and slithering off toward the continued fight. *The death-dealers are headed into the heart of the city.*

"We'll check there first," she said, nodding her head toward the organic buildings inside another interlaced wall of branches. At three stories high and surrounded by not only a wall, but ten-foot high thorn bushes, she suspected at least something—or someone—important enough inside to protect, or keep from getting out.

"What about them?" Sahib asked.

Nya followed his line of sight to the remaining Virid soldiers in the courtyard. Glassy eyed and walking in circles, their hands moved up and down in a vain effort to conjure up even a bud from the gooey black and brown soup of plant material. Even their personal weapons—snaking vines and thorn projectiles—had liquefied, dripping down their arms and legs in a useless mess.

"What about them?" Nya replied back.

Kaden explained the situation to the confused young warrior. "There's nothing in range for them to attack us with."

Favored fools, Nya thought, stepping out from cover.

As soon as the Virid soldiers caught sight of her, they shrieked, throwing their arms in her direction to somehow dredge up something living from the tarry heaps.

Laughing, Nya ran toward them with her swords raised, and in less than five cuts, finished off the last remaining soldiers in the area.

"You shouldn't have forgotten the old ways," she whispered, staring at one of the felled soldiers as she wiped off her swords on her pants and re-sheathed them.

Nya let out the breath in the lungs, feeling charged and fantastic. Whatever Sulo had given her to counter the effects of the flower killed her hunger and hyped her senses while dulling the pain of her injured ankle. Like this she could take on all the Virids, the Nezra. *The entire Realm.*

Ignoring the shouts and the rumbling ground as the Nezra's attack continued up ahead, Nya made her way over to the three-story structure situated behind the wall and thorn bushes. Kaden and Sahib joined her, searching for a safe way through the thick brush.

"This isn't going to work," Kaden said as he hacked away at the thorn bush with his axes, only to have it regrow and tighten into knots. "And we'd better make a decision fast."

Nya looked to where he pointed with his axe. Disoriented Virids stumbled out of the forest, trying to flee the horror unleashed by the Nezra. Civilians pulled at their hair and fell to their knees, babbling nonsensical words and reaching out to invoke plants already turned to mush. The soldiers, not differentiating friend from foe, used combat vines snaking up their arms to attack one another, even the civilians. A few mobile plants—bird-eaters and tree walkers—charged behind, summoned by their specialized handlers to take down anything standing in their way.

"*Shy't,*" she muttered, pulling the two other warriors with her as she circled around the building and took shelter behind the half-rotted stump of a massive whitewood tree.

"We'll wait them out; let them kill each other off," Nya said, keeping her swords out and staying low to the ground.

"Oh no…"

"'Oh no' what?" Nya said, not turning to see what Kaden had spotted.

"Sen!" Sahib shouted, breaking cover as the young girl ran right out into the courtyard, in full view of the infected Virids.

Nya pulled Sahib by his shirt back behind cover. "Stay down."

"We have to help," Sahib said, notching an arrow and taking aim at a Virid soldier advancing on the Outlier girl.

Nya allowed him to shoot the arrow, hitting the soldier in the head and knocking him back, but didn't let him notch another.

"She'll draw them away—we can try the thorn bush again," Nya said, eyeing the wall.

Kaden grabbed her by the wrist. "She came back, Nya."

"So what, she's—"

"She's not as weak as you think."

The rush of heat to her cheeks surprised her. She shouldn't feel anything for the girl—especially not guilt for making the right survival decision for an Outlier that wasn't really part of their clan.

"Fine. You two get back to the wall—find a way in," she said as she took off to intercept Sen.

Vines shot out at her from every direction, and no matter how many she struck down, more came snaking at her from the arms of ashen-faced soldiers.

"Get down!" she shouted at Sen as the girl pulled at the vines wrapped around her legs.

Leaping up into the air, she evaded an attack from the vines slithering across the ground and came slicing down, full force, with her twin blades on the vines tethering Sen to a pair of soldiers. The soldiers shrieked, retracting their weapons only to whip around for another strike.

"Go," she said, picking up Sen by the armpit and hacking at the subsequent jabbing attacks.

She managed to drag the girl no more than ten feet before a specialized soldier joined the fray, aiming his tree walker at their position.

Her stomach dropped at the sight of the eighty-foot tall tree tromping toward them with its gigantic, multiple wooden limbs dragging through the plant debris. The horizontal splits in its upper trunk gave it half a face—or at least one caught in a permanent grimace. Leaves shook from its wiggling twig fingers, and bark peeled back from around what could have been its eyes, revealing hollow black pits that seemed to track her movement.

I really hate those things. Gritting her teeth, Nya sheathed one of her swords and unpinned the electro trap on her belt, readying it for the assault. It didn't carry much of a residual charge, but she hoped it'd be enough to at least fry off a limb or two.

"Nya!" Sen said, pulling on her leg as Nya counted the treewalker's steps and prepared to jump.

"Get to Kaden," she said, kicking Sen off and pointing to the two other warriors searching the guarded structure for an entrance. "Help them find a way in."

"But—"

"Go!"

Without looking back, Nya sprinted toward the treewalker, dodging vines and its swinging limbs. The treewalker roared as she anchored onto its back foot with her sword and hauled herself up to its lowest branches.

Skirting around the wayward vines still shooting up from the soldiers below, she sheathed her sword and unbelted the electro trap. With a grunt she pried open the electric jaws, keeping her hands away from the buzzing sensor in the middle. As a vine shot up and grabbed at her boot, she slammed the trap into the tree, triggering the bite. The treewalker bucked and twisted as blue bolts shot down its trunk and out of its limbs. Nya held tight until the behemoth fell forward onto its upper limbs, allowing her a straight shot to its head.

With smoke pouring out from around the teeth gouges of the electro trap, she scrambled her way toward the top of the tree. Branches batted at her face, but she dodged and ducked, keeping light on her toes. Unsheathing her swords, she cried out as she drove the twin blades down into its nape with all of her strength, severing the vital electrical bundle that linked the tree to its handler.

The treewalker pulled itself forward a few more feet on its upper limbs. A great sigh, like the last puff of air escaping a bellows, escaped from the horizontal splits in its bark before it collapsed against the exterior wall of the three-story structure.

That works, she thought, climbing up the rest of the dead treewalker and peering over the wall. To her satisfaction, Kaden and Sahib were already inside, weapons drawn, backs to the wall.

Scanning the area, she spotted what would have made her suspect a jail or government institution: prickly thorns on the inside of the walls, deterring any kind of escape, and tired footpaths in the low-cut grass, worn by repetitive circles. The rest of the interior, drab and uninteresting—especially considering the Virid flare for organic beauty—bespoke of the chilling nature of whatever lay behind the sod-covered walls of the structure.

What the—?

A shadowy figure, big enough to blot out the bioluminescent bulbs hanging from the tops of the wall, descended from the sky, landing just behind the warriors with only a whisper.

Akoto.

She couldn't believe it. The dumb animal could fly. Or at least glide. *And is strong enough to carry two people...* she thought as Sen and Sulo slid off his back. *At least he's useful.*

As she dropped down from the felled treewalker, Sen gaped. "Nya! Ohmygod—did you see that? The treewalker—you took it down—and then—wow!"

"Yeah, I was there." Ignoring Sen's continued exuberance, she jogged up to Sahib, Kaden, and Sulo. "Report."

"We saw a few guards, but they all ran toward the fight up ahead," Kaden answered.

"Good, then let's get inside."

"You won't find your people here," Sulo said as Nya surveyed the best possible entry point.

"Is this Sanctum or not?"

Sulo crossed his arms and looked her dead in the eye.

"We just saved your life, *kapu't*," Nya said, keeping one eye on the felled treewalker that served as a bridge over the wall. A few disoriented Virids scampered up, but slinking vines stole them back before they could make it over. "You owe us."

"Sen and Akoto saved me," he growled.

"So did Natsugra's medicine," Kaden argued.

"We don't have time for this," Nya said as a bundle of vines spilled over the wall.

"Please," Sen said, touching Sulo's elbow and looking up at him with her big hazel eyes. "She just wants to help people."

Sulo grunted, shooting Nya a heated look. "This is Sanctum, but it's the East wing, where they keep all the old-timers. You want the interrogation holding cells, four buildings down."

"Let's go," Nya said, picking up her step toward the western buildings. The shouts and the sounds of splintering trees made her push even faster, despite the crunching and popping of her ankle. Not that any injury, not matter how grievous, would stop her now.

Cutting off the heads of any curious flowers turning to their position, she led them to the leafy canopies hanging over the entrances to the East wing. As she ran to the moss-covered fountain separating the East building from domed structures in the next yard, she noticed some of her party lagging behind.

"Keep up!" she shouted at Sen as the girl and her beast stayed by the entrances to the East building.

Sen shook her head and fidgeted with her hands, not budging.

"Of all the stupid—"

"Her uncle's in there," Sulo said in his usual flat tone.

"Her uncle?"

"Go on," Sulo said as a Virid soldier launched over the wall and crashed a few feet from them. Despite the greenthumb's broken neck, his legs and arms continued to twitch as black sludge oozed from his mouth. "I'll catch her up."

As Kaden and Sahib finished off the infected Virid soldier, Nya grabbed Sulo by the shoulder. "Tell me why you care so much about that girl."

A low growl vibrated up from his chest and through her arm. She felt his muscles tense as thick hair fibers broke through his skin and tickled her hand. On the verge of shifting, he only managed a few grunted words. "Tell me why you don't."

Shoving off of her, Sulo ran back to Sen and Akoto, giving her no time to respond. After shouting something at the girl, he kicked down the bamboo doors to the East wing entrance, and ran inside. Sen looked to Nya, but the warrior woman only stared back at her, angry and frustrated for reasons she couldn't explain. A second later, Sen and her beast ran inside the East wing entrance, disappearing into the dark building.

"What now?" Sahib asked, wiping the green Virid blood from his knife onto his pants.

By the nervous expressions on both Kaden and Sahib's faces, she could guess their reactions: *No bully bear, no midnight beast.*

"We didn't need them before, we don't need them now. We are Chakoa."

"Aye," Kaden shouted, slamming the butts of his axes into the ground.

Sahib joined in, craning back his neck and shouting to the stars. "Aye!"

As humans and trees shrieked, and fires lit up the night sky, Nya pointed her swords toward the chaos, into the heart of death and decay.

"Let's go free our people."

▲▽▲

CHAPTER 15

Sen took only a few steps inside the East wing of Sanctum before screeching to a halt.

"Sulo!" she cried, unable to take her eyes off of the dozens of white-haired men and woman sitting around tables, in wheelchairs, or on couches in the atrium. Blank-faced, they didn't show any recognition of her presence, or make any noise. Not that any of them could. Plant roots threaded into their arms and legs, up their nose, and down their mouths.

"You can't help them," Sulo said, trying to turn her chin toward him.

But she looked back, wanting to reconcile the horror.

"This is how they're fed, sedated, and kept alive," Sulo explained. He pointed to glistening pink stalks in the middle of the atrium under the glass ceiling. In the center, a yellow, undulating mass expanded and retracted liked great lungs.

"Come on," he said, pulling her down the hall.

"H-how do you know this?" she asked as they passed more of the vegetative elderly rooted into the plants. Bioluminescent flowers, hanging from support beams, cast eerie shadows over their expressionless faces.

When he stayed silent much past the expected time to respond, she thought he wouldn't tell her. *Did I make him mad?*

As they passed into a quiet hallway lined with spiny plants and glowing orange flowers, he finally answered in gruff tones. "I've worked under a very powerful Virid elder for the last fifteen years."

"So you protect him?"

"Yes."

"Don't you need to get back to him now?"

She regretted asking the question as soon as she saw his fists flex and muscles bulge, blanching the many scars that crisscrossed his back.

"Do you think I, or any of my kind, wants to serve the other denoms?" he said, turning to her, his cool green eyes piercing straight through her.

Frightened of his tone, she took a few steps backward until she stood underneath Akoto.

Sulo turned over his forearm, revealing the symbol of the Virids branded into his skin. "They can try to indoctrinate us, murder our families, torture us until we're stripped to the bone, but we will never be their servants."

Sen heard something more buried between his words. A horrible loss, something that strained each syllable and stole his breath. Despite her fear, a greater need prompted her to ask the obvious question: "Then why stay? Why not join the Shadowless in the outlands?"

The bully bear Shifter, intimidating in size and presence, bent forward a little bit, as if someone had kicked the wind out of him. Instead of answering her question, he ground his teeth together and looked over his shoulder. "Let's get going; this place isn't going to stay quiet for long."

Keeping close to Akoto, Sen followed Sulo down another hallway lined with flowers and undulating stalks. Something didn't feel right. *Why aren't there any guards?*

It made sense that some of them would have left to join the fight, but not all, especially in an institution.

Sulo went over to the abandoned nurse's station and tore through the desk and file cabinets. As he tossed charts and flung around papers, countless questions burned through her mind. *How could anyone hurt someone like this?* she thought, turning around and around, still trying to absorb all the ghostly faces and limbs infiltrated by pulsating roots. *Why would they keep all these Outliers alive like this? What are they doing to them? Would my parents have sent me here?*

The last question sent shivers down her back.

No, not her father. He wouldn't stand for such a disgrace. She'd be better off dead than—

Akoto grunted, offsetting her balance so she had to hold on to his face to steady herself. "Hey!" she said, giggling as he drowned her in a sloppy lick to the face. "Stop that."

Sulo found whatever he wanted and leapt over the desk. "I think this is him; room A95," he said, jangling a key in one hand, "down that hallway. Hurry."

Fear squeezed down on her fragile hope. "Are you sure? My father said he…"

The rest of the sentence died at her lips. *…killed himself.*

Not that her mother ever confirmed the story, but she didn't deny it either. And knowing how she felt now, after finding out the awful truth about herself—being shadowless, a lowly Outlier—she garnered enough bleak insight into why someone would choose such an irreparable path.

"You can't believe everything other people tell you, Sen." When she didn't reply, he sharpened his tone: "You want to turn back?"

"N-no," she whispered back.

"Then keep up."

Sen followed along, Akoto padding behind, as Sulo led them deeper into the East wing. The glass ceiling disappeared as Sulo unlocked a series of red-marked doors, replaced by a roof of barred sequoia-oak and some kind of corrugated metal.

That's not right, she thought. Virids didn't use any kind of metal in their architecture, only organic material, and the occasional use of natural rock formations and other landscape phenomena. Or at least that's what the pompous Virid proctor at her school used to drone on and on about at some of the interdenom lectures. *"The pride of the Virids, the most harmonious, God-favored denom of them all,"* she could still hear him saying. *"We live in true accord with nature, celebrating only what she intended."*

"Hold up," Sulo whispered, stopping her in her tracks. Lost in her thoughts, she hadn't noticed Akoto's concerned growl, or the two figures at the end of the hallway. With some of the bioluminescent flowers raked from the walls, she could only make out their hunched outline, and the oblong shape of their arms.

Sen looked at the doors to her left and right. *A90, A91.*

That means that those things are right outside my uncle's door.

One of the bioluminescent flowers sputtered overhead, enough to give them a glimpse of the bodies lining the end of the hall. Patients, tore apart at the limbs, lay in decaying, bubbling heaps.

Clinging to Akoto, Sen whispered to Sulo: "You think my uncle—?"

He made a slicing motion across his neck, indicating for her to shut up, but she couldn't help herself. Memories of the battle near the Spires—of the rot, the disease, the inhuman attackers—the terrible whisper beyond the dying woman's lips—*"save me."*—or any of the carnage they had witnessed made her pull on Sulo's arm. "Let's find another way."

"There isn't any." Sulo eyed the knife on her belt. "You've got to fight."

He didn't wait for her response. With a furious roar that transformed him from man to bear, Sulo dropped down on all fours and charged, his body cracking and expanding with each step toward the two dark figures at the end of the hall. In the heat of his charge, the sound of his thumping paws echoed off the metal walls, rattling stone tiles and shaking the sensor flowers blooming on the walls.

"No!" she screamed as the bully bear swiped at the darts shooting out from the shadows. Within seconds his roar turned into a fading guttural sigh, and he collapsed against the wall, several feet away from the two figures, next to the dead patients.

Akoto tried to paw her back, beneath him, away from danger, but Sen wrestled her way in front of him and ran to the bully bear.

"Stay away from him," she shouted as the two figures moved toward the bear with rickety steps, as if walking on broken bones.

Even when she caught sight of their mangled faces, she didn't stop.

Are those—?

But as she tripped over a mushy, severed limb, her brain made the connection.

Nurses—oh God—the nurses—what's wrong with their hands?—

(those aren't hands—)

In the far reaches of her memories, she recalled her mother telling her about the more advanced Virid healers, how some of them could sprout roots or other plant appendages from their hands in order to physically connect to their patients. But what she saw—jagged stems with hollow, pointed tips instead of fingers, dripping with a black, viscous fluid—portended less palliative intentions.

Something whizzed past her face, grazing her ear. Terrified, she dropped to her hands and knees, taking cover behind Sulo's massive body.

"Akoto!" she exclaimed as her companion, only a step behind, went bounding past her, his teeth bared, hackles raised.

The nurses continued their assault, shooting darts from their mutated finger tips. Instead of Sen, then concentrated their attack on Akoto, as he closed the distance between them with each long stride.

"No!" she screamed as his footsteps faltered, and he slowed.

Seeing him drag his paws across the floor, his head getting lower and lower to the ground, she snapped. Springing out from behind Sulo, she ran straight at the nurses. She didn't care about their colorless faces, or the way their mouths had been frozen open in a scream. The blood splattering their cream-colored aprons and prim hats, or the fatal wounds cutting across their throats didn't register, only the whimpering cry of her best friend.

"Stop hurting him!"

As she cut in front of Akoto, putting herself between him and the assailants, she felt more than the sting of the darts as they punctured her arm and thigh.

"You've got to fight."

She heard Sulo's voice, and remembered the feel of the leather grip of the knife in her hand from her forced practice session with Nya. The knife, hot against her hip, lit up like a beacon in flaming hues of red and orange.

Nya's face appeared before her, her dark eyes livened by violence. *"Fight back."*

This isn't right, she thought as her eyelids grew too heavy to hold open.

Gritting her teeth, she focused on the rattling stems of the nurse's fingertips, and the steaming breath pushing out of the holes in their chest. Their faces ballooned out, then twisted in on themselves, as they reached out for her with mutated hands.

Poison. They've poisoned us.

Thoughts pulled apart, turning to wisps of smoke. Her arms and legs became distant things attached loosely to a wooden core.

Have to…fight…or we'll all…die…

A hardened fingertip raked her cheek, then pressed into it, piercing the flesh.

Akoto, she cried out. In the distance, she felt her left hand grip the fur of his chest. *Help me.*

Fire poured through her left arm and up into her neck and head, burning away the fog blanketing her thoughts. Her eyes flew open, wider than she thought she could stand. Taking in the faces of the nurses before her, she saw past their tortured faces and grisly flesh, into a dark space that shouldn't have existed.

"Save us."

Still pierced by one of their fingertips, the fire moved from her head, funneling through her cheek and down through the nurse's fingertip. She roiled alongside it, her mind stretching across conceived boundaries, bombarded by sound and light.

"What's happening out there? Where did all the guards go?"

A woman, no older than thirty, with auburn hair and light green skin looked back to her, eyes wide with fright. Patients, peeking out their doors, looked to them for guidance.

"You stay here; I'll go look outside."

"No, I'll go with you."

Incredible pain lanced through her cheek, and she cried out, but couldn't pull away as the next scene unfolded.

"Who's that?"

The other woman leaning out the window with her pointed to the dark figure slinking through the bushes, crooked fingers stretched out in front of him.

"I-I don't know," she said, trying to make sense of anything: the putrid smells, the screams and cries echoing out across the courtyard—the way the bushes and trees cracked and fell apart as the shadowy figure neared.

"Look!" the other woman cried, pointing to the missing guards writhing on the ground, their combat vines wrapped around each other's throats.

"Get back," she said, trying to pull the other woman inside the nurse's station.

But when she looked back, bloodshot eyes gazed back at her, and black-tipped fingers wiggled in her direction.

Sen resisted, trying to free herself from the awful feeling invading her body. Someone or something stole the breath from her lungs, drained all the blood from her face and limbs. Even as she tried to pull away, she couldn't escape the caustic fingers digging through her sternum to seize her heart.

The violation didn't end there. Left only with pain, she could not recall enough to remember who she was, or what other purpose she had as a terrible voice whispered out across her mind, erasing all but her animal fear: "Ennari."

Sen bucked back with a scream, freeing herself from the connection to the decaying nurse. In the confusion, she lashed out, kicking the nurse in the chin, sending her crashing into her companion.

"Get away from me!"

Light exploded from all around her, inundating even the darkest corners of the hallway. In that brief moment, Sen saw the two nurses, their faces no longer mangled, but pinched in confusion as she stood over them. With tears in her eyes, one of them reached out to her, black streaks fading from her mutilated limbs, whispering words Sen could not hear.

What did I just do?

The light vanished. Everything wobbled and see-sawed. She couldn't tell the floor from the ceiling, or how her feet could possibly end up over her head.

Akoto...

As the world spiraled away, she used the last of her strength to reach out for her friend, not letting go of his coarse fur, even as her mind pulled apart.

▲▽▲

CHAPTER 16

Nya ducked behind a fallen gray oak, batting the smoke from her face. Dead Virids, putrefied plants and twitching bird-eaters lay strewn about the yard in steaming piles. Up ahead, flames and black smoke chugged out of two of the four clay and wood structures comprising the central Sanctum buildings.

"Fire's spreading," Kaden said, pointing to the third building starting to smolder. Squinting, Nya could make out the prisoners slamming themselves against the barred windows, trying to break free before the fire consumed the building.

Out of the corner of her eye, Nya caught Sahib grinding his knuckles into the tree bark. She waited longer than she wanted to, just to see if he would say it. Even after his initiation into the Chakoa, he held on to undesirable emotions, making him a liability to the clan. Outliers couldn't afford compassion, especially not bleeding hearts. However, after a hunting expedition with Sho a year ago, the boy came back shaken, and changed, no longer willing to throw himself away for anyone but his clan.

Don't suggest we save them, too, she thought. *Or I will cut your throat right here.*

Sahib didn't look at her, his eyes fixed forward, awaiting her command.

"Side entrance. Stay alert," she said, climbing over the tree and heading for the cloister connecting the third and fourth building. Hugging the moss-covered wall, she ran toward the string of guttering orbs over a birchpine door, keeping an eye out for any movement. Kaden and Sahib stayed close behind, weapons drawn, covering her blind spots.

What's this? she thought as she tested the brass door handle. Locked. Even worse, reinforced metal plating secured the frame and backing, making it impossible for any Virid—or any of the other favored—to manipulate or destroy. *Sanctum guards must really want to keep their prisoners from escaping.*

Examining the nearby windows and exterior structure didn't give her much hope. From what she could tell, wood and plant material just served as a veneer for a metal superstructure.

Kaden racked the back of his axe against a barred window. "Thought those greenthumbs hated metal."

"Yeah, it's a load of *shy't*," she mumbled, running her hands along the walls and slats, trying to find some imperfection that would allow them to break through.

"Nya," Kaden whispered, alerting her to the movement down the alleyway.

Nya signaled for the other two to mimic her as she pressed herself against the wall, trying to keep out of sight.

"Whoa."

Nya smacked her hand against Sahib's chest and threw him a dirty look for breaking silence. But when she saw the gross disfigurement of the Virid soldier's face, she had to keep herself from exclamation.

Another infected, she thought, her insides tightening. She didn't like the way his eyes roamed in their bloodied sockets, or the way his yellowed skin shriveled together like desiccated fruit. He dragged his right leg across the ground, the foot crunching down at an odd angle, making her aware again of her own ankle injury.

Uckkk… She didn't like the black sludge spilling from his mouth, or the open wounds across his neck. If not for the competing smoke, her nose and lungs would have been filled with the dead animal stink she'd now come to associate with the dark liquid. Rotten bastards.

As Nya paced out when to spring out of her hiding spot and deal the Virid his death-blow, Kaden nudged her. She didn't look back until he grabbed her elbow, lowering her sword. Before she could yank her arm back, he drew her attention to the keyhole above the door handle.

"We need him alive," Kaden whispered.

Nya didn't understand what he meant until she examined the keyhole closer than before.

It's not meant for regular keys, she thought, seeing the rim of green plant scrapings lining the inside of the hole. *They snake in their combat vines to manipulate the inner cylinder.*

"*Shy't,*" she muttered as smoke pumped out from the adjacent building and other Virid soldiers, battling each other in the front yard, screamed past the alley. Every passing second counted. *Killing is so much easier.*

"Hide," she said, shoving Kaden and Sahib back around the corner.

"What are you—?"

Before Kaden could finish the sentence, she pressed the blade of her right sword against her left forearm and pulled back. Biting pain streaked up her arm, but she pushed it aside and embraced the adrenaline rush that charged her senses.

The infected solider paused, tipping back his head and emitting a ravenous cry as she pressed her bloody arm against the door, saturating the keyhole.

"Come on," she whispered, staying as long as she dared before retracting her arm and dashing around the corner.

"Hurry," she said, shoving her lacerated arm into Kaden's face. The warrior looked at her in confusion, but didn't hesitate to apply the staunching herbs from the pouch on his waist belt. As soon as he finished, she ripped one of the yellow flowers from a supportive trellis and rubbed its pollen along the wound bed.

"What are you—?" he started.

"It's attracted to blood."

"But he's a Virid."

"Not anymore."

The infected soldier hissed, lurking forward with excited gurgles. Nose upturned, he sniffed the air and pinpointed the blood smear on the birch-pine door.

"*K'thei,*" Sahib whispered as the soldier pressed his face against the keyhole, snorting and lapping at the stain with a withered black tongue.

On the opposite end, a bird-eater, severely damaged in the fray, turned one of its three heads into the passageway between the buildings.

"Sahib," she said, stepping back for him as the massive plant zeroed in on the infected soldier.

In one fluid motion, the young warrior sprung out from behind the corner, kneeling as he pulled and notched a bow, took aim, and shot an arrow at the mobile plant tromping toward their mark. The arrow struck one of its rosette faces, stunning the creature and sending it stumbling into the wall.

Nya pulled Sahib back out of sight as the soldier, transfixed by the fresh blood, fed his combat vines into the keyhole.

Come on, she thought, waiting for the precious sound of the vines aligning the pins to spring open the lock as the bird-eater shrieked.

Yes—

Over the infuriated cries from the rallying bird-eater, she heard the telltale click, and leapt out from behind cover. Before the soldier could retract and battle the three-headed beast charging at him, Nya hacked off his vines plugged into the keyhole.

As the bird-eater snapped down on the infected Virid's head, Nya turned the wiggling vines and unlocked the door.

"Nya!"

She heard Kaden's shout as she tumbled backward, head over heels. Strong arms grabbed her by the chest and pulled her away from the stampede.

Disoriented, it took her a moment to comprehend the door swinging on its hinge, and the dozens of men and women in blue gowns streaming out from the building. Piercing cries rattled her back into action as the bird-eater, still stuffing its pink oral cavity with the Virid soldier, focused a new attack the escaping prisoners.

"Let go," she said, pushing herself out of Kaden's arms and back into the fight.

The bird-eater swung its bladed leaves left and right, sending bits of blue material and warm blood spraying through the air. Nya carved her twin blades through the chaos, cutting down leafy limbs until she reached the primary stalk. Digestive fluids dripping down from their ribbed gullets slimed her face, but she didn't hesitate. Swinging around on its spines, she chopped off one head after another, until its last head mewled in pain and fell forward.

Nectar perfumed the air, mingling with the wretched smells of rot and blood as she delivered the death-blow to the bird-eater. Still, she reveled in the moment, standing over her kill, feeling the only satisfaction she ever allowed herself anymore.

"Chakoa!" Sahib shouted as more prisoners poured out of the unlocked door. "Any Chakoa?"

Nya didn't bother trying to be heard over the cries. "Hey," she said, grabbing one of the fleeing men and pinning him against the brick wall. Circumferential scars covered his bald head, some still inflamed and red with root-like stitches. "Where are the Chakoa?"

The man looked away with a crazed expression, his eyes never connecting with hers for more than a second. "C-Chakoa?"

"Where are my people?" she said, showing him the black and red tattoos along her neckline bearing the Chakoan symbols.

Red and orange flames belched from the second-story windows of the opposite building. The man tried to free himself from her grips, but she slammed him again against the wall. "Where is Sho?!"

The man pointed a shaking finger back at the door. "Dangerous."

Irritated, Nya shoved him away and reconvened with Kaden and Sahib near the side entrance. "Anything?"

"It's too hard to see now," Kaden said, fanning the smoke from his face with a cough. "They could have gotten out with the others. We should follow them."

Nya looked back at the open door, seeing into the sterile reception area of white tiles and metal bars. The strange architecture coupled with the blood-stained walls and dead bodies made her override his suggestion.

"They could be trapped in there. Let's go."

Kaden and Sahib followed behind her, checking the overturned furniture and dead bodies for clues. A few of the fallen prisoners appeared sickened, their faces ghostly white. Just like the *Soushin*...

And the Virid guards looked just as grotesque and deformed as the ones infected in the yards, their combat vines wrapped around each other or other prisoners, black sludge caked around their mouths.

Nya reached a control station at the end of the hall. Someone or something had ripped off all of the safety bars from the partition. Ignoring the blood splatters, and the Virid guard smashed against the desk, she hopped over and went right to the building maps carved into metal plates hanging on the wall.

As she looked over each one, Kaden chopped out a bigger hole in the crisscrossing bars for himself to wiggle through, and joined her side.

"There's too many floors; we don't have enough time to figure out which lockdown they're in."

Nya racked her knuckles against one of the maps. "Sho's the most wanted Outlier in all the lands. They wouldn't keep him with the general populace. They'd isolate him—"

Visions of him tied to a rack, Virid guards taking turns lashing him with their combat vines, flashed through her head. She had to clear her throat to keep her voice from faltering. "...pump him for information."

Kaden coughed more violently this time, his eyes watering as smoke drifted down the hallway. "What about records?"

Nya eyed the broken file cabinets to her left covered in black ooze and wet plant debris. Papers, shredded and stained, littered the ground. "Not an option."

"What about there?" Sahib said, shouldering his way through and pointing to the basement level. Red warning signs and high-level containment notices covered the smaller map.

"Good enough. Let's go."

Nya backtracked out of the control station, winding through the hallway and toward the stairwell at the end of the reception area. Through the barred windows she could see the battle unfolding in the front yard as Virids and their mobile units attacked each other. Gigantic tree walkers, bird-eaters, and other vegetative monstrosities clashed over the soldiers in the blanket of smoke, not discerning friend from foe.

"It's locked," she said after testing the door handle to the stairwell. Old demons stirred as she slammed her fist against the metal door.

"We can't stay here," Kaden said, crouching low to the ground to get out of the smoke.

"I'm not leaving."

"We don't know if they're even in here."

"Nya," Sahib said, drawing her attention back to overturned table near the reception. A prisoner lay crumpled underneath, her blonde hair covered in dried blood. "She's still alive."

Nya ran over to the woman and knelt next to her head. Battered from head to toe, she raised her head just enough to look Nya in the face. Blue eyes and fair skin bespoke of her northern origins, but the spread of red freckles across the bridge of her broken nose made her think of the ice forest dwellers. In another setting, they might have been enemies, vying to cut each other's throats.

Are those plants sewn into her arm? Nya clenched her jaw at the sight of the yellow roots sticking out of the woman's forearms and bare shoulders, not wanting to imagine what horrors the woman had endured in Sanctum.

Sensing that intimidation would get her nowhere, Nya set down her swords, but kept a firm voice. "Where are the Chakoans?"

A weak laugh escaped her lips. "Dead."

Nya persisted, unwilling to believe. "All of them?"

"Dangerous," the woman said, fighting for each word. "Tried to...break out. Killed guards...started riots..."

"There were six of them," she said, holding the woman's chin up. "How many are left?"

The woman coughed, sending her entire body into a spasm. Blood spurted out of her nose as she gasped for breath, clawing at her throat. Sahib and Kaden held her down as Nya tried to get what little information she could out of the woman.

"We'll help you get out," she said. Sahib looked at her in shock, but Kaden, knowing the conditional nature of that kind of promise, didn't react.

The woman grasped Nya's arm. Even in her debilitated state, the woman's blue eyes reminded her of the hottest part of the fire. In some remote part of her awareness, Nya felt herself pull away as her mind drew unwanted parallels to her own life.

"One..."

"Who?" she demanded, gripping her shoulders.

The woman grunted, arcing her head and pointing a finger at the stairwell. "Him."

Nya grabbed at her swords as the stairwell door flung open. Black smoke plumed out, obscuring her sight. Still, the effects of the occulrum enabled her to recognize the outline of the man running toward them at full speed, and she restrained Kaden as he made to throw his axes.

"Sho!"

Covered in plant debris and soot, the runner came to a halt a few feet in front of them, chest heaving. Nya held tight to her swords, unsure if the man standing before her, dressed in a tattered guard uniform, bore the same Nezran illness. She recognized his brown eyes, but only in shape and contour, not the violence-cut expression that trapped the breath in her lungs.

"Sho..." she tried again, trying to connect.

Something changed. Familiarity melted the icy sheen to his eyes. "Nya."

Sheathing her swords, she ran up to him, ready to fling her arms around him, but stopped short when he faded back a step.

"We came to rescue—"

"The others are dead. Help me with these," he said, handing her the black, wicked bulbs he carried in his arms.

No hello, not even a hint of a smile; nothing like how she had secretly imagined their reunion playing out. Hurt and disappointment squeezed down on her heart, but she rationalized his behavior. *This is my fault. What was I expecting? He's a warrior.*

She took a few of the bombs and lashed them to her belt, as did Kaden and Sahib.

"Sho, I—"

"I made some modified explosives," he said, cutting her off. Ripping off a strip of cloth from a fallen captive, he tied together a sash to hold the black bulbs against his chest. "We need to destroy this place."

"The fire's doing a pretty good job," Kaden said.

Sho shot him a vicious look. "We leave nothing to chance."

"Wait," Sahib said as Nya followed Sho out of the building. "What about her?"

Nya looked back at the dying blonde woman. Pain shuttered her eyes halfway, but she did not plead, did not look to her for sympathy. Nya looked to Sho, but he ignored all but his objective, arming himself with whatever he could find from the broken furniture and dead guards as he set down the bombs against support pillars.

This is no place to die.

"Carry her outside," she said, surprising all of them, even herself, at her decision. "Then it's up to her."

Following Sho outside, she covered up her nose and mouth with the back of her sleeve, her lungs burning with the smoke. Firelight and the bioluminescent bulbs strung along the paths guided them back down the cloister and to the same shelter behind the grey oak.

As Sho removed a few bombs from the sash, Kaden and Sahib caught up. Nya gave a cursory glance to see where Sahib had dropped off the blonde captive, only to see her limping off down the floral path between the fountain.

Dammit, she thought, unsure if she should be pissed at Sahib, or about the chance of another ice-dweller surviving to hunt her later.

Refocusing her attention, she tried to get something out of Sho. "What's the plan?"

"We'll throw the rest into the burning buildings," he said, pointing to the blazing structures ahead. "Finish the job."

"What the hell would survive the fire?"

Gripping bombs in both hands, Sho spit out each word as he stared into the fire. "The worst kind of evil."

The look in his eyes withered any retort, or any remote doubt of his authority on the matter. Even Kaden held his tongue and waited for Sho to give the command.

"What about the others?" Sahib asked, pointing toward the East Wing.

Sen. She quickly reprimanded herself for thinking of the stupid girl first, and not Sulo or even the midnight beast. Given the fast-spreading battle, Sen had probably already gotten herself killed.

Still...

A blinding flash made her crouch back behind the grey oak, followed by a thunderclap that rattled her teeth and bones. When she peered back over, great rags of white fire shot up from the fourth building they had recently escaped from, followed by a burgeoning mushroom cloud. Smoke rings rose in twisting, writhing shapes, drawing lightning from the agitated sky.

"Sho, wait!" she said as he took off toward the third building, bombs in hand, ready to take down the next structure. Kaden followed, loosing a great warrior cry.

Ears ringing, she turned to Sahib and pointed to the East Wing. "Run!"

The young warrior took off, his long, lanky legs speeding him away faster than a deerkat. She watched him only for a moment, until he disappeared in the consuming smoke. With a cry that summoned her greatest anger, she armed herself with Sho's explosives, and ran into the fire.

CHAPTER 17

"Hello?"

The voice came from afar, down an impossibly long tunnel.

"Wake up; you can't stay here."

Gentle hands searched Sen's face and then descended to her shoulder.

"Please, get up. You have to go."

Footsteps shuffled away.

Father?

No, the voice wasn't harsh enough.

Sen opened her eyes, trying to make sense of her surroundings with a head stuffed full of cotton. Faint beams of moonlight trickled in through a boarded-up window, giving her a sense of the objects across the room: A single bed, a sagging shelf with aging books and a few odds and ends. In the opposite corner, bioluminescent bulbs hung from a dehydrated stalk, illuminating a policy and notice board detailing the strict procedures for all East wing residents.

"What's going on…?" she muttered, holding her head as she inched her way onto her elbow.

It came back to her in a rush: Sulo charging at the nurses and collapsing. When she tried to help, she put not only herself, but Akoto as well, in danger.

I can't do anything right.

Her mind snagged on an important detail: *Wait—the poisoned darts—*

She tried to find the projectiles that had struck her arm and thigh, but only a tiny hole in her clothing, ringed with purple ooze, remained.

How did I survive?

"Akoto," she whispered, looking every which way for her friend.

"Who's Akoto?"

The voice. Sen darted her eyes back and forth, her feverish imagination populating every shadow with the monsters of death and decay.

"Don't be scared. I pulled you in here to keep you safe."

Despite his benign overtures, she yelped when she saw the man in the threadbare robe shuffling out from the corner. The shock of white hair atop his head matched the stubble on his chin and neck, though as he approached, she couldn't reconcile his age. A few wrinkles and liver spots decorated his forehead, and if not for his hair, she would have guessed him in his late thirties.

"I saw you out there," he said, pointing a shaking finger in the vicinity of the door.

Squinting, Sen took another look at his face. Even in the relative dark she could discern the colorless irises, and the way his pupils stayed dilated, even as he shuffled into a beam of light.

He's blind.

"...So bright, like the sun. Like in my dreams."

Sen collected herself off the floor, but took a few steps back from him, running into the decomposing wood dresser. "Who are you? Where am I? Where are my friends?"

The man held his hands out in front of him, feeling for any objects in his path. "You mean those big furry things in the hallway?"

"Yes—are they okay?" she said, dodging him and getting up on her tip-toes to peer out the eye slit in the door. From what little she could see, she could make out Akoto and Sulo's massive bodies, and the regular rise and fall of their chests. She also spotted both nurses, unmoving and face down on the floor.

"I guess. The giant one snores worse than you."

Sen considered what he implied and turned back to him. "So that wasn't poison?"

"Poison? No. The nurses are mean, but they shoot tranquilizers, not poisons." A lop-sided smile brightened his face. "At least not yet."

As he chuckled to himself, Sen asked again: "W-who are you?"

"Ah, of course, forgive me; I'm out of practice for visitors. I'm Haebi."

Sen clapped her hands together. "Haebi?! As in Haebi Mor?"

The white-haired man recoiled a bit, a frightened look upon his face. "J-just Haebi."

Sen looked at the number underneath the eye slit on the door. A95

"It's Sen!" she said, opening her arms up wide and making her way over to him. "I can't believe you're alive!"

"Sen?"

The confusion in his voice, and the rigid way he put out his hands in front of him, made her pause.

"Sen. Senzo, really. Your niece; Lyn's daughter."

"Lyn..."

His voice faltered, and his breath came in short, quick bursts, as if anticipating a vicious attack.

"I-I came to rescue you, get you out of here," she said, trying to get back his attention as he mumbled to himself and fiddled with his hands.

"No, no; can't speak of such things."

"Uncle Haebi?"

With a nervous laugh, he paced the room, bumping into the bed and shelf as he ran his fingers along his few possessions.

"What's wrong?" she asked as he crammed himself into the corner farthest away from her.

"Don't want to sleep again, please," he said, covering his head with his arms.

Not knowing what to do, Sen got down on her knees and crawled over to him. "Tell me what to do."

Whimpering and mumbling, Haebi worked himself even farther into the corner, his joints cracking and popping as he made himself as small as possible.

As she watched her uncle cower, her mind replayed the awful sights of the residents infiltrated by the plant roots, and the nurses with tranquilizer darts shooting from their stemmed fingers. "Why are they hurting you?"

Without thinking, she reached over and touched his knee. Haebi gasped, then looked up at her, his white eyes jittering in their sockets. "Sen... Senzo."

"Yes," she said, surprised when he grabbed at her hand and pulled it close.

"You're real?"

"Yes."

"I thought...they told me Lyn never came by, that she didn't bring you to see me the day after you were born."

Curious delight filled her heart. "You saw me when I was a baby?"

"I-I thought so. But the doctors here told me my radiant little niece was all in my head. Then they did something to my eyes; they said they were tricking me, that they could not be trusted."

Still caught in Haebi's grasp, Sen could only look away as he pulled down the scarred lid to one of his blanched eyes. "But I know what I just saw; I saw everything—when you were shining."

"Uncle, no, I can't—"

"I saw *everything*," he insisted, tightening his hand around hers. "These ugly walls, the dead nurses and patients, your friends. For the first time in fourteen years, I could see. You did that, Sen." His voice reduced to a whisper: "Do you know what that means?"

"It's Akoto," she said, deflecting his inference. "He's special. He's doing all this."

Haebi's tone sharpened, turned hard. "Don't listen to the people that limit you, Sen, especially that cursed father of yours. Embrace all that you are, believe in what you can become. *Lucente.*"

"*Lucente?*"

"Shine."

Grunting, snarls. Behind the closed door, Sen could hear Akoto starting to stir. Part of her wanted her friend to rush to her rescue, but another part, transfixed by Haebi's blind gaze, needed something in her uncle's bizarre words.

"The Nezra are attacking; we have to go," she said, tugging on her hand. "Come with me. We'll be safe in the outlands."

"No, I'm no good, not anymore," he said, half-laughing, half-crying as he withdrew his hand from hers. "But I can help you, little star."

Reaching inside his shirt, he pulled out a necklace. Sen recognized the blue spherical bud of the Scylan twig tied to a hemp string. "Now's your chance. Do what I couldn't. Follow your own light."

Does he think it's glowing? Sen didn't know if she should accept the necklace dangling from his hand. Syclan buds only lit up when charged by a lightning strike, and not when broken off from the tree.

"Take it," he said shaking it in his hand.

"But it's not…" She couldn't finish the sentence, not when his tenuous smile hinged on her acceptance.

"Not glowing? Of course not. That's up to you."

"Huh?"

An outside explosion rumbled through the building, rattling the walls and straining the bioluminescent lights. Though the violent reminder of the war raging on in the Gardens spiked Sen's anxiety, it didn't seem to effect Haebi one bit.

"The Scylan trees are very special, Sen—more special than those stiff Lightning Guild elders understand. The trees react to all kinds of energy, not just lightning."

"Like what?"

Another explosion rocked the building, but when she yelped, he grabbed on to her arm again to keep her attention.

"When I was very quiet, when I listened to the deepest parts of myself, the bulbs would light up, even when I held a twig broken off from the tree."

Uncomfortable by the thought, Sen didn't know what to say. *It's not possible,* she kept telling herself, taking in his disheveled appearance and station in the asylum as proof of the fallibility of his words.

"But that was a long time ago…when I was young like you, before this place."

"Uncle Haebi, I don't—"

"Keep this close to you," he said, pushing the necklace into her face until she took it from him and put it around her own neck. "Don't lose sight of yourself. Don't end up like me."

A third explosion, this one much closer than before, shook dust and debris from the ceiling. Sen covered her head as plant material and metal fittings rained down from above.

"Please, uncle—you have to go with me," she said, freeing him from the rubble and taking his hand. "Akoto and Sulo will protect us!"

"Sulo?!" Haebi retched his hand away from hers. "Stay away from that mutt!"

"What?"

"Sulo nearly killed your mother—and you—when he found out she had Kajar's child."

Sen didn't understand. In the short time they'd been together, Sulo had never aggressed her, and even helped her find her uncle.

Maybe he is crazy, she thought. But her father hated bully bears, enough to banish them from the Guild. And she remembered Sulo's odd inflection when they met up in the Gardens: *"You don't recognize me, do you?"*

Her confusion deepened as she thought of the scars on her mother's neck, arms and chest. *Father always said mother was attacked by a coguar, not a bully bear...*

(Did Father lie to me?)

Another explosion slammed through the building, knocking Sen off her feet. Smoke and debris filled the air, making it nearly impossible to see or to breath.

"Uncle!" she cried between coughs, spreading out her arms to sense her surroundings and steady herself on the debris-covered floor. Light trickled in from the hole blown out of the side of the exterior wall. As some of the particulates settled, she could make out a long and skinny figure peering through the damaged section. Petrified, she tried to call out to Akoto, but the breath left her lungs.

"Sen?"

Joy fizzled through her fear at the sound of the young warrior's voice. "Sahib!" she said, tripping and scrambling her way to him. He greeted her with a big, goofy smile and an awkward hug.

"We gotta go. We found Sho, but he's blowing the place up."

"Huh?"

"We'll figure it out later. Where's Sulo and Akoto?"

"Wait," she said, as he pulled open the door leading back to the hallway. "My uncle—where'd he go?"

"Wake up," Sahib said, shouldering the bully bear. The giant Shifter groaned, then shook his head, still groggy from the tranquilizers. Sahib moved to Akoto, shaking him until he popped open his eyes and growled.

Sen kicked over broken tiles and wedged herself under fallen bookshelves, desperate to find Haebi.

"Anything?" Sahib asked, returning to her side as the beasts got to their feet.

Sen bit her lip and looked back to the gaping hole in the exterior wall. "Did you see anyone running from here?"

"There's a lot of people running around outside; it's chaos."

Sen ran into the hallway, searching the dead bodies for any remnants of her uncle. When she found the nurses, she gasped. Under the flickering light of the bioluminescent bulbs, she saw no disfigurements, no black veins streaking up their necks and down their arms. Terrified but curious, she crouched down and turned one of their shoulders, enough to get a look at one of their faces. *She looks…*

The rest of her thought finished out deep in her subconscious, where her own prejudices could not impede the observation. *…At peace.*

Sahib pulled her up by the arm. "Sho's going to blow this place up, whether we're in it or not."

"But my uncle—"

"He's not here, and we've gotta go!"

Bewildered, she allowed Sahib to guide her back through the hole in Haebi's room leading out to the side yard. As soon as they set foot outside, a brand new nightmare unfolded. The ground, scorched from death and fire, cracked open in places to swallow up entire trees. People ran in every which direction, in and out of the smoke and fallen buildings, away from the screeching creatures that sought them out.

"Stay close!" Sahib said, pulling her away from the East Wing. Sen did her best, her feet catching on dead vines and broken ground. Still fighting the lingering effects of the darts, Akoto and Sulo followed behind as they made their way toward the hedges.

Sen clutched to Akoto as Sahib armed his bow and shot at anything that neared. Ground quaking, she held up her hands over her eyes as a white-hot column of fire blazed up toward the sky from a building up ahead.

"Where's Nya? Where are the others?" Sen shouted against the fray.

If Sahib heard her, he didn't answer. Brow furrowed, the young warrior looked less confident with each passing second.

"Sahib!" she cried as a vine lashed around his shin. Before he could react, the vine retracted, dragging him off.

Roaring, Sulo charged after him, disappearing into the smoke.

"No…"

Still holding on to Akoto, she looked every which way, her mind unmooring in the havoc.

Run away,
but
Uncle Haebi—
Sahib
—Nya.

A vine shot past her face, trying to grasp onto Akoto, but the midnight beast bit down on it, and yanked. The Virid soldier flew past them, whipping into the side of the demolished fountain.

Run!

Sen mounted Akoto, and spurred him toward the only path not blazing with fire. Vines shot out at them from every direction, but she batted them away and kept low, pressing herself as close as she could to Akoto.

A break in the smoke allowed her a clear sight of the edge of the Maze wall, but as she redirected him toward the opening, a hoarse howl, followed by a blast wave that threw her from Akoto's back, derailed her escape. Tumbling through a gooey mass of plant debris, she landed hard against someone or something, collapsing them on top of her.

Thrashing about, she felt cold, waxy skin, and caught glimpses of blood-shot eyes, and a gaunt face. The putrid smell of death overpowered her nose, making her gag.

Nezra—

Sen screamed. As the Nezran grasped her neck with its blackened fingers, her entire body turned to ice. It hissed, bringing its hideous face closer to hers, exposing her with malice, digging into the marrow of her bones with disease-ridden intent. Raked open by invisible fingers, she felt her body crumbling, seconds away from death.

Akoto howled, jarring her senses. In some remote corner of her mind she was aware of him charging toward her, but in the brief time it would take him to reach her, she'd already be putrefied.

The knife at her belt. She felt it hot against her skin, a beacon shining out to her as the world fizzled away.

"Fight back!"

Nya's words, though she couldn't be certain if real or imagined, rose above the chaos. In the clutches of death she reacted, survival instinct guiding her hands to shoot down, grab the knife and thrust upwards, into the Nezran's gut.

Oh God, I'm so sorry—

Only a sucking sound escaped the Nezran's lips at it stumbled back from her. Regaining enough feeling in her limbs, Sen scrambled away just as Akoto swept up around her, roaring at the death-dealer.

—I didn't mean to hurt you—

"Sen—"

Sen snapped to the right. Surrounded by Virid soldiers and a bird-eater, Nya tried to fend off her attackers while protecting the unconscious man at her feet. At first the Virid uniform confused her, but by the fierceness and desperation of Nya's defense, and seeing no greenish tint to his skin, Sen guessed his identity. Sho.

Shrieking, the bird-eater dove its heads at Sho. The woman warrior spun to the left, managing to slash and hack off spiny protrusions. But as she dodged its sharp rows of teeth, a spray of thistle spikes snagged her leg. When she tried to compensate, she rolled onto her injured ankle with a sickening crunch, and fell forward. Combat vines snapped around her arms, pulling her taut. As she tried to free herself, other soldiers concentrated their attack on Sho. Vines snaked around his chest while infected Virids shot each other with forearm-mounted thistle cannons.

"Sen—help him!" Nya screamed as she kicked up and fought against her tethers.

Before she could climb atop Akoto, her friend took off, barreling after the injured Nezra slinking off into the smoke. "No, come back!"

The bird-eater, serum seeping down its stalk from open gashes, reared back around, this time angling toward Nya. Distracted by the vines slapping her face, Nya grabbed onto Sho's foot and tried to keep the Virids from stealing him way. "Sen!"

Nya—

No Akoto, no knife. No way to protect herself, let alone help anyone else.

I can't do anything—

(Run—*)*

One of the bird-eater heads bit into Nya's side. Fresh blood peppered the air, sending all the infected into a frenzy.

"Nya!" she screamed, running straight to the woman warrior. One of the bird-eater heads turned to her, spraying her with a face-full of nectar. Coughing and spitting, she dove on top of Nya, kicking the bird-eater latched onto her side until it let go.

"Sho…" Nya gasped, trying to hold on to Sho's boot as the Virids' combat vines heaved and jerked his flaccid body.

"Let go!" Sen pulled her off as the bird-eater sliced down with its bladed leaf, nearly chopping off Nya's head.

"Let me go!" Nya said, wrestling against Sen to get to Sho as the Virids continued to thrash each other to get at their prize.

Sen felt Nya's hot blood soaking into her own shirt as the woman warrior bucked and rolled over. Pushing her away, Nya crawled on her hands and knees toward Sho.

In the confusion, one of the Virids attacked the bird-eater, shooting one of its faces full of thistle spikes. As the mobile wailed and redirected its fury, Sen caught sight of bloodshot eyes emerging from the smoke. Not one pair, but two. Then three. Four.

Death-dealers—

Sen's heart leapt into her throat. Scrambling back over to Nya, she grabbed her by the shoulders and yelled. "Run, we have to r—"

Words stripped from her mouth, she felt a familiar chill seize her intestines, and grind down into her bones, this time with tenfold force.

Akoto, help us!

Aware of the burgeoning emptiness inside her, Sen crawled back on top of Nya as the woman warrior rolled over, desperate to protect her from the attack.

"Sen..." Nya said, her voice choked by the same invisible force. Blue eyes expressed pain that awoke the deepest parts of her as the surrounding flowers, plants, Virid soldiers—even the bird-eater—collapsed. "What's happening...?"

Something bright caught her eye. A soft glow buried under her shirt, small and round.

Haebi's necklace—

Shining.

Like—

No, not me. Not without Akoto. He's the one—

As death firmed its grasp, Sen clung to Nya, abandoning all thought, all hope, and cried out.

CHAPTER 18

As the death-dealers tore her apart, Nya held on to her pain, clinging to the only thing that ever kept her grounded. Ice hooks dragged down her spine, splaying her open, exposing her to frigid hands that reached in and pulled her inside out. The temptation to let go, to release into the encroaching black numbness, crossed her mind.

(So much easier…)

No. I must save Sho.

Her anger returned; she remembered the attack from behind, Kaden getting swept up by a tree-walker, Sho getting knocked out by one of the flying vines. With the effects of the flowers she'd eaten waning, the pain of her ankle returned with a vengeance, and she couldn't go after Kaden, let alone bear Sho's weight to haul him away from the infected Virids.

But she had stood her ground and fought off greater hordes before.

Not against Nezra.

The black numbness inched its way down her fingers and toes, into the distal parts of her limbs. The absence of feeling frightened her more than pain. Pain meant she was alive, could still put up a fight.

Sho…

Pinned on her back by the girl and stricken by the Nezra's dark touch, she could do nothing but watch as the death-dealers slunk toward them, blackened fingers outstretched, whispering in their moribund tongue. *"Ennari…"*

Do something, she tried to will herself, but the pain icing her veins kept her trapped.

Sen's face pressed against hers, the girl's hot tears wetting Nya's cheeks. *Sen…*

As annoying as she was, the girl didn't deserve such a grisly death.

Nya closed her eyes, terrified of the void washing away her pain and eating at the mortal coils tethering her to the world. Anger and hatred paled; strength, skill and ferocity dissipated. Stripped away, she faced the bleakness of her own heart, and all that she had sacrificed in fear.

My clan—

My family.

Myself.

"Lucente!"

Sen's cry erupted across her fraying nerves, sending a shockwave of light and energy coursing through her body. Inhaling sharply, Nya filled her lungs with more than just air, but vibrating coruscations that illuminated the farthest reaches of her soul. In that moment she could no longer distinguish Sen's face, or any other living being around her, as each person, every blade of grass, turned into shimmering points of light.

No, she thought, fighting against the vision. The light frightened her, made her feel more vulnerable than ever before. Never in her life had she seen herself, or those around her, with such unabashed clarity. Sen, no longer weak and wimpy, shone brighter than a star. Even her own light, a burning sun beaming from within, surprised her. *What's this?*

As she took in another breath, the corporeal barriers between herself and Sen vanished. Bodies pressed together, Nya felt each pulsation of girl's heart as if it beat in her own chest.

No! She tried to push away, break Sen's hold.

This is a trick, she convinced herself, unwilling to accept what she saw or felt. The implications threatened the world she had created for herself, the warrior that could endure the severest pain, stave off love and attachment. She couldn't survive in this place, not as she was.

As the light exploded across the battlefield, Nya saw the Nezra shield their faces with their cloaks. Mewling like injured sheepkins, they retreated, scattering across the yard. Foreign feelings of grief and pain pressed up against her mind, but dissolved like a dying echo before she could turn her full attention to them.

"Nya!" No longer enshrouded in light, Sen's face reappeared over her, hazel eyes wide with concern. "Hey, are you okay?"

No, she wanted to scream. Tears pricked her eyes, but her body, still not under her command, would not obey her orders.

Sen lifted the damaged armor plate over Nya's abdomen, inspecting the gaping wound left by the bird-eater. "I-It's okay, I'll get us out of here."

It's bad, Nya guessed by the shakiness of Sen's voice. Not that she needed the girl's cursory inspection to know that. Returning with reignited fury, pain sapped at her mind, denied her strength to do much more than move Sen's hands away from the wound.

"Akoto—over here!"

Despite the tears blurring her vision, Nya spied the gigantic beast galloping through the smoke, the head of the original Nezran attacker in his jaws.

"Help me," Sen said to her beast, pulling at his neck to get him to stoop lower for Nya.

She hated the girl lifting her up at the waist, and the involuntary cry that escaped her lips when she folded over the bite wound.

"I'm fine," she muttered, stars wheeling through her brain as Akoto and Sen struggled to get her lifted and positioned onto his back.

"Wait—" she blurted out as Sen climbed up behind her and steered

Akoto back to the Maze. Lancing pains shot through her stomach with each rise and fall of the beast's shoulder blades. "Sho…"

"I'm sorry—we can't stay."

Nya looked out across the Sanctum yard. With the Nezra gone, the Virid soldiers regained consciousness, and the tree-walkers and the bird-eaters stirred. Vines wiggled on the ground, and the bird-eater heads opened and closed their razor-sharp petals. She would have braved the reviving infected, or the thickening smoke from the building fires blotted out the entire sky, but not the streaks of lightning blazing across the sky.

The Guild is coming.

And with the way Kajar commanded, everything and everyone in his path would be killed to abolish a threat, even if his own daughter happened to be on the battlefield.

What just—?

Sho—I failed—

Sulo—Kaden—Sahib—

The light—what was that light?

—I should never have let you go—

Overcome, Nya allowed herself to slip into the comfort of darkness as lightning streaked across the congested sky.

CHAPTER 19

As Sen reached the sloping buttes and layered outcrops of the Koori lowlands, the first sliver of the white sun awakened the sky, casting solemn yellow rays into the sleepy darkness. Sen pulled on the hair of Akoto's back, making him pause at an overlook just before the Spires.

"Nya?" She touched the woman warrior's back, waiting to feel her chest rise. About two miles back she'd stopped moaning, but they couldn't stop now, not after what happened in the Gardens.

Nezra, death creeping inside—
(No other choice)
—call the light—
(but Akoto isn't near)
Brilliant and filling, casting away all shadow—
(Did I do that?)

A chilly breeze from the north brushed against her face, blowing the loose strands of her hair into her face.

Get Nya back, she told herself, spurring Akoto as soon as she felt Nya's ragged breathing against her fingers.

Bracing Nya with one hand, Sen held on to Akoto, wanting him to go faster than his limping gallop would allow. Still, she couldn't help but lose herself in his remarkable speed, in the feeling of almost-flight with each step. Never in her life had she felt such freedom, even as the wind whipped her face, and tears froze to her cheeks. Any notion of hunger faded, and the aches of her exhausted body surrendered to the joy she never thought possible.

Whistles and yips. Sen recognized the warrior calls and pulled back on Akoto's hair, making him slow to a trot as they wove through the Spires.

"It's me, Sen!" she said, looking every which way for signs of the Chakoa. Save for the soft padding of Akoto's feet in the sand, and his customary low growl, the entire desert fell silent. "Nya's hurt—please help us. Where are you?"

Osan emerged from behind a boulder, his arms raised. "Where are the others?"

"I'm sorry," she whispered, shaking her head and pulling Akoto to a stop.

Other Chakoans appeared from behind their hiding spots, weapons still drawn until Osan waved them down. Natsugra, waddling up from the side, lifted Nya's floppy head and frowned.

"Get her to my tent," the medicine woman said, pointing to a cluster of Spires up ahead.

Sen did as instructed, helping the other Chakoans carry her and place her in the tent, but when she tried to stay inside and help, Osan pulled her away and sat her on the dried-out bough of a bristlepine.

The clan chief assumed his most austere tone. "Tell me everything that happened."

Sen looked at the star-shaped scars on her hands, not knowing what to do or say. She didn't plan on lying to him, but how could she tell him the truth? Phantom electrocution pains traveled through her arms and down her legs as she remembered her father's equally horrible punishments for choosing either.

"Start from the beginning," he said, slapping his walking stick against her boot.

Akoto, curled up underneath the shade of another bristlecone tree close by, looked up and growled.

He's not your father, she reminded herself, glancing up at Osan and then back at Akoto.

"It's okay, buddy," she murmured. Then, with a sigh, started from the beginning.

Over the next hour Osan listened with his brow pinched together as Sen recounted the disastrous rescue attempt in Virid territory. He didn't stop her when she told him about the infected Guild and Virid soldiers, the beserker tree walkers and bird-eaters, the horrifying sights within Sanctum, or losing the other Chakoans and the Shifter in the fray. But when she came to the part of Nya's rescue, his whole demeanor changed, and he leaned forward with renewed interest.

"The Nezra…were everywhere," she said, voicing faltering. Bloodshot eyes and gaunt faces flashed through her mind, her limbs tingling as her nerves recreated their deathly touch. But when she tried to recall the next part, something inside her hitched.

The Scylan necklace, glowing underneath her shirt.

Abandoning all hope—

—resorting to all that was left—

Her voice carrying out across the battlefield, lighting up all that surrounded her. "Lucente!"

Fright stole her words, and she glazed over all that she couldn't believe. "…b—but I got Nya out before the Guild struck. Then we came back here."

Osan looked at her with the scrupulous eye of a battle-worn elder, a man who would not be fooled by the prevarications of a child.

"You just pulled Nya out of an attack like that? Surrounded by Nezra and infected soldiers?"

"Akoto helped," she said, stretching for the truth.

Shame and embarrassment swamped her heart, and she teetered on the verge of tears. How could she lie to Osan, especially after he took her, a shadowless nothing, into his clan?

Because what happened can't be real, she told herself. She saw the light again, a brilliant halo that originated from her core and expanded outward, illuminating herself and Nya—the entire battlefield—before vanishing.

Akoto was nearby, that's why—

"Embrace all that you are..." The memory of her uncle's voice rattled her self-denial, gave pause to the usual criticisms that kept her locked away. *"...believe in what you can become..."*

"Sen," Osan said, taking the seat next to her with a grimace. Turning to her, he gazed at her with the rising sun at his back, highlighting the gold flecks in his brown eyes. "You saved Nya."

"But she's—"

Osan placed his hand on her shoulder. "Can you not take praise, child?"

Looking back at her scarred hands, she shook her head. "Sorry. I'm not used to it."

A sharp whistle broke their conversation. One of the Chakoans hooted at the top of his voice: "Warriors approaching!"

Osan moved faster than she could react, knocking her sideways as he ran to the other clan members gathering near one of the Spires. Trotting over, she alternated standing on her tip-toes and crouching down to spy between clan members as the dark figures in the distance closed in on their position.

"Is that—?" someone started.

Other clan members chimed in:

"—Looks like a bear."

"—Someone's running beside it."

Squinting, Sen could make out the familiar outlines of the lost warriors. Sulo, in bully bear form, ran at a full sprint toward them, Kaden and another man riding on his back. Alongside the bear, the wiry Sahib kept up, his legs pumping at a furious pace.

They're alive! she thought, feeling happier than she expected.

"It's Kaden and Sahib—Sho!" someone shouted as the party neared.

The entire clan erupted in cheers, some running out to greet the arriving party, others crutching or tottering along as best they could.

"Thank you; so good to see you all again."

As soon as Sen caught sight of the speaker still sitting atop Sulo as Kaden dismounted, she recognized him from the battlefield. Sho. The dark-haired man in the stolen Virid uniform. Without realizing it, she wrinkled her nose and took a step back as the other clan members crowded around. Even Sahib and Kaden, after receiving blankets, fresh water, and greetings from the clan, returned their attention to the man atop the bear.

"Sho," Osan said, greeting the warrior with a firm grip to the forearm.

Sho returned the gesture, adding a slight bow. "Forgive me, chief, for my delayed return."

Protecting his ribs, Sho accepted help sliding off Sulo, and used a younger Chakoan's shoulder to keep upright. He appeared worse off than Kaden and Sahib, covered in soot, his visible wounds caked with blood. Still, a charismatic smile adorned his face, and his confidence overshadowed the breath of his injuries. "Many thanks to my brethren for the rescue. I wouldn't have made it without you," he said, nodding to Kaden and Sahib.

The bully bear shuddered and grumbled as he transformed back to his human form. Wiping the clear film from his eyes and stretching out his back, Sulo glared at Sho. "You're welcome."

"Sulo, you've always helped the Chakoa," Sho said, placing his fist over his heart and bowing to the Shifter. "We're in your debt."

"Nya, wait—you're in no condition—" Natsugra's admonitions got her nowhere as Nya, half-naked and cradling her injured side, burst out of the medicine tent, the unsecured bandages and poultices falling off her as she hobbled toward the arrivals.

"Sho!" she cried, breaking through the crowd. Stumbling into his arms, she embraced him hard enough that they both winced, but neither let go.

"You wicked fool," Nya said, grabbing his hair and pulling his head forward.

Sho smiled and pulled her in harder until their two foreheads touched. A hush fell over the Chakoa as the two struggled against each other, their faces turning red.

Confused, Sen looked to the other clan members. *Are they happy to see each other—or fighting?*

Then again, with all she knew about Nya, perhaps wrestling made more sense than greeting someone she cared about with a hug and kiss.

"Nya!" Natsugra scuttled in behind them, and slapped Sho on the arm until he loosened his hold on the woman warrior. "Get back to the medicine tent, now."

"Please Natsugra," Sho said, still holding on to Nya with one arm as he faced the medicine woman. "Can Nya not stand and receive her praise? If not for her leadership, I would not be here before you, ready to serve my people."

Cracking his walking stick on a rock, Osan answered in a booming voice. "Defiance will not be praised."

Sho's eyes darted between Osan and Natsugra, then to Nya. "I ask for her pardon in exchange for the news I bring you from the Realm."

The other clan members traded nervous whispers as they waited for their chief's decision. Sen didn't know what to make of any of it, especially the quiet fire in Sho's yellow-grey eyes or the way he wouldn't lower his gaze.

"My orders were clear," Osan said, motioning for Nya to go with Natsugra to the medicine tent. "Now is not the time to divide our clan."

"I agree. That is why in light of the new war, I want to repledge myself to the Chakoa, to our great clan, and that I will do everything my power to take down the denom elders of the Realm."

The other clan members erupted with questions and exclamations:

"New war?"

"Slay the denoms!"

"What's happening?"

"Why are the Nezra attacking?"

Sho held up his hands to quiet to the clan, but Osan interceded. "Sho! This is not the time."

"We don't have time," Sho said, pointing back to the northwest. Stacks of dark clouds and swirling smoke filled the skies above the burning Gardens. Explosions, off in the distance, denoted the continuing battle. "The Nezra are attacking the Virids, spreading their death and disease. Listen!"

Another peal of thunder echoed across the desert.

"The Guild is in the fight. With the denoms divided, we have our best opportunity to take out the world leaders and end their barbaric reign."

"No!" Sen shouted. When the entire clan turned to her, she almost lost her voice. "Y-you can't do that."

"Who's that?" Sho said to Nya.

Nya looked at Sen, blue eyes narrowing. "Sen. New kid."

The other clan members parted, leaving her standing alone. Wringing her hands together, she couldn't look Sho in the eye as he stared her down.

"Do you know what the favored do to us Outliers in Sanctum?" he said, his voice sharpening. Sucking in her breath, she turned away as he revealed zig-zagging scars descending his chest. "They *pity* us shadowless; they justify their torments by saying they want to bring us into God's light."

Before Sen could think of a response, he continued, anger quickening his words. "It wasn't just the greenthumbs, either; Swarm and Guild physicians came to Sanctum to perform their own experiments on us, to see if maybe they could convert us to one of their own. As if there was something wrong with us because we don't have their powers."

Clan members spit on the ground, some shouting expletives as Sho continued. "Is it not bad enough that they cast us out of the Realm—but to experiment on us, to turn men and women into abominations—"

The memory of the East Wing residents, infiltrated by plant roots, blazed through her mind. *All those people...was that some sort of experiment?*

"—we cannot sit back and let them make us into monsters!"

As the clan members hooted and shouted, Sen thought about the veracity of what Sho had said, especially if the Swarm, Virids, and Guild had come together to form Sanctum.

That's why I saw metal in the East Wing, she thought. A chill ran down her spine as her mind took it one step further. *Does my father know what they do there?*

Fear carved into her belly. Her father was austere and impossible to please, but he wasn't evil. She bit down on her lip ...*Is he?*

No, she thought, fighting against her gut. Besides, how could murdering someone be the answer? "Y-you can't kill the elders."

"Watch me," Sho said, unsheathing his knife and holding it up to the sky.

As the others cheered, Sen despaired.

"Save me."

The words rang out across her mind, gaining momentum as her memories pulled her back. She remembered connecting with the infected Soushin woman, hearing her weakened voice amidst the turmoil. Fast-forwarding, she recalled the nurses in the East Wing, feeling their terror as the Nezra gouged their minds and sickened their bodies, all the while whispering a single word: *"ennari."* And the halo of light, brilliant and powerful, bursting out from her chest and illuminating the world around her as the Nezra descended upon her and Nya.

The Nezra...

In that moment on the battlefield, she had known nothing but her own fear, but as her mind layered the events against each other, she realized something beyond herself. She saw the death-dealers again, pale and cadaverous, their reddened eyes sunken into their skulls. As the light touched their faces, she felt herself dip beneath their skin, into the poisonous blood running through their veins.

They're sick, too.

The revelation made her forget herself for a moment, and she shouted out above the cheers. "We have to warn them!"

"Warn who?" Sho scoffed.

"Everyone. I—I think the Nezra are infected, too."

Sho laughed. "The favored persecute you, little girl—do you not understand that? They would shoot you down before you even reached the wall, if not worse."

Cheeks turning red, she looked to Nya for help, but the woman warrior stayed fast at Sho's side. "But we can't just let people die—"

"Without a shadow, I seek only the comfort of darkness, and the freedom of its emptiness," Sho said, reciting the Chakoa credo. "You are weakened by your attachments, girl."

Feeling all of the eyes of the Chakoa on her, Sen wanted to run away and hide, or call for Akoto, but her legs had rooted themselves into the ground. She stood there, mouth clamped shut, unable to do anything but shake.

Seeing that she had no retort, Sho continued: "It doesn't matter if the Nezra are sick, or if they want to seize world power. Now is the time for vengeance—and for the rise of the shadowless!"

Clan members bumped into her as they rushed Sho, applauding and praising his valiance. Even Nya, injured and fatigued, managed to lift a fist to the air and shout.

As she backed away, Sen noticed Osan and Natsugra on the periphery. The two clan elders watched the commotion with placid expressions, seeming to confer with each other with a few exchanged glances, but otherwise showing no reaction.

Why aren't they stopping this? she wondered, but the answer came in the twist of her gut as the clan joined together in a war-time chant. *Sho...*

Handsome and powerful, he commanded the passion of the clan, even in his debilitated state, bringing out the fire and fight in a decimated people.

Distraught, Sen ran back to her dozing companion, and climbed up on his back. "Akoto, go," she said, urging him to take off as fast as he could. Anywhere but here.

But after only a few steps, Akoto grumbled and groaned, stretched out his back, and then leaned back and forth as if to shake her off.

"Akoto!" she yelled as she slid off and landed on her side, sand shooting in her mouth and eyes.

A cold nose sniffed at her neck, followed by a slobbery tongue that licked her cheek as she coughed and sneezed. Finally, after she cleared most of the red sand from her face, she saw him retreating back to the bristlecone tree and curling up again in its shade.

Fine, she thought, brushing off and running off toward a spire. Heights usually terrified her, but right then she needed to get away, even if it meant climbing up to the stars.

Sen grasped the first red-rock handhold and looked up. From her vantage point, the top of the spire scraped the cloudless sky.

Coward, she told herself, cursing her shaking limbs.

Gritting her teeth, she put one hand in front of the other, pulling herself up with her heart lodged in her throat. The eastern winds picked up, blowing her hair in her face and finding every hole in her shirt and pants, bringing goosebumps to her skin. But with every finger scraped inside the porous rock or knee racked against the unforgiving vertical surface, she spurred herself forward, too afraid of what would happen if she stopped.

Once on top she collapsed, not caring she lay only inches away from a treacherous fall. Hungry, exhausted, and overwhelmed with questions and feelings she couldn't begin to translate, she lay on her side and stared out to the west. The glowing blue wall, once a beacon of her exclusion, appeared less vibrant than usual, as if the Guild soldiers hadn't replenished its electrical defenses. Farther north, she saw the same dark clouds and smoke above the Gardens, but she turned her gaze back toward Hirak mountain, to the Guild fortress.

Ennari...

A Nezran word, the call of death, of consumption.

The Nezra's sickness will spread. The thought of more fighting, spreading death and disease, made her heart ache. Even if the denoms regarded her as shadowless, that didn't mean that they deserved to suffer, or for entire cultures and nations to be eradicated. *What can I do? If the Nezra are sick, they won't stop.*

"Haebi... Mother..." she whispered. Succumbing to exhaustion, she brought her knees to her chest and rest her head on her arm. As she drifted off, Akoto's howl rose up from the desert sands, a doleful cry that called out to the deepest parts of her. With tears in her eyes, she added: "...father."

▲▽▲

Sen woke to a darkened sky and a blanket wrapped around her body. Rubbing the crusts from her eyes, she couldn't discern the figure sitting next to her until her vision adjusted to the evening light.

"Nya?"

The woman warrior sat next to the edge of the spire, gazing out to the east. Below them, great bonfires lit up the clan grounds, and Chakoa, young and old, celebrated the return of their lost member.

"Here, eat this," Nya said, keeping her eyes trained to the activity below as she pushed a wooden bowl toward Sen.

Propping up on her elbow, she took one sniff of the steaming bowl of stew before guzzling it down.

"How did you get this up here?" Sen asked, wiping her mouth with the back of her sleeve. Given Nya's bandaged arms, ribs, hands, and splinted ankle, she wasn't even sure how Nya managed to haul herself up, let alone a bowl of soup and a blanket.

Sen expected a biting remark, or at least some form of sarcasm. Instead, Nya kept an even tone and picked at her shirt stained with globs of stew. "I like to improvise."

Unsure if she could laugh, Sen hid her smile and set the bowl down. "Thanks."

"Sure."

Silence fell between them as they watched the dancing below. Finally, Sen conjured up the voice to ask: "Why aren't you celebrating too?"

"Osan sent me to find you."

Sen raised an eyebrow. Without looking at her, Nya picked up Sen's skepticism.

"I know you're upset," she said, her voice softer this time.

Not knowing what to say, Sen held her breath, waiting for Nya to add something harsh.

"Our ways are difficult to understand, at least at first. But you'll learn the difference between attachment and loyalty. One will get you killed. The other gives you family, a purpose. And to for us shadowless, it's the only way we can survive."

Is this real? For the first time since they had met, Nya spoke to her without anger lacing her words, or her hands in fists.

"What you did back there…in the Sanctum yard…" Nya's voice faltered, and her brow pinched together. Even in the low light, the woman warrior's gaze held the same intensity, vivid blue eyes connecting with Sen's. "I can't remember much, but I do remember seeing that light. Your light."

Sen turned away, unable to hear her words. "I don't know what happened."

Grunting, Nya readjusted herself on the edge and looked back down below. "I don't believe in *nasci*. I don't believe in legends, and least of all hope."

Sen didn't know how to take her statement, especially by the waver in her voice.

"But you're not the girl I thought I met in the Dethros. You and that beast—Akoto—you two are worth your skins."

If anyone else had said it, she probably wouldn't have taken it as a compliment, but coming from Nya, she beamed.

"No-no-no," Nya said, blocking her attempts at a hug.

"Sorry" Sen said, pulling the blanket back up over her shoulders.

"Time to get back. You should come, too. Sho's receiving a new row of tattoos." Nya pointed down to where Sho sat bare-chested and cross-legged in front of the largest bonfire. Osan held up a ceremonial box and chanted a blessing over Sho's head as the other clan members got down on their knees.

"Why?"

"We use tattoos to honor our clan members, tell their stories. Sho survived a nightmare. We can't forget what he, or any of the others, sacrificed."

"What about you, Sahib, and Kaden? Will you get new ones, too?"

Nya shook her head, her expression hardening. From her silence, Sen guessed that Osan still held her in contempt.

Before she could stop herself, Sen blurted out: "Will he punish you?"

Gaze narrowing, Nya looked out across the desert, past the star-speckled horizon. "You make your choices, Sen. I can live with pain, but not with myself if I didn't do everything in my power to rescue my family."

Nya's words sunk deep, sending an involuntary shiver through her body and awakening the memory her own physical punishments. Exit wounds on her hands and feet tingled, and she heard her father's disappointed words. *"Senzo, why are you always running?"*

"Not again," she whispered.

"Huh?"

"Nothing," Sen said, peeling off the blanket.

"Come down," Nya said, turning around and beginning her descent. She paused, her head still poking up above the lip. "It's time to get you properly initiated."

Sen smiled, but didn't follow her down right away. Crawling over to the other side of the Spire, she looked for Akoto under the bristlecone tree. When she didn't see him, she sat back on her heels and closed her eyes.

Where are you?

As she thought of her friend, other feelings drummed up from her subconscious, procuring their voice from Nya's words: *"I can live with pain, but not with myself if I didn't do everything in my power to rescue my family."*

Everything in my power...

A single word whispered up from her heart, conjuring memories of Akoto's howl, and the transcendent light she saw on the battlefield.

Nasci...

All her life, she had wished herself different, a warrior like Nya, wise like Natsugra, or at least brave like Sho; someone who could speak their mind and not freeze up or run away. Someone strong, and powerful; someone who could make a difference.

A light formed in front of her closed eyelids. When she opened her eyes, she saw the lucent orb beneath her shirt, shining like a star.

"When I was very quiet, when I listened to the deepest parts of myself, the bulbs would light up..."

Thumbing the Scylan necklace, more of her uncle's counsel came to mind: *"Embrace all that you are, believe in what you can become."*

Maybe it didn't matter if she was or wasn't nasci, if the radiant powers she experienced came from Akoto, or came from an unknown source. I still have something to offer, she thought, looking at the glowing bulb in her hands.

Two eyes, different colors, flashed before her as a shadowy giant landed next to her on top of the spire with little more than a whisper.

"Akoto!" she exclaimed, kissing his nose. The black-furred beast growled, but allowed her to squeeze his neck.

Climbing on top of him, she gave one last look to the Chakoa below as they danced in the firelight and sang their war songs. Even Nya, distinct at a distance with her shaved head and braids, joined the celebration, imbibing with Kaden, Sahib, and a newly marked Sho. Once enough of them healed—maybe sooner—the clan would go to war, tearing down what they could inside the Realm while the Nezra lay waste to the denoms.

"I don't know what I am," she whispered into the night, turning her gaze back to the glowing blue wall of the Realm as she clung to Akoto. Nudging him with her heels, he took a few steps and jumped off the spire, opening his wings to catch the winds.

"Akoto!" she cried, terrified and enlivened as he glided through the air.

As he weaved in and out of the spires, she dared herself to let go. Holding on with just her legs, she spread her arms wide, allowing the cold rush of air to wash over her face and body, and fill her lungs. The great expanse of the unknown filled her, endless possibilities and whispers of a future she could not comprehend in her wildest dreams.

I may be shadowless, I may be nothing, she thought as she set her sights on the fires still raging in the Gardens. Firming her grips back on Akoto's black fur, she made a promise to herself, and to whatever God might be listening: *But I will do everything in my power to save those I love. I am not running away anymore.*

THE ADVENTURE CONTINUES IN SHADOWLESS – VOLUME TWO: BATTLE AT HIRAK MOUNTAIN

W14 Productions presents *Killymuck* in association with the Bunker Theatre, London 26 March – 13 April 2019 with the following cast and creatives:

All characters	Aoife Lennon

Writer	Kat Woods
Director	Caitriona Shoobridge
Designer	Minglu Wang
Lighting Designer	Joe Price
Associate Lighting Designer	Gareth Weaver
Sound Designer	Benjamin Grant
Movement Director	Louise Kempton
Vocal Coach	Josh Hunter
Production Manager	Zara Janmohamed
Producer	Annabel Williamson, W14 Productions
Stage Manager	Micaëla Corcoran

Killymuck has been generously supported by Arts Council England and The Carne Trust.

Thank you also to Aidan Carroll, Exchange Theatre, nabokov, Marlowe Theatre, Paines Plough, Platform and Sarah Simmons without whose support this production would not have been possible.

CAST

AOIFE LENNON

Recent theatre credits include *Mule* (Edinburgh Fringe Festival, Northern Ireland tour, Omnibus); *XX* (Theatre503); *Autumn Fire* (Finborough) and *Romy and Julian* (tour).

Film and television credits include: *Oh Be Joyful, Palestine Lost, Online & Inlove* and *Room Service.*

Aoife was shortlisted for the Filipa Braganca Acting Award, Edinburgh Fringe in 2018.

CREATIVES

KAT WOODS | WRITER

Kat Woods is a writer and director from Co. Fermanagh in Northern Ireland. She has a particular interest in staging works that provide a platform for those from the underclass/ benefit class background. Works that are representative of her community. Works that redefine the discourse surrounding the poverty stereotype.

Kat is an Associate Artist at The Pleasance and an Associate at Omnibus Theatre. Kat is a Royal Court/Kudos TV writers group alumnus.

Kat's work has been performed in England, Ireland, Scotland, Wales, Finland, Baltimore, Washington DC, Connecticut and New York. Theatre writing and directing – select credits include *Killymuck* (Edinburgh Festival Fringe, the Pleasance, Omnibus and Foyle Arts Building); *Wasted* (Northern Ireland and International tour, One Act Festival Savoy Wales, King's Head, Soho Playhouse, Edinburgh Festival Fringe); *Mule* (Northern Ireland tour, Omnibus, Edinburgh Festival Fringe); *Belfast Boy* (Catalyst Festival, Lantern, Omnibus, Edinburgh Festival Fringe, the Tampere Festival Finland); *Lost* (the White Bear, Blakes of the Hollow Enniskillen, Foyle Arts Building, Up Three and Ten, Etcetera Theatre); *Dirty Flirty Thirty* (Blakes of the Hollow Enniskillen, the Playhouse, the Pleasance, the White Bear) and *Skintown* (the White Bear).

Awards: *Belfast Boy* – The Stage Award for Excellence, The Fringe Review Award for Outstanding Theatre.

Killymuck, *Wasted* and *Mule* – The Peggy Ramsey Award.
Belfast Boy and *Killymuck* – longlisted for the Amnesty International Freedom of Expression Award.
Wasted – selected for the Encore series Soho Playhouse New York (Best of Edinburgh).
Skintown – longlisted for the Bruntwood Royal Exchange Award.

CAITRIONA SHOOBRIDGE | DIRECTOR

Caitriona is a recipient of the Genesis Future Directors Award and will direct *Ivan and the Dogs* at the Young Vic in 2019. She was a Jerwood Assistant Director at the Young Vic and directed the parallel production to the main house production, *Yerma*. She has worked as an Associate/Assistant Director at Headlong, the Almeida and the Young Vic and trained on the NT Studio Director's Course.

MINGLU WANG | DESIGNER

Minglu Wang is a scenographer who explores the body, space and performance in a bold, ritual way. With a background of BA Theatre, Film and TV Art Designing, she graduated from MA Scenography at Royal Central School of Speech and Drama with distinction in 2015. She has been working with collaborators for many productions internationally, and also has been actively engaged with her works at renowned festivals, Prague Quadrennial of Performance Design and Space 2011, London Art Biennale 2015 etc. She was a finalist of the Linbury Prize and winner of Taking the Stage in conjunction with British Council Ukraine in 2015, and a selected designer at World Stage Design 2017.

JOE PRICE | LIGHTING DESIGNER

Joe trained at the Royal Welsh College of Music & Drama and received the 2015 Francis Reid Award for Lighting Design.
Credits include: *My Name Is Rachel Corrie* (Young Vic); *The World's Wife* (Welsh National Opera); *Redefining Juliet* (Barbican); *Heads Will Roll* (Told by an Idiot); *Kite* (The Wrong Crowd); *Conditionally* (Soho); *Mrs Dalloway* (Arcola); *Heather* (Bush); *Breathe* (Bunker); *Goldfish Bowl* (Paper Birds); *This Perfect World* (Theatre Royal Bath); *Fossils* (Brits off Broadway NYC); *This Must Be the Place* (VAULT Festival); *Let the Right*

One In (Arts Ed); *Magnificence* (Finborough); *How to Date a Feminist* (Arcola); *Some Girl(s)* (Park); *Around the World in 80 Days* (Theatre Royal Winchester); *Some People Talk About Violence* (Barrel Organ); *Dry Land* (Damsel Productions); *Alternative Routes* (National Dance Company Wales); *The Duchess of Malfi* (Richard Burton Theatre Company); *Animal/ Endless Ocean* (Gate) and *Y Twr* (Invertigo).

BENJAMIN GRANT | SOUND DESIGNER

Benjamin Grant studied at Royal Central School of Speech and Drama and has experience designing for Theatre, Dance and Installation, often working on devised work and new writing.

Recent sound design credits include: *The War of the Worlds* (Rhum & Clay); *The Road Awaits Us* (Sadler's Wells); *Education Education Education* (The Wardrobe Ensemble).

Other credits include: Associate Sound Designer for *Beware of Pity* (Schaubühne) and Associate Sound Designer for *The Kid Stays in the Picture* (Royal Court).

LOUISE KEMPTON | MOVEMENT DESIGNER

Louise is an actor, movement director and choreographer. She trained for her BA (Hons) in Acting at Rose Buford College and later progressed to the Guildhall School of Music & Drama where she completed a masters in Movement for Actor Training.

As a movement director and choreographer her practice covers a broad spectrum of disciplines including pure movement, devising and theatre making, period dance and historical movement etiquette. She is also a skilled puppeteer, having trained in Bunraku style puppetry for performance whilst a member of the *War Horse* company for the National Theatre.

Movement direction and choreography include: Tobacco Factory, the National Theatre Connections, Old Red Lion, Southwark Playhouse, Merely Theatre and Oval House.

Acting credits include: the National Theatre, Storyhouse, Trafalgar Studios, Litchfield Garrick, Tobacco Factory, New Victoria, Mercury Theatre, The Unicorn, York Theatre Royal and the Dutch National Opera. Louise is also a regular visiting practitioner at accredited drama institutions including Guildhall School of Music & Drama, Northampton University and St Mary's University.

ZARA JANMOHAMED | PRODUCTION MANAGER

Zara trained at the Royal Academy of Dramatic Art in Stage and Production Management.

Recent work includes: Production Management *Mrs Dalloway* (Arcola); RADA Festival, *Dramatic Dining Cabaret* (RADA), *Grotty* (Bunker) and *Rotterdam* (RADA).

Stage Management: *Dick Whittington and his Cat* (Oxford Playhouse); *80th Anniversary Gala* (Oxford Playhouse); *A Passage to India* (Tour and Park); *Raising Martha* (Park); *Scapegoat* (St Steven's Church) and *Kill Me Now* (Park).

Other: *Fabric* (Soho and Community Tour), Edinburgh Fringe (Mick Perrin Worldwide).

MICAËLA CORCORAN | STAGE MANAGER

Micaëla has worked as a freelance Stage Manager both in the UK and abroad. Previous credits as Stage Manager include: *Crazy for You* and *American Idiot* (Mountview); *Fiddler on the Roof* (Frinton Summer Theatre); *Hare & Tortoise* (Pied Piper Theatre Productions); *Bloomsbury Songs* (Bloomsbury Festival); *Girls* (HighTide Festival and Talawa Theatre); *Finding Mr Paramour* (Theatre of Europe and Kinoteater (Estonia)); *Our Street Our Stage* (Assemble Fest); *139 Copeland Road* (Abby Normal Theatre Company); *L'Incoronazione di Poppera*, *Albert Herring* and *La Périchole* (Opéra de Baugé (France)); *Spamalot* and *Oliver!* (Bournemouth Musical Theatre Productions).

She has also worked as Production and Tour Manager on *Caterpillar* (Small Truth Theatre Company); Production Stage Manager on *Happy Warriors* (WT Stage); Company Manager on *Dickens' Dictionary* (RCSSD); Stage and Tour Manager on *Playing Mathilde* (Quorum-ETC, France) and as Assistant Stage Manager on *Il Barbiere di Siviglia* for (Grange Festival).

ANNABEL WILLIAMSON | PRODUCER

Annabel Williamson is the founder of W14 Productions, focusing on new plays with a strong social conscience. Most recently: *The Political History of Smack and Crack* (Edinburgh Fringe Festival, Soho, Mustard Tree); *31 Hours* (Bunker); *Jam* (Finborough); *The Brink* (a co-production with the Orange Tree); *The Late Henry Moss* and *Upper Cut* (Southwark Playhouse).

With four concrete pillars marking out a large thrust performance space, an eclectic mix of audience seating on three sides of the stage, and a craft beer bar, The Bunker is a visceral and unique performance space with a character of its own.

The Bunker believes in artists. We give ambitious artists a home in which to share their work with adventurous audiences. We are champions of each piece that we programme and we want to ensure our stage is filled with exciting, exhilarating, and contemporary theatre featuring artists that represent the world that we live in.

The Bunker was opened in October 2016 by founding directors Joshua McTaggart and Joel Fisher. The theatre's first year of work included the award-winning sell-out show *Skin a Cat*, Cardboard Citizen's 25th anniversary epic *Home Truths*, and the world premiere of *31 Hours*. In-house productions have included *Abigail*, *Eyes Closed, Ears Covered* and *Devil with the Blue Dress*.

In September 2018, Artistic Director Chris Sonnex joined Executive Director David Ralf to lead the theatre's small but dedicated team, several of whom were involved in the original conversion of the space. Bunker Theatre Productions CIC is a not-for-profit theatre, which currently receives no public subsidy.

Find Out More

Website: www.bunkertheatre.com
Box Office: 0207 234 0486
Email: info@bunkertheatre.com
Address: 53a Southwark Street, London SE1 1RU

THE BUNKER TEAM

Artistic Director: Chris Sonnex
Executive Director: David Ralf
Head of Production: Hannah Roza Fisher
General Manager: Lee Whitelock
Front of House Manager: Ed Theakston
Marketing Manager: Holly Adomah Thompson
Duty Manager: Samantha Smith

New Work Co-ordinator: Matt Maltby
Associate Directors: Debbie Hannan & Sara Joyce
Resident Companies: Damsel Productions & Pint-Sized
Founding Directors: Joel Fisher & Joshua McTaggart

Bar Staff: Kevin Bouasy, Grainne Pearson Cockrill, Eleanor
Greene, Tiffany Murphy

Interns: Geo Barcan, Samuel Hackney-Ring, Florence Taylor

Volunteer Front of House Team:
Jida Akil, Julien Annet-Short, Danai Archonti, Verity Bate,
Harry Brierley, Emily Dixon, Beatrice Hadjipateras Dodgeon,
Serene Goodridge, Ashley Hodgson, Eleanor Huggins, Weronika
Kubak, Jaimie Leung, Øystein Lode, Dylan Manning, Skylar
Mabry, Ella Mark, Savithaa Markandu, Alexia McDonald,
Cesar Melo, Sophia Meuer, Sam Palmer, Daria Phillips, Samuel
Phillips, Naima Sjoeholm, Eliana Skoul, Márcia Lopes Tavares

As a registered Community Interest Company that does not
receive subsidy, Bunker Theatre Productions CIC relies on generous support from individuals, foundations, and companies to
help us make relevant and ambitious theatre. If you would like
to support the work that The Bunker creates, you can find out
how at www.bunkertheatre.com/support-us

KILLYMUCK

by Kat Woods

ıl SAMUEL FRENCH ıı

samuelfrench.co.uk

ISBN 978-0-573-11638-4

www.samuelfrench.co.uk

www.samuelfrench.com

FOR AMATEUR PRODUCTION ENQUIRIES

UNITED KINGDOM AND WORLD
EXCLUDING NORTH AMERICA
plays@samuelfrench.co.uk
020 7255 4302/01

Each title is subject to availability from Samuel French, depending upon country of performance.

Acting Editions

BORN TO PERFORM

Playscripts designed from the ground up to work the way you do in rehearsal, performance and study

---

Larger, clearer text for easier reading

Wider margins for notes

Performance features such as character and props lists, sound and lighting cues, and more

---

+ CHOOSE A SIZE AND STYLE TO SUIT YOU

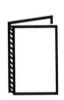

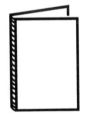

STANDARD EDITION

Our regular paperback book at our regular size

SPIRAL-BOUND EDITION

The same size as the Standard Edition, but with a sturdy, easy-to-fold, easy-to-hold spiral-bound spine

LARGE EDITION

A4 size and spiral bound, with larger text and a blank page for notes opposite every page of text – perfect for technical and directing use

| LEARN MORE | **samuelfrench.co.uk/actingeditions**

MUSIC USE NOTE

Licensees are solely responsible for obtaining formal written permission from copyright owners to use copyrighted music in the performance of this play and are strongly cautioned to do so. If no such permission is obtained by the licensee, then the licensee must use only original music that the licensee owns and controls. Licensees are solely responsible and liable for all music clearances and shall indemnify the copyright owners of the play(s) and their licensing agent, Samuel French, against any costs, expenses, losses and liabilities arising from the use of music by licensees. Please contact the appropriate music licensing authority in your territory for the rights to any incidental music.

USE OF COPYRIGHT MUSIC

A licence issued by Samuel French Ltd to perform this play does not include permission to use the incidental music specified in this copy.

Where the place of performance is already licensed by the PERFORMING RIGHT SOCIETY (PRS) a return of the music used must be made to them. If the place of performance is not so licensed then application should be made to the PRS, 2 Pancras Square, London, N1C 4AG.

A separate and additional licence from PHONOGRAPHIC PERFORMANCE LTD, 1 Upper James Street, London W1F 9DE (www.ppluk.com) is needed whenever commercial recordings are used.

IMPORTANT BILLING AND CREDIT REQUIREMENTS

If you have obtained performance rights to this title, please refer to your licensing agreement for important billing and credit requirements.

AUTHOR'S NOTE

When I was eight years old my primary school teacher daily reprimanded me in front of the entire class for my "appalling handwriting". She equated it with intelligence and humiliated me so much that I felt scared to present her with any work, so I didn't. I wore an eye patch and was immediately placed in a lower reading group. I could read perfectly...just couldn't see! I was highlighted from a young age as being disruptive and disobedient in class and would often be excluded from activities, trips and competitions or quizzes. The school certainly did not want a dinner ticket wielding, council estate residing, second-hand uniform wearing daughter of an alcoholic benefit claimant to represent them in any capacity. Or at least this was how I was made to feel. I was lost and traumatized by the socio-economic circumstances of my childhood. I began to act out and dislike school and so disengaged. I needed help, not to be shunned and isolated.

Killymuck is a fictitious housing estate based on my experiences growing up in Northern Ireland during the Troubles and entering a post conflict society. It is a call for change. A call to recognise that a meritocratic society can only be achieved if we have a level playing field to begin with.

Equity coupled with equality.
It is my battle cry.

Killymuck was first produced by Kat Woods at the Omnibus Theatre on 19 July 2018 and later transfered to the Edinburgh Fringe 2018.

Performer	Aoife Lennon
Writer/Director/Producer/Lighting/Sound	Kat Woods
Stage Manager/Operator	Matt Part

ACKNOWLEDGEMENTS

My family: Mammy, Maureen, Paul, Timothy, Sheila Woods; Austin, Tamzin and Imogen Cronin; Katie Park, Jenny Large and Aunty Geraldine, without your love, support, accommodation, generosity and guidance this would never have happened.

Lisa Fitzpatrick, Tom Maguire, Carole-Anne Upton, Adrian O'Connell and all at the University of Ulster Drama Department, you pushed me to pursue my dreams when I had no one else to do that.

Chris Sonnex, David Ralf and all at the Bunker Theatre. A fortune teller once told me a Chris would change my life...it might have taken ten years but it's happening!

Annabel Williamson, Monsay Whitney, Stef O'Driscoll, Redd Lily Roche, Ella Corcoran, Minglu Wang, Joe Price, Ben Grant, Louise Kempton, Amy Mae Smith, Zara Janmohamed; for being my first but also the greatest co-creative team ever!

Cat Shoobridge, from script support to the enormity of your directing talent and for giving me faith in my work.

Louise Stephens for the constant encouragement, script feedback, attendance at my plays but most of all for your friendship.

Marie McCarthy, Felicity Paterson and all at Omnibus Theatre.

Sam Devitt at TCH for the support and flexible rota arrangements in the old rent paying job.

Christine Gamble (Gambini) you are just awesome!

Mr Collins (Science teacher) and Mrs Cunningham (Sociology) for not giving up on me.

Claire Millar, Sally Rees, Martin Hall, Julie Cohn, Will Hearle, Serena Jennings, Tanya Singh, Joyce Greenaway, Kayleigh Llewellyn, Patricia Fivey, Geraldine Cooper, Ben Galpin and Harrie Dobby; Dan Jones, The Peggy Ramsey Foundation, To all who donated to our Edinburgh fringe fundraising campaign.

Aoife Lennon, without you this play would not exist but most of all thank you for being a friend at my lowest points when I needed it the most.

In loving memory of my dad.

RIP.

Kitchen. Northern Ireland 1979.

Womb sounds.

Helloooo can you hear me... I think I'm ready—

We hear muffled noises in the background. Two people saying goodbye to each other. There is a third voice telling the second voice to hurry up.

No no no, why's he...he can't leave, I'm done in here. Fed up.

Jumps up and down whilst speaking.

Need to come out now.

Splish.

Oh no what was that? Oh...is this supposed to be...oh...can I just go through here?

Splash.

I think if I just sliiiiiiiide my shoulders and my head a bit.

I can just squeeze through here.

Muffled noise, same voices as before. They forgot something.

Splosh.

Oh I think she peed herself. Here I come.

Whhheeeeeeeeee.

Splat.

Baby cry.

Boom.

Out.

Ready.

Born at 5.40 in the pm, just slid right out.

Mum said, "Took 'bout twenty mins, door to door or even womb to floor."

"You came into this world fast like you were on a slide or something, couldn't wait, seven weeks early and 5lbs. Your father just left to help Uncle Pat with a fallen tree, I was on me own, thank God he came back."

She thinks that's why I like going fast.

"An adrenaline junkie," she calls me.

Roller coasters.

Swings.

Spinning.

Twisting.

Tumbling.

Jumping.

Jumping out.

Jumping in.

Jumping high.

Jumping low.

Jumping any fuckin' where.

OTHER VOICE *(This could just be the performer's voice.)* There is no factual or evidence-based algorithm that can dictate why we are born. Why you were born you or why I was born me. Or why we are born into the circumstances that we are born into. Although, depending on individual dogma, we may see this as a divine act of God or Gods or simply a random occurrence. However, what I can state without doubt is that no one is born equal.

The class structure within the UK and Ireland is an omnipresent entity, which serves to reinforce this concept.

I have always been aware of class from a young age.

My father was a snob, a middle-class snob who fell down the social mobility ladder with an addictive alcoholic-induced

thud, landing at the doorsteps of the people that scared him the most. Queuing for benefits on a Monday morning only to squander them on drink by Monday night, leaving a young family in a housing estate bereft of finance.

My birth year coincided with the "Winter of Discontent of '78/'79".

Labour were ousted as betrayal merchants by those that voted them in in '74 and in rolled Margaret Thatcher and the Conservatives.

Maggie T, all guns a-blazing for the welfare state and the scourge of society.

Austerity.

Austerity.

Austerity.

Punishing the poor for the mistakes of the rich meant growing up within the benefits structure was to become a cocoon for hand-to-mouth existence, lack of educational opportunity, social mobility stagnation and the materialisation within these households that the trickle-down economic ideology does not work.

Now more than ever I don't quite know where I fit within the social strata, this class hierarchy that exists. So, I started to create this piece, using my own experiences as a model, exploring class and what effect that has had on me whilst trying to navigate and function in a world where money affords opportunity.

Is it just a fact that we the underclass have to work twice as hard to get our voice heard in comparison to those from a more privileged background?

Where does it start?

Who contributes to it?

How can we change it?

(End of OTHER VOICE.*)*

"Niamh, are you comin' to the swimmin' club after school the day."

"Nah I eh...I em I don't feel well.'

"What's wrong with ya?"

"Just feel a bit sick."

"I can lend ya the mon—"

"I don't feel well."

My best friend on the estate was a girl called Ciara. I used to think she was a proper richo, her da had a job and a car, a navy blue one. Don't know the make but it had all the doors, you know, the ones where you can get in the back and the front. They had a fridge freezer stuffed with food like Alphabites and frozen chips and frozen burgers. We didn't have a freezer at ours. First time I tasted a Petits Filous was in Ciara's. They had Sky and a video machine. Not many had them on the estate. Her da worked though. Earned a bit more then us benefit bastards.

Siobhan Carey, the other girl that hung about with us, was the same, her ones even had a French exchange student to stay for a week one summer. Her mum had bought in the Camembert and Brie and went full-blown French for the duration of her stay. She even accented Siobhan's name when calling her in...

(in a French accent)

SIOBHAN

SIOBHAN

Her ma was scared shiteless that we would get Marie from Paris pregnant or lure her into a world of stealing or fucking and cunting with every mouthful. Full of airs and graces, she was.

Siobhan wasn't allowed to play with us after the "White Lightning Incident". Not that I wanted her to hang with us as she fuckin' touted to her ma that we spiked her drink

when she was the one that bought the cheapest cider in the shop in the first place. Sure we didn't even have any money.

Puking your ring on yer ma's good carpet is one sure way of being found out.

My da couldn't work as he was the victim of a hit and run accident, left for dead on the roadside, had pins in his legs holding them together so he couldn't walk that well. Disability Living Allowance or DLA is what he got. And straight it went into the register of his local. Pity presents would follow when he'd lash out.

Mammy said that he banged his head that day. Damaged his brain. They separated and she had access to the money for the first time.

Income support, family allowance or whatever it was called.

£105.28 weekly for five people.

"Niamh, are you comin' or wha?"

"Are you deaf or something? I said I don't feel well."

I didn't like gettin' a lend of money cuz I knew that I couldn't pay it back.

The swimming club didn't have us benefit kids in it. I went a few times and I...I eh I liked it, I really liked it, but it was just y'know em such a mare, what with getting home and scabbin' money for it in the first place.

Anyways I didn't like gettin' money off Ciara.

We had a fight this one time when Siobhan was there and she spat the words out.

"Your mammy doesn't even have any pots and pans."

It wasn't even true, we had at least two.

"We fuckin' do."

"No youse don't and you get all your clothes from the Sally Annes."

The elements of truth in her retorts just switched up my rage from a five to a ten.

The Sally Annes was the Salvation Army.

"It's food parcels we get from them, not clothes."

The clothes came from Mum's friends at her Al-Anon meetings and it wasn't any of her fucking business where we got our stuff from.

"It's a free country, isn't it?"

So I ran after her and booted her in the shin.

She went home crying and her ma dragged her round ours after.

"Look what your Niamh did to our Ciara, Look at her leg."

My ma says:

"Jesus, Maura, I'm so sorry. What have you got to say for yourself, Niamh?"

"I'm sorry, Mum, but she said...she said em..."

"She said what, Niamh?"

"That we had no pots or pans."

"Did she now...where would she be hearing something like that?"

Me ma looked Ciara's ma dead in the eye, told her to leave.

Ciara's ma stormed out.

"Don't you dare kick anyone again, you hear me now, I'm warning you. I don't bloody care what the hell they say."

She only took that tone when she was really angry and you knew the wooden spoon would be coming out if you backchatted her.

So I scarpered upstairs as quick as I could, that sorta run that you do with your hands on the stairs as well, pushin' ye faster like a wee dog. *(We see her do this.)*

But eh as I...

As I got to the top...

I could hear her cry.

So I stayed and just listened for a bit.

I shouted "Sorry".

She didn't say anything.

Nothing.

It was just silence.

Beat.

I *hated* myself for that.

Beat.

I hated the fact that she could feel so shit for havin' nothin' and that I couldn't help her. I just wanted to go round Ciara's house and fuckin' piss all over her pot cupboard.

Well, maybe steal the good ones first then piss all over the rest.

Me da hated Killymuck. When he was younger he wasn't allowed to play with people on the green. That's what the people from the housing estate were called. He wasn't a Nordy, he was from over the border. He was always banging on about how the council used Killymuck as a dumping ground. How they rounded us all up and dumped us on the outskirts of town.

Like we were the misfits that didn't fit anywhere else.

Me and my sister thought there may be a curse on the estate.

Hexed.

Doomed.

We made a list once, it detailed the houses that had kids our ages and their imperfect circumstances:

Number 14: Parents: Separated.

Number 16: Parents: Divorced.

Number 18: Alcoholic ma.

Number 20: Alcoholic ma and da.

Number 22: Suicide.

Number 24. Leukaemia.

Number 28: Alcoholic da.

See, cursed!

Gummy Bears theme tune plays. NIAMH *sings along.*

"Roisin, hurry up, it's on."

In he walks. Straight to the TV and turns it over.

"Right, out. Homework now."

"We were watching that."

"I said out."

The kids TV stuff clashed with the Channel 4 racing. He'd usually be already perched on his chair in front of the TV watching it but he wasn't there this time.

"But I—"

"Don't you dare answer me back!"

Roisin jumps up and leaves, thinking that I would follow but I sat on so he yanked me up by the arm pushed me out of the room and switched it over.

I go get my school jotter and go back in, I knew it would piss him off.

Today in class Mrs Smyth said that Killymuck was a Paupers' Graveyard and that it was to do with the famine and the workhouses or something and that all the dead people were buried under Killymuck. Is that why this place is cursed. Me and Roisin think it's cursed.

"Either come in or go out."

He's glued to the TV.

His horse is nose for nose with another in the final furlong and he's cheering it on.

"You said to do my homework!"

"Exactly. You, not me. That's what the encyclopaedia's for."

"Photo finish, is it?"

"GET OUT AND DO YOUR HOMEWORK!"

He needed that win. There was no money in the house.

"Don't be in there annoying him."

"It's not fair, we were watching the TV and he just stormed in and turned it over—"

"He'll be gone now soon."

And he was, that was him won enough for a few days of a bender. Mammy was relieved to have him out of the way. Peace, no longer have to tiptoe around him.

We had these red leather-backed encyclopaedias with gold writing on the front that me da got off some salesman and paid him like a quid a week, but the firm went bust after a month and we more or less got them for free.

My da was crazy about education.

The goal was always to get a degree and get a good job.

Education.

Education.

Education.

Job.

Money.

Exit shithole life.

In Ciara's house they didn't have an encyclopaedia, they didn't need them, they had Sky, so she'd come round and

borrow ours although she was only allowed in our house if my dad wasn't there. He didn't like people in the house, he had a thing about it.

"Right, Ciara, we can both use it, but we are only allowed to read it like three times each then close it and then write our work."

Little did she know that when she left I would go back and double-check to make sure that I hadn't left anything out. Ciara was only in my tier at school for the subjects that you weren't tiered for like History, Art, PE, Home Economics or things like that. There were five tiers, top tier was one... I was in that class.

Actually, I was thrown out of class more times then I was allowed to stay in. Although, Karen McIntyre was far worse than me. We always got grouped together. One time she got 2% on her Science test and pulled the teacher by the hair and scraped her face with her nails. The information whoshed through the school like a strong wind.

Karen battered Mrs G.

Karen battered Mrs G.

Karen battered Mrs G.

Karen battered Mrs G.

The Internet had just been rolled out to schools and we had three computers for the entire school. The corridor that our classroom resided on had one. Four classrooms filled with thirty-five to forty students and one computer. There was a programme set up to talk to a school in America and we took it in turns to chat to them but any time it would come to swapping out to us, Mrs Smyth would bang out:

"We've ran out of time today, girls."

"You said that last time."

"Well, we are doing it by the roll book and your surname is at the end of the register."

"But that group had Claire Burns, Ann O'Reilly and Shauna Tapster, that doesn't make sense, they are at the start and at the end of the register."

"That's enough, Niamh."

She did that every week until the summer holidays then used that as an excuse.

Bus noise or beep of a horn.

So, we pile on this bus.

One of those education school buses, rusty, yellow and white, a tin thing, on wheels.

The boys from the Protestant school were on it already as the bus went past them first.

They all snarf and giggle and titter as we get on.

Ciara's on first and she holds her hand up and I sit next to her.

Not often we get to mix with boys and less often we get to mix with the Prods, so excitement was palpable through the bus.

One of the many cross-community initiatives as the Enniskillen bomb had went off the year before.

Jesus, day it happened, we were on our way to Mass in our neighbour's car. Me ma had not long had our John so she couldn't go and me daddy, well let's just say he was a lapsed Catholic.

He was always on a come-down on a Sunday anyway and Mum used to think it was best if we weren't in the house annoying him. So she sent us with Micky and his kids.

Me, our Roisin and Micky's two in the back. I was trying to steal the money outta the Mass envelope Ma had given us, there was only a pound in there but it was two fifty pees, so I thought one for me, one for the church roof.

I had it near prized open when— *(bomb sound)*

The car lifted slightly off the ground, we didn't know what was happening and Micky did a 360 in the middle of the road and pelted it home. Once the bang hit then it was silent for a few minutes, then the sirens came. It was on the news already, what with it being Remembrance Sunday and the first live news feed or something. Me ma was hysterical by the time we got back. Eleven reported dead, many injured. She hugged us and we went inside the house.

That got us out of Mass for a few weeks.

Anyway, this one school trip was a barn dance thing. A joint venture for the Catholics and Protestants. Off to the Ulster American folk park to "immerse ourselves in the story of the brave immigrants who made the journey across the Atlantic to America hundreds of years ago."

Yawn.

Yawn.

Yawn.

Boring.

Boring.

Boring.

Was the general consensus on the bus. We were too interested in how we were going to chat to the boys who had occupied the back seats and they were too interested in what they would say to us.

"Which one do you like?"

"Dunno not sure, think the one standing up second from the back."

"He keeps lookin' at you."

"You sure?"

"Yeah, course I am."

So I look behind me and he shouts up:

"What the fuck are you lookin' at? Seen the state of that one in the green coat, wee Fenian. That's a Fenian scabby gipsy coat that even your granny wouldn't be seen dead in."

I didn't have any grannies they were all dead.

So, I tell him to "fuck off" and Ciara calls him a prick, the rest of the girls stand up, as do the boys and a mini stand-off breaks out.

At that the teachers and nuns go crazy because all they hear is fuck, prick, fenian and dead grannies all in one go and come running down the bus to break it up.

They think I started it:

"I didn't do anything."

They call off the dance but we go to the folk park anyway. Be a whole handling getting us all off the bus and back in for lessons so we just bate on.

Ciara tells me she likes my coat and that:

"He only said that cuz he likes you."

I don't believe her and when I get home I take the coat off and in a rage throw it on the ground. Ma asks what's wrong but I run upstairs screaming that I want a new coat.

"Just a black one like everyone else has, not a shitty green thing from the nuns or Al-Anon or wherever the fuck you got it. I want one from a shop with the tag still on and the shop bag and the receipt. Can you not just buy us something new from a shop for once in our lives."

I never told her why I was upset and I never got a new one. So I would take it off before going to school and be cold rather then be seen with it on.

Beat.

I didn't understand how hard it was for her.

Beat.

I hate myself for that.

My da was still in and out of ours even though they were separated and he had his own flat. The summer before the eleven plus he enforced a rule of a practice test a day and I passed all of them. I even passed the mock. But he was relentless, somewhat obsessive. He hated the secondary school and was in my head constantly. He had this spiel about going to the grammar, getting a good education and getting a good job. Roisin had passed it the year before and he used that as a bartering tool.

"Your sister did it.

"Your sister passed."

"You don't want to be the stupid one now, do you?"

Sister passed. Fucking passed. Passed.

Stupid. You're stupid. Stupid.

She passed, you're stupid.

Thicko thicko stupid stupid. Stupid fucking test.

Night before I couldn't eat.

Couldn't sleep.

So, Ma got Leo Gorden to pray with me. He was a healer man, had the cure for various ailments, warts, anxiety. It was done over the phone and he made me feel relaxed for the duration of the call. Maybe he was better at warts than calming anxiety and nerves. Cuz when he hung up I felt sick. Sick to the pit of my stomach. This one exam. This was our way out.

Go to the grammar get a good education get a degree get a good job.

Fuck fuck fuck.

This just kept repeating in my brain.

Pass the exam.

Go to the grammar.

Get the good education.

Get the degree.

Get a good job.

Go to the grammar.

Get the good education.

Get the degree.

Get a good job.

Go to the grammar.

Get the good education.

Get the degree.

Get a good job.

Get the fuck outta here.

DING.

DING.

DING.

PENS DOWN.

HEADS UP.

PAPER OVER.

Before I knew it, I ran out of time, I hadn't even got through a third of the paper

I fucked it.

Proper fucked it.

OTHER VOICE Is the education structure equipped to handle children coming from different households, different economic structures and different cultures? Research from

the Institute of Education suggests that children from disadvantaged backgrounds are more likely to be perceived by teachers as less able than their more advantaged peers, despite getting equivalent scores in tests.

There have been numerous studies and research polls with the conclusion that living in poverty corresponds to losing fourteen points of IQ. Children from poorer backgrounds, who receive free school meals, are statistically less likely to achieve five or more GCSEs. It has led sociologist Diane Reay to assert that this present Conservative government "is making inequality in education worse not better". She states that the schooling structure "is still educating different social classes for different functions in society". Author and MOBO Award-Winning hip hop artist Akala speaks extensively on race, class and education. He reinforces Reay's point by suggesting that, "we are not interested in turning kids from impoverished areas into rocket scientists...kids from these estate structures do not have the same life opportunities as those from privileged backgrounds."

Private tutors, books, extra curricular cultural activities, drama groups, dance classes, theatre excursions, these are all things that aid the learning process and these are all things that the underclass and a number of working class children cannot afford.

End of OTHER VOICE.

The secondary had a maroon jumper and grey skirt. I couldn't borrow any hand-me-downs off Roisin as she was at the grammar, so St Vincent de Paul helped out with the new uniform.

"Joseph, come and look at Niamh in her new uniform, doesn't she look smart."

"If she fuckin' looked that smart she wouldn't be going to the secondary for the thickos now, would she. I don't want to see her."

He was sat watching the racing. But he'd been in one of his moods all day. The living room door was ajar and I could see the fireplace and my grandma's clock that sat on top. Just above that sat a picture. It had a blue cloudy sky background with a forest of trees that had shed their leaves and emblazoned on it in gold writing were the words:

God grant me the serenity to accept the things I cannot change

Courage to change the things I can and

Wisdom to know the difference.

"He doesn't want to see me, Mummy."

"Let me just go in and talk to him, he doesn't mean it. Joseph—"

"You see, this is what you do, pick pick pick."

"Awk, Joseph, she's standing right outside."

"I fucking told you I didn't want to see her, NOW GET THE FUCK OUT!"

He was often like that. Usually when there was no money. I think he was always worse when he was sober and craving than when he was intoxicated and falling about. Either way he spouted abuse.

Car horn sound.

"There's me lift, I've to go on here to my meeting, the boys are in bed, Nicola will be here in five minutes"

Ciara's older sister Nicola babysat us every Thursday night. There was a group of girls that hung around with each other on the estate, best friends, Nicola, Tracey, Mary and Sinead. They were "the babysitter gang" but we always got Nicola cuz we liked her the best.

On a Thursday night Mammy would go to this thing called Al-Anon, she called it "her meeting", we knew what it was and even though the other members were supposed to be

secret we knew who they were too. It was like a group to help those who had family members who suffered with alcohol addiction. I loved when Nicola would babysit, she would let us stay up past our bedtime to watch *Desmond's* on Channel 4 and would bring sweets with her, Wham Bars, Frosties and penny choos. She was only a few years older than Roisin, but Roisin was still too young to mind us. Nicola had a part-time job in our local shop as well. You could work there from thirteen back in the day. So, she always had the nicest clothes.

Sometimes I would stare at her and then look at myself in the mirror and wonder when my boobs would look like hers. Try and pull them out, stretch them but there was nothing there. She caught me at it one day and told me they would come when I was her age.

Nicola dated the best-looking guy on the estate, Paddy ye called him, and sometimes if she babysat us he would call to our house. Roisin and me would just sneakily watch them kiss on the sofa. Dreaming that it was us. Paddy built a tree fort at the top of the estate and because Ciara was Nicola's sister he would let us use it during the day.

It was made out of old laminate flooring and had a swing made out of an old piece of wood that hung from yellow rope precariously off a branch. The swing had graffiti written all over it.

Ciara wuz ere,

Niamh is a skiller.

I was pretty skillful to be fair.

Someone wrote that Nicola was a slut... She wasn't. So me and Ciara got a permanent marker and wrote PRICKS in capitals over it.

They wrote that Paddy's da was in the Ra, which was a bare-faced lie. Cuz actually it was Paddy's ma that was in the Ra, well, Sinn Féin. She was like a political speaker,

went to America and stuff to raise money for the cause, the United Ireland cause.

His ma was apparently on the board who commissioned some type of peace graffiti thing. Paddy even helped to paint it, he was proper arty, said he was inspired by the Aztecs and painted an Orwellian big brother eye on the side. Started as a political art piece that we actually didn't give a fuck about at the time cuz all we cared for was that it was brightly coloured and cheered up the drab cream monotony of the housing estate gable walls. Me da said the mural was painted after the Enniskillen bomb. Represents the coming together of two tribes, the Taigs (us Fenians) and the Huns (the Prods from the Proddy estate). Not too sure the Prods knew we were trying to get on... We still got crab apples fucked at us every time we went to the shop on that green, white and orange bike Santy got us for Christmas.

One time I kissed one of them during a game of letter torture; he tasted like Jaffa cakes... For ages after I thought that's why they were called Orange Men!

The older ones used to drink and smoke and have mini raves up at the fort and sometimes we would drink the leftovers the next day if there was any still knocking about. This one time Nicola was barred from seeing Paddy after the "Ouija Board Incident". It was such state scandal.

Y'see you can't burn the Ouija board. Well, I mean...like em...I've never tried but but Nicola and her mates did it up the tree fort one night. They got freaked out and threw it on the fire and the fire went straight out. Apparently her mum took her to the local priest, Fr Moore, because she was hysterical.

"I've seen him, I've opened up the portal, he's coming for me, he's coming for me. Donna said she seen him already, he's half pig, half man. Hooves for feet and a snout for a nose. The Pigman is coming.

"PIGMAN"

"PIGMAN"

"PIGMAN"

She was all crazy exorcist eyes, trying to crawl under her bed. So Fr Moore prayed the rosary and threw holy water on her and said to snap the board into seven pieces, bury it and put more holy water on it, in order to break the curse so no bad spirits come out.

Anyway, they did as the priest said, dug a hole and buried it. I'm not sure Nicola was right after that y'know.

When we were old enough and Nicola and her friends had other jobs it was mine and Roisin's turn to babysit. Well, Roisin was always first choice. I was only the go-to if there was absolutely no one else to ask. My favourite thing ever was babysitting. Sure, it was pure easy, the kids'd be in bed and no one wanted to make a show of themselves, houses be immaculate. All you'd have to do would be just sit there, watch TV and if the kids wake up send they back to bed, threatenin' them with the robin in the garden watching for Santy.

See that robin there... It could be any bird that you seen, just call it a robin... Well that robin there watches and goes straight back to Santy if you have been a bad boy. Now go on back to bed. Off they'd go and I'd give it 'bout twenty minutes to be on the safe side and if I didn't hear anything I would sneak off to the kitchen and rob the biscuit jar.

The babysitting jobs, eh, let's just say em the pay fluctuated ever so slightly and it would be like hittin' the jackpot if you got the call for the prostitute next door. She paid between £10 and £15 whereas some only gave you £3 even if you had been there from 7pm to 3am, that's not even 50p an hour like. But it was better then nothin' and you could always rob their food.

She didn't know that we knew she was a prostitute and I guess there was no hard-core evidence, apart from what we thought we knew. We just put two and two together.

She always had money but no job, different men at least twice a week and a few times we were spying on her out the bedroom window and seen the men give her money. Notes not coins. Sharon, ye called her.

My mum was a wee bit competitive with Sharon when it came to her garden. She had often taken slips of rose bushes from over growing plants from the rich people's gardens on our walks back from Mass on a Sunday and planted them in our garden and they would grow. Like magic.

The Mart was on every Thursday. It was like a trading place for farmers and their animals and also some market stalls. You could get everything from a hundred loo rolls for £5 to shell suits to flowers. Mum would buy sweet pea and maybe another pot of cheap something, usually pansy. We had a fence around our little front garden and the sweet pea would scramble up intertwining the wire looping in and out until it reached the height of the fence. The pansy although cheap was not to be outdone, it held its own beside the voluptuous sweet pea with a huge head of flower in vibrant purple and yellows.

I heard Sharon say once:

"You're fierce green-fingered, Mrs Maguire"

Mum would go all coy and shy and retreat back into the house.

"Do you think her rockery is nicer then mine?" she'd say.

Never had the heart to tell her that the prostitute next door had the edge on her when it came to flower arrangement.

She had seasonal flowers like daffodils and snowdrops and bluebells in spring.

When summer came she had marigolds, beardtongue, oxalis, day lillies, zinnia and sunflowers.

It was as if the rainbow birthed a flower patch. There was no competition.

We daren't let on though.

Wise up, Mammy, you know ours is better. We'd say.

"Can Roisin babysit the night?"

"I think she's booked for the O'Briens."

"Awk is she, that's fine then."

"Eh...Niamh's free."

"Erm."

"Sure I'm only next door, I can keep an eye?"

"Ok that'll do, send her in at 7.30pm"

"Ma did well to secure that job for me."

So, I'm all set. Just brushed me teeth. I always like to brush me teeth before babysitting, it gives the impression that I care about hygiene, that I'm serious about the job afoot.

I go round, she isn't off until 8pm.

"They're in bed but if they wake up tell them about the robin."

"Don't give them anything more to drink as Cara might wet the bed."

"Your mum has the details of where I am going, if you have any problems go get her."

Ok.

And off she went. She smelt of musk but in a nice way, not the stinky one, high heels, black trousers and black top.

It was just me in the house alone...well apart from the two kids sleeping upstairs. At 9pm I raided the biscuit jar. She always had the best biccies.

Trios, Viscounts, Orange and Mint Club, Gold Bars, Wagon Wheels, Penguins.

In a proper biscuit jar, not an old Family Circle biscuit box, a proper ceramic jar filled to the brim. I started on the Gold

Bar. Had two. Liked them. Then worked me way through a few more, ending on a Mint Club.

By 10pm I was bored. I'd already seen Dirty Dancing and all the Disney videos Sharon had on display.

Nothing on TV, except The Kelly Show. It was always shite. Same old comedians, same old music, same old guests.

Boring.

Boring.

Boring.

Him and his curly hair, belly and beard.

The thing with the sugar high is the epic low that follows. *(yawn)* So. I decided to have a wee nap. Her sofa was soft like a bed ours was a second hand thing from some woman who lived at the park.

So I lie down, shuffle myself into a good position when I spot a video under the TV.

It's shoved right the way to the back.

Oh, maybe this is one I haven't seen before.

I go and get it.

It's a blank tape with the words Predator scrawled in block capitals across the front. I haven't seen Predator, it's that Arnie one, right?

It's not fully rewinded so I figure if I watch a bit and like it then I can rewind it fully after.

So, I slot it in—

Orgasm noises.

Oh shit...oh shit ah fuc— What the fuck is this?

They're in a...a gym.

Two men, one woman, ah Jesus cocks and fanny everywhere. One has a tash and is licking her out, the other is putting his cock in her mouth.

I'm too scared to watch anymore, I mean I can't, it's against the Cath— I mean sex is— I don't even know if they're in love or if they're married ahhhh nooo...

But if I don't I'll never know what happens.

So, I go to watch on when I hear a creak in the floorboard above.

Fuck I'm babysitting.

The kids start to clamber down the stairs whilst I frantically try to get the tape off and back under the TV. In the chaos I accidentally turn the volume up instead of down, moans and groans on stereo.

Shit shit shit.

Off off OFF!

I run towards the door *(She runs towards the door.)* and hold it with my foot, stopping their entry.

"I want Mummy."

"She's just away to the shop."

"I can't sleep."

"Y'see that wee robin outside?"

But the robin didn't help, they were too startled and were crying and crying.

I had to go and get me ma and in a frenetic purge of Catholic guilt and shame I spill the beans that I think I have watched porn. She asked me where I got it from. I pointed to under the TV.

I've never seen her so angry.

She sent me on home and stayed herself until Sharon came in. Good job Sharon was drunk because I don't think she

remembered fully what Mummy had said to her. Roisin was ragin' with me cuz we weren't allowed to babysit for her anymore.

Next day me ma made us all go to Mass.

The problem with twelve o'clock Mass was that there was only a bus there but no bus back. So you'd have to walk the three miles home.

Ok, ok, I suppose the walk was nice if it wasn't raining. Sun shining.

We would walk the shortcut home, it took you off the main road, so away from the cars and other traffic. Up past St Michael's and St Joseph's, the boys' secondary and grammar schools, they sat on a hill, the secondary was at the foot of the hill and the grammar was at the top.

Lookin' down.

The houses along this route were like something you would see in a movie. Big plush gardens with gorgeous flowers in bloom, doorways with arches and drives with cars.

I did a paper round once in the area but got sacked because I flung the papers into the gardens instead of going and placing them on the doorsteps.

The Bensons house was at the end of the shortcut and it was usually manned by two Doberman Pinscher dogs. Salt and Pepper. They were fierce and would come running at ya (barks) only to be choked back by a great big lead. If we were walking back on our own we usually ran past the entrance at high speed but Mum was with us, so we walked it and took the chance.

The dogs were nowhere to be seen.

"Salt, Pepper."

No one in, so, ma went to the side of their garden and snipped a bit of the hydrangea that she so envied every time she had passed the house.

"Great I'll plant that now when we get back. Bloom for next year," she said.

We've another fifteen minutes of walking left and Mum carries it carefully in her hand.

We go by the place where they built the telephone poles. The smell of black tar suffocates your nostrils as we walk by. On past the Protestant estate, footpaths laced with red, white and blue, Union Jacks adorn the lampposts, and past the shop, then up the back alley to the house. We didn't always go the back way to the house, but it had started to rain, it was slightly longer but it offered more shelter.

We get to the other end and we see Sinead, Mary and Tracey all sat on Nicola's door step crying. Me ma told us to go on into the house and she went and spoke to them. Next thing we know she has asked all the girls round ours. Me da wasn't there so it was fine this time to have people in. Ma puts the kettle on. We watch as she fills it and switches it on at the wall.

Right, girls, upstairs and do your homework.

I don't have any, I said.

Just go up stairs and read. Now.

We ran up stairs but then we crept back down to listen, the third step from the bottom creaked so we double stepped it to make sure we wouldn't be heard. Roisin was in front and I was perched on the step behind.

Whispering.

"I can't hear, Roisin."

"Would you shut up."

"What's an abortion?"

"Shhh, they are going to know we're here."

The girls were crying.

Beat.

We start to cry.

Tracey speaks first. She tells Mum that last night Nicola had overdosed on some pills.

She was doing her GCSEs, wanted to be a vet.

Nicola's funeral happened on a school day and we went and formed a guard of honour with others from the estate and her form year in our school uniforms. Her older sister sang as the funeral procession left the chapel.

The girls followed the family and all dropped a single rose into the ground as the coffin was laid in. We went back to school for afternoon class and no one spoke of it. No school announcement, no counselling offered.

I got put on detention after for leaving the class when I shouldn't have and telling the teacher to "fuck off".

OTHER VOICE The women of Northern Ireland continue to face the harshest abortion laws in the world. We are continually being denied the same rights as women in the rest of the UK and the Republic of Ireland. Northern Ireland is considered one of the most conservative societies in western Europe, with the Church still maintaining say in societal norms.

Northern Ireland, and in particular areas of deprivation and poverty, continues to have the highest rate of suicide in the UK, per head of population, according to the Office for National Statistics. Those from the lower class structures tend to be more at risk. Northern Ireland is also unique as it is a post-conflict society with one of the highest PTSD rates across the globe. The findings of a Samaritans report stated that the number of men taking their own lives in Northern Ireland has increased by 82% from 1985–2015. To date Northern Ireland has no sitting assembly to secure funding when financial cuts continue to deplete mental health resources.

OTHER VOICE *ends.*

"Roisin, Niamh, John, Pat. In now for your tea."

When he was in the house my dad was really strict about us coming in at 7.30pm every night. We'd be ragin' as that was the time the good games like out and after or letter torture would be kicking off. But he didn't want us "taking drugs or getting impregnated". Like we didn't have a choice or a mind of our own. Think it was his chance to exert his "Fatherness" over us to make up for his absence, some sort of residual guilt parenting play.

The words "Horse Head", "Fat Bitch", and "Roisin, Niamh, John and Pat" are chanted and repeated, reverbed, building to a crescendo so that they end after the last sentence in the below sequence.

He'd embarrassingly call us in in age order. Which of course set off the lads in the estate. They would mimic him and shout it at us everywhere. *(in reference to the end of the sound effect)* FUCK OFF!

This one time we were all out in the square playing red rover. I was the fastest runner so always got picked no matter how much the boys hated me. It was all good if I was on their team but if I wasn't they would chant the words horse head at me and this time one of them smacked me a headbut cuz I had told him to fuck up. My nose started to bleed and they all ran away. Me ma called the police and the lad got a warning but that didn't stop them.

Valentine's Day that year they all stood outside my house and as I left to go to the shop to get milk, one shouted:

"Why the fuck did horse head think that it's ok to send you a Valentine's Day card?"

"I don't know, as if I would fancy that, ugly fat bitch."

"Neiiigghhhhh horse head horse head."

I ran back in and closed the door tight and started to cry.

"They don't mean it," Ma said.

"They say it all the time."

"Just ignore them."

That night we agreed that Ma would cut my hair and that I wouldn't wear it in a half ponytail anymore. Turns out Siobhan and Ciara had sent him a Valentine's card from me. A handdrawn one that had a red heart on the front and on the inside declared my undying love for him. They knew the boys hated me.

The next day I went to school and got put in detention for fighting with the class prefect. She had said that my hair was nicer longer. I kicked her in the shin and called her a dickhead.

Ciara became closer and closer to Siobhan and we just kinda drifted apart as the months passed by.

When Christmas came I decided that we would try and raise money to buy each other presents. We didn't believe in Santy anymore so it was hard to ask for anything when you knew there was little money. We used to get these logs for the fire from a relative who had trees on his land that he would cut, chop and discard. Well discarded to us.

We had been saving our birthday money and anything that we got and I persuaded Roisin to use it to buy candles. I had this idea of making Christmas logs, I'd seen them in a shop and they looked easy enough.

I thought everything through. We could get the holly from the bush at the top of the football pitch, the one up after the roundabout; we had the logs already and icing sugar for the snow.

Ma and Da were in town that day, doing bits of Christmas stuff. So we had the house to ourselves. Like a proper functioning business, pre-orders were essential so we knew how many to make. Roisin did that bit as the neighbours liked her better. So, off she went, door to door. Ten on order and we had only went around thirteen houses. At £2 each we were already in the profit zone.

Out the back I search through the logs to find the driest, most aesthetically pleasing ones and set about bringing ten into the house. Lay them on the table in the kitchen with the rest of the kit. And we are ready.

On went the holly, berries facing front ways.

A dust of icing sugar for fake snow.

And the candle in the middle.

Shit, we need a hole.

I didn't think about that.

We didn't have a drill. We try sellotape but it didn't work and looked shit. We try tying it on but that didn't work and it also looked shit.

Ping!

Brainwave.

Let's melt the bottom of the candle over the fire and stick it on, let it set and cover it with icing sugar.

So, I'm on my knees *(kneels down)* bent in front of the fireplace, the flames are too high and the first candle burns quickly and in a panic I pull it away and the wax skits up and hits the Serenity prayer picture. Roisin says, "God grant me the serenity to accept the things I cannot change apart from the candle wax which is now part of the frame."

I hated that picture anyway. We let the fire die down a bit and start again.

Pause.

I didn't hear him come in.

He's drunk.

Probably drunk all the Christmas money.

"What the fuck are you doing?"

I'm crouched over the fire, candle in hand, melting it in the burnt down embers.

Roisin explains that we have a business and that we are selling Christmas logs so that we can get everyone gifts this year.

"No child of mine will go around this estate fucking begging."

Mum runs in and tells him to calm down, that it's ok.

"It's not fucking ok."

He lifts his hand and smacks her away. He kicked her down the stairs once, black eyes, broken teeth, stomach, face, head, Punch Slap Bang.

"I'm so clumsy," she would say.

He was embarrassing.

I hated him.

In that moment I hated him.

I did.

"We have two more to do and I'm finishing them."

But with that he came hurtling towards me as Mum tried to grab him, he lifted his foot and with one kick.

Smack.

I put my hands out to save myself, they hit the back of the fire place, the hot chimney breast.

He kicked me head first in.

Hands burnt.

I started to scream.

God grant me the serenity to accept the things I cannot change

Courage to change the things I can and wisdom to know the difference.

He retreated upstairs, calling me for all the fuckers under the sun.

"Bringing shame on the family, begging for money."

Mum rang the police and he was escorted from the house.

The neighbours were outside, all listening.

The boys that called me horse head stared and sniggered.

More fucking ammunition for them, I thought.

When he left we finished the logs.

We had an order to complete.

The next day I went to school and got put on report for a month for not doing any homework.

The teacher asked to see my book because I was being "more disruptive then usual."

There was nothing in it.

I mumbled fuck off.

She told me she had enough of my backchat.

"Get out now, report to the principal."

Insolent behaviour was capitalised on the top of the report card.

Insolent behaviour.

Insolent fucking behavior.

I never knew what that meant.

The prostitu – em Sharon from next door moved out my GCSE year. Me dad had broken the back window lookin' for money the same day the housing executive woman was out interviewing ones in the estate, asking about the soliciting that had gone on.

A barring order was placed on him and he wasn't allowed within five hundred yards of the house and in a separate turn of events Sharon got evicted.

My mum refused to answer any questions in the interview and pretended she had not seen any exchange of money or gentlemen callers come and go. A rumour went round that it was Siobhan's ma that touted on her.

I was going out more and more. Getting drunk on White Lightning and Buckfast most nights. I was so drunk one time that an older boy finger fucked me so hard I can barely remember it but the next day I woke up in hospital. Mum cried as the nurse went into detail about the blood they had found all over my pants. "It's not a big wonder she gets in these states dressed like that," she said.

I had eighty denier tights on, a skirt and a T-shirt.

It's usually a few weeks between one going and a new family moving in. The council go into the house and clean it. They return the property to what it looked like originally so all the new shelves and cupboards that Sharon had bought offa her prostitute money were all ripped out and replaced with the orange shite ones found in all the council estates.

They ripped her rockery to shreds too.

Concrete, in place of the flowers.

Me ma was ragin' about that.

One day a van pulled up.

They were English.

Mother and daughter.

Rachael, you called her.

Same age as me but taller, much taller.

We became besties.

Thick as thieves.

One time we decided to bunk off school. Me and her just. She had stolen the Art room CD player the day before and we played The Cranberries full pelt whilst downing cheap vodka.

(*"LINGER" by The Cranberries* plays.* **NIAMH** *sings along.*)

She takes out her deodorant.

Sprays it in the bag and inhales it.

So I do the same.

Not sure I liked it, felt weird, light-headed, and in the haze my worst nightmare, hallucinating Siobhan.

Except I'm not.

And she's real.

She's stood right there.

"What the fuck are you skip rats doing?"

Where the fuck did she even come from. I tell her to piss off.

"Are you sniffing glue?"

"It's not glue."

"Does your ma know?"

"Fuck off."

"Who you telling to fuck off, what's it they call ya...horse head?"

"What did you say?"

"You deaf or somethin', I said horse head!"

I don't know what came over me but I jump to my feet and punch her straight in the face. She falls to the ground, pulling me with her.

She's on the ground.

She's got my hair but I don't feel it.

I'm on top of her.

---

* A licence to produce KILLYMUCK does not include a performance licence for "LINGER". For further information, please see Music Use Note on page xiii.

Punches.

Bash.

Smash.

"Don't you fucking call me that."

Rachael pulls me off her.

Siobhan goes home.

We never speak again.

I was on report for most of the rest of my school years, getting into fights, lashing out, stealing, drinking, skipping homework. Mr Collins said that, "I was the one of the most intelligent pupils that he ever had." He never once used the "I have my GCSEs" pep talk, don't know why anyone thinks that works, reverse psychology bullshit just makes me angry.

He gave me extra notes, photocopied work that I had missed. Helped me to get the grammar grades needed to do A-levels.

The new uniform was navy, purple and green. It felt right. It felt good.

It didn't help me to settle down, that was Mrs Cunningham... the Sociology teacher. She gave me hope and belief and taught me to read and question everything.

When it came to uni, Rach and me went to the same place and shared a house with some others. I was studying a BA in Sociology and she was doing Communications Advertising and Marketing, or CAM for short. One of the girls in the house share was in a Christian group so she would invite them all around once a week to watch a video. Patch Adams with Robin Williams. Looked absolutely pish and I wasn't wrong!

Halfway through the film I got a pain so fierce in my side that I ended up in bed.

The next morning the pain was still there.

I thought it was appendicitis.

As I was getting ready to go to the doctor, my phone began to vibrate.

An old Nokia 5210 with a little aerial sticking out.

It said, Home.

Hello

Who's this?

Why are you ring—

Put my Mother on the phone.

Put her on the phone.

PUT MY FUCKING MOTHER ON THE PHONE!

Daddy?

But he didn't have any hear—

What?

Is he dead?

IS. HE. DEAD?

My legs went to jelly as I fell back on the bed.

I told them I would get the bus home. Fr Jim said he would send the local priest to lift me. He played Shania Twain's album with Man I Feel Like A Woman on it the whole two-hour drive. Maybe he thought it would take my mind of it. It didn't.

I thought he was a weirdo. All the while my head was rushing with final memories... I can't rem— I think we were fighting.

Not talking.

I asked, was it sectarian.

They said no.

A random attack.

Random.

Attack.

The pain I had in my side the night before subsided as the day went on. I would find out later in the coroner's report that it happened at similar times to the first knife wound.

He was stabbed eleven times.

Top of the Pops had been taped the Thursday night. All Saints' "Pure Shores" was number one. We all sat in the living room listening to it on repeat. Huddled together, not talking.

Not long after, I dropped out of uni.

He made it impossible to love him.

But I did.

Epilogue

There is no blueprint or model that can be applied here to other families who grow up in impoverished circumstances. "Here's how you get out, here's the social mobility answer", because everyone is different and each circumstance unique. But then again that isn't the point of why I have written this play. It's about opportunity. It's about giving those who aren't as lucky as me a chance.

So, I have struggled here a bit to offer a finish, an end, and to be honest I've had a few different endings mapped out to this play. The first dissected the characteristics of children of alcoholics and detailed that impoverished families have a higher rate of addiction problems. Which inevitably lead to other situations, such as crime and suicide.

The second ending highlighted the nature of imposter syndrome and how that has affected me through navigating a world where money affords opportunity. Especially throughout the education structure, this is where I felt the most out of place due to my circumstances and obvious bias from teachers. One teacher I had solely taught extracurricular Irish to the rich kids. Did she think we wouldn't notice?

Mr Collins's actions had a ripple effect. That simple affirmation of intelligence gave me belief in myself. For example, I didn't have that encouragement with language. I studied French, didn't take an active interest in it because I didn't believe for one second that I would have the ability to leave my hometown, let alone the country, as I had never been on holiday before. To me it was a redundant thing.

This negative ideology is reflected in the theory developed by psychologist J. B. Rotter which he terms, "Locus of Control". It explores the degree to which we believe we can directly control the outcome of events in our lives as opposed to external forces beyond our control. Positive teacher–student relations and indeed positive educational surroundings such as home life help to achieve this.

I've decided to settle on the third ending. Which is actually an illustration, originally penned by Angus Maguire. The first drawing he presents depicts three people of varying heights standing on boxes trying to view a game restricted by a fence. This side represents equality, as all the boxes are the same height. But not everyone can see the game. The other scenario, equity comes into play. With equity we want to give everyone the appropriate tools in order to help them succeed. From the illustration the smallest person is given what he requires to reach the same eye level of the tallest person so in the case of the drawing, extra boxes.

Say we use this model in the class argument, so instead of arguing to *have* access to the same things like education and cultural opportunities etc. we *make* these things more accessible for people from different economic, cultural, ethnic and minority backgrounds. Do we need to start thinking about equity before equality in order to see change happen, well guys that is why you are here, listening and watching. Next time there is a general election ask your local MP what they have in place for the underclass in terms of social mobility, what support and outreach programmes they are planning and, if there aren't any, petition them to make a change.

I'm done with talk.

All we do is talk.

By challenging the norm we can evoke change!

Blackout.

"PURE SHORES" by All Saints.

---

* A licence to produce KILLYMUCK does not include a performance licence for "PURE SHORES". For further information, please see Music Use Note on page xiii.

VISIT THE SAMUEL FRENCH BOOKSHOP AT THE ROYAL COURT THEATRE

Browse plays and theatre books, get expert advice and enjoy a coffee

Samuel French Bookshop
Royal Court Theatre
Sloane Square
London
SW1W 8AS
020 7565 5024

Shop from thousands of titles on our website

 samuelfrench.co.uk

 samuelfrenchltd

 samuel french uk